W.E. COLLIN was professor of romance languages at the University of Western Ontario from 1925 until his retirement in 1959.

GERMAINE WARKENTIN is a member of the Department of English at Victoria College, University of Toronto.

The White Savannahs, originally published in 1936, is the first study of Canadian poetry from a modern point of view. It contains essays on Archibald Lampman, Marjorie Pickthall, E.J. Pratt, Leo Kennedy, A.M. Klein, A.J.M. Smith, F.R. Scott, Marie Le Franc, and Dorothy Livesay. The contributions are based on a series of analytical essays originally published in the *Canadian Forum* and in the *University of Toronto Quarterly*. Professor Collin's work added much to the establishment of a new climate of opinion among readers and publishers of poetry in Canada.

Literature of Canada

Poetry and Prose in Reprint

Douglas Lochhead, General Editor

The White Savannahs

W. E. Collin

Introduction by Germaine Warkentin

UNIVERSITY OF TORONTO PRESS
TORONTO AND BUFFALO

©University of Toronto Press 1975
Toronto and Buffalo
Reprinted in paperback 2015
ISBN 978-0-8020-2141-0 (cloth)
ISBN 978-0-8020-6241-3 (paper)

Library of Congress Cataloging in Publication Data

Collin, William Edwin
  The white savannahs

  (Literature of Canada; 15)
  Reprint of the 1936 ed. published by Macmillan, Toronto; with new
  material added.
  Bibliography: p.
  1. Canadian poetry — 20th century — History and criticism. I. Title.
  PR9190.5.C6 1975   811'.5'209   73-92516
  ISBN 978-0-8020-2141-0 (bound) ISBN 978-0-8020-6241-3 (pbk.)

The White Savannahs was originally published in 1936 by the
Macmillan Company of Canada Limited, Toronto.

This book has been published with the assistance of grants from the
Ontario Arts Council and the McLean Foundation.

Preface

Yes, there is a Canadian literature. It does exist. Part of the evidence to support these statements is presented in the form of reprints of the poetry and prose of the authors included in this series. Much of this literature has been long out of print. If the country's culture and traditions are to be sampled and measured, both in terms of past and present-day conditions, then the major works of both our well-known and our lesser-known writers should be available for all to buy and read. The Literature of Canada series aims to meet this need. It shares with its companion series, The Social History of Canada, the purpose of making the documents of the country's heritage accessible to an increasingly large national and international public, a public which is anxious to acquaint itself with Canadian literature — the writing itself — and also to become intimate with the times in which it grew.

DL

Contents

William Edwin Collin, 1893-

Germaine Warkentin

Introduction

W.E. Collin's *The White Savannahs*, first published in 1936, is a critical study of nine Canadian writers. Usually regarded as a work of the modernist movement, in actuality it escapes easy categorization. Though its chief emphasis is on what was then very recent poetry, it begins with a nineteenth-century figure, Archibald Lampman. Its principles arise in the aesthetics of the English philosopher T.E. Hulme, but it contains an appreciative essay on Marjorie Pickthall, a Canadian poet Hulme would have loathed. Though it praises the value of critical knowledge, and is organized unconsciously around the powerful motif of resurrection, *The White Savannahs* begins with a poet about whom we have recently discovered we did not know as much as we thought,[1] and ends with one who has almost disappeared from Canadian literature. Despite these paradoxes, *The White Savannahs* is one of the central works of modern Canadian criticism. Of it, A.J.M. Smith stated: 'Professor Collin's contribution to the establishment of a new climate of opinion among readers and publishers of poetry in Canada can hardly be over-estimated.'[2] And fourteen years after its publication, Desmond Pacey still called it one of the 'two good books on Canadian poetry.'[3]

The other study Pacey had in mind when he made this remark was E.K. Brown's *On Canadian Poetry* (1943). The two books are frequently considered as a pair, and with good reason: Brown wrote one of the more intelligent reviews of *The White Savannahs*, and Collin responded when it came his turn to review Brown with a respectful but brilliant challenge to all that *On Canadian Poetry* represents.[4] The contrast between these two

Canadian critics is instructive. Both were academic students of literature, but Brown's temperament was historical and normative, whereas Collin is a visionary whose writing seeks a virtually poetic persuasiveness. Though Brown spent time in France, as Collin did, *On Canadian Poetry* belongs to the judicious, Arnoldian tradition of the pre-war *University of Toronto Quarterly*. *The White Savannahs* emerges from a French tradition in which the critic aims to identify and reveal, in an iridescent and subjective prose, the central motifs of a writer's art. In attacking what he believed to be the weaknesses of Brown's study — his historical determinism and the timidity of his taste — Collin wrote:

> What guarantee have we that analysis and comparison will yield the truth of poetry? Is poetry a matter of literary elements, formal beauty, influences, and reputations? Are these not things imposed from without by the contemplating critic? Is poetry merely expression? Is it not rather an inner experience wearing a garment of words?[5]

It is this inner experience which Collin seeks in each of the essays which make up *The White Savannahs*.

The White Savannahs was the first book-length work on English-Canadian literature written from a purely critical standpoint. Those studies of writing in Canada which had been done before its appearance had been primarily historical and biographical. Works like Archibald MacMechan's *Headwaters of Canadian Literature* (1924) and James Cappon's studies of Roberts (1905) and Carman (1930) were essentially genetic: they attempted to draw the outlines of a pioneer literature, or to sketch the growth and achievement of a single talent, but rarely developed an analysis which brought the reader into close contact with the text or carried him into general problems of poetics. Lionel Stevenson's *Appraisals of Canadian Literature* (1926) broke the strictly historical pattern by attacking certain central problems, but apart from this, analytical criticism was the province of the reviewer and literary journalist. Collin's book was the first to attempt such a task for its own sake and at any length.

With one or two exceptions, reviewers of *The White Savannahs* were courteous, but puzzled, and even today it is a book more respected than understood. In *The Making of Modern Poetry in Canada* Louis Dudek and Michael Gnarowski class Collin as a mandarin, typical of the 'minority culture of embattled intellectuals' to which modern poetry chiefly speaks.[6] James Steele recently suggested that Collin's criticism had affiliations with the Marxist attempt to break down classical ideology in criticism. But he observed that the 'myth criticism' Collin developed was intellectually inconsistent with his left-wing sympathies.[7] Neither of these comments reflects Collin's real personality as a critic. Although Collin understood the originality of his task when he began to put the book together in the early thirties, he was not setting out to establish a new way of looking at Canadian poetry. Rather he was characteristically responding in a personal way to the impress on him of a group of poets he recognized as cohesive and principled. These were writers who were not part of the genteel literary establishment then dominant in Canada. His book is not theoretical, but its point of view is plain: admiration for art and disdain for artifice, compassion for failed aspiration combined with an ironic and clear-sighted view of its results.

Collin's special situation in Canadian literary history emerges clearly when we realize that Collin is our only major critic to have undergone the immigrant experience which our writers have dwelt on so obsessively. It was this experience that led to the deep sympathy of his article on that other exile, Frederick Philip Grove.[8] It informs his criticism with a tension created by the pull of two separate but insistent realities, as well as by the struggle to articulate the act of transformation which results from their engagement. For Collin, language, style, and vision are all branches of some creative experience whose single root (despite his skeptical view of Frye, Collin would call this root 'myth') originates in unexplored wildernesses of the human psyche. In his essay on Marie Le Franc he writes: 'Even a barren, useless and forbidding land can be absorbed into one's soul and issue forth again metamorphosed into a memorable picture of psychic experience.'[9] *The White Savannahs* represents just such a metamorphosis. The effect on Collin's personal culture and critical method has been necessarily somewhat unusual, and *The White Savannahs*, as it had no predecessors, has had no posterity. But this is perhaps as it should be, for W.E. Collin is the least doctrinaire of men. Though he was the first to draw public attention to the 'McGill School' of poets, he has never pretended to a school of his own, and so far is he from creating an *oeuvre* that *The White Savannahs*, published in the midst of the Depression, is in fact his most recent book. His life for eighty years has been, like his criticism, a principled response to the challenge of the particular moment. Today he lives in thoughtful retirement at London, Ontario, secluded from the lively Canadian literary scene of the sixties and seventies, a merry but uncompromising figure in his privacy.

William Edwin Collin was born in Oakenshaw, near Durham, England, on 9 May 1893. His father was a mining official and

Methodist lay preacher, and he grew up in an atmosphere which, while cultivated, was quite outside the Tory, Anglican, Oxbridge world which later came to be called 'the establishment.' The Methodism of Collin's family was not of the astringent sort he was later to meet in Ontario; rather than a legacy of prohibitions, it left him the energy of its hymns and sermons, the language of his preaching father and of the Bible. Collin went to King James I Grammar School in Bishop Auckland. Eventually he matriculated at the University of London, but did not go directly to university, since an illness intervened, and then the First World War, in which he served some time in the Royal Naval Air Service.

At the end of the war, he was a clerk in the military service in London, working each day in an office in Bedford Square, not too far from the stream of faceless City men in *The Waste Land* who

> Flowed up the hill and down King William Street,
> To where Saint Mary Woolnoth kept the hours
> With a dead sound on the final stroke of nine.

'It was T.S. Eliot,' Collin later wrote, 'who found the "verbal equivalent" for our spiritual mood immediately after the war. He saw the human mart and thoroughfare change into a desert; and because his face shone with that vision he led a numerous band of pilgrims through a spiritual wilderness which offered neither bread nor water, nothing but deceptive mirages.' (*WS* 158).

Among this 'numerous band' Collin is interesting for two characteristics. First, he took energetic measures to secure his own map of the desert, haunting Harold Monro's Poetry Bookshop, searching *avant-garde* magazines like *The New Age* as each issue appeared, and tracking down where he could such figures of the current literary scene as F.S. Flint and later Arthur Machen. Collin's taste, though alert, was typically Georgian. Like that of many men of the early period of English modernism, it had been shaped by the pre-Raphaelites and their twentieth-century heirs, and his interests encompassed poets like James Elroy Flecker as well as the Sitwells. Then, as later, he saw poetry as fundamentally a living experience which the notion of 'schools' could only hinder.

Second, he was at work finding his own way out of the desert, in part through Eliot's own methods and even before Eliot found the way himself. In an article published early in 1931 (and which clearly indicates that he had either not heard, or not assimilated, the fact that Eliot had become an Anglo-Catholic) Collin was to write:

> Our life is a dry death in a desert — as it was in the time of Ezekiel, and the Kings from the Orient, and the Fisher King in the West, as it always was and will be — where we raise stone altars to our gods. If we are led towards Life the way will be hard and voices will sing in our ears saying that it is all folly. It will be hard but we would do it again for the joy of seeing Life. Once we have looked on Life we shall have no more ease in the cactus land among a benighted people whose souls, through fear of life, have become sticks and stones. We shall always be in exile there, wishing for death, wondering about the other kingdom across the dark river. A certain static mood of emptiness, disappointment, impotence, doubt, but also of waiting as if something might come about, a breath to make our bones live, a possibility of life.[10]

For Collin, the clearest kind of affirmation in a time of despair was not to leave the desert, but to turn back and make a garden there. This position, which Collin was able to articulate fully only in the late twenties, had begun to develop a decade earlier. It evolved out of a thorough but intensely personal reading of Eliot's own sources, T.E. Hulme and Sir James Frazer, by a temperament essentially life-seeking and quite without Eliot's reserve and melancholy.

Like many others of his generation, Collin responded enthusiastically to Hulme's rejection of Romanticism; the effects may be seen in his essay on Lampman. But more interesting was Hulme's doctrine of art. Hulme proposed a renovation of poetry founded on the creation of new images which would, as Hulme described his 'analogies,' 'enable us to dwell and linger upon a point excited.'[11] To strip poetry of its accretion of habit, to seek in 'geometric art' the techniques of abstraction which make symbolic art possible, and out of this to create a new excitement, all seemed a plausible program for poetry. But Hulme's notion of history, and its attendant political position, was less attractive to Collin. Hulme's rejection of much of human culture since the Renaissance was based on his distaste for its accompanying belief in progress and human perfectibility, illusions which he scornfully termed 'humanist.' 'What is important,' he wrote in 'Humanism and the Religious Attitude,' 'is what nobody seems to realize — the dogmas like that of Original Sin, which are the closest expression of the categories of the religious attitude. That man is in no sense perfect, but a wretched creature, who can yet apprehend perfection.'[12] And in 'Romanticism and Classicism':

> Put shortly, there are the two views, then. One, that man is intrinsically good, spoilt by circumstance; and the other that he is intrinsically limited, but disciplined by order and tradition

to something fairly decent. To the one party man's nature is like a well, to the other like a bucket. The view which regards man as a well, a reservoir full of possibilities, I call the romantic; the one which regards him as a very finite and fixed creature, I call the classical.[13]

Hulme was definitely on the side of the classics.

'Hulme,' Collin was to write, 'made possible a return to religious poetry in England'[14] because his essays provided an alternative to the doctrine of evolution and to mechanistic and positivistic views of human nature. But the doctrine of original sin Collin could not accept. Though he writes approvingly of Hulme in his 1930 essay 'Beyond Humanism,' he does not use the term humanism as Hulme would have used it except in his review of E.K. Brown. Instead, he attempts to salvage a more optimistic (Hulme would have said 'romantic') view of human nature, through an investigation of the structures of myth and the imagery of the religious imagination. The foundations for this were laid in his early reading of Frazer, whose work suggested to him a way of integrating past and present, the old garden and the new desert, through a marriage of the modern discipline of anthropology with the ancient arts of literature. Frazer's study of vegetation myths provided, in fact, the dominating pattern by which Collin was to organize his own perception of cultural history throughout his career. Because of it, he is more interested than many modernists in investigating the meanings 'nature' might have for a poet. And when he tries to estimate the character of a poet's originality, he thinks not merely in Hulmean terms of the austere and purified but of something primal as well. The most singular and persistent characteristic of his criticism emerges from this; it is his fascination with life, rather than death, and with the personal, the immediate, and the dynamic, rather than the fixed and canonical.

This flourishing intellectual growth began during Collin's sojourn on the edge of post-war London's literary world. It was continued when he went to France as a scholarship student in 1919, and encountered not Eliot, but his *'semblable,'* Baudelaire, not Hulme, but his master, Remy de Gourmont. He studied Romance languages, first at Rennes and then at Toulouse, where in 1922 he took his *license ès lettres* as a student of the eminent *provençaliste* Joseph Anglade. In doing so, he was widening the distance between himself and the central traditions of English culture, to which as a non-conformist and a northerner he already felt peripheral. But he was, of course, plunging himself directly into the continental stream that fed modernist thought. His stay in France did nothing to change the direction of Collin's development, but everything to broaden his range of literary experience, and to give him a technique with which to deal with it. He was introduced to the origins of European vernacular literature in the mediaeval poets of Provence, and at the same time in the lectures on Verlaine at Toulouse was taught contemporary poetry as a living body of knowledge. Out of his reading of Sainte-Beuve and Gourmont there emerged a method which enabled him to apply his thinking about the ideas of Frazer and Hulme directly to the study of texts. It was the method of the *'causerie,'* the epidiectic discursive essay that seeks to discover the central experience of a poet's work. And walking about France and Spain in his holidays, he made literary pilgrimages in search of his poets and their places, just as in Montreal in the forties he was to search out John Sutherland and his printing press.

) This uncommon amalgam was to find an unexpected niche in life. In 1923 Collin, after a year as French master in an English prep school, crossed the ocean with his copies of Hulme and Mallarmé and came to stay in the Department of Romance Languages at the University of Western Ontario in London.

In his solitude in that first winter, the campus of Western with its few buildings and meagre library seemed yet another waste land, the genteel and stifling Ontario world which it served 'a climate ... where water longed to be ice.'[15] Perhaps Ontario would have been easier for Collin to understand had he emerged from the English 'establishment' rather than from a non-conformist background. Like many other emigrants, he might have settled in, deceived by the pious imitation of English life which late colonial society fostered. Or like others he might have rejected the place outright as delusive and stagnant, and returned home. Collin did not give in, but the pain of his struggle can be gauged in some words he was later to write about Frederick Philip Grove:

> Seul un déraciné, seul un homme qui appartient par ses origines à la vieille culture européene et qui a été transplanté dans la civilisation de ce nouveau monde, peut savoir quelle dut être la nostalgie de Grove au cours de ces années.[16]

This first contact with Ontario was to prove one of the shaping notions of *The White Savannahs* ten years later; revulsion at its creative consequences burns through the essay on Lampman which begins that book, and provincial repression of vitality forms the image with which the book concludes, the image of new life still sleeping beneath the blanket of snow that is the Canadian savannah.

Collin's sensibility, however, was of an independent sort. Bred on the Bible and trained on the troubadours, Breton lays,

Mallarmé, and Baudelaire, his head filled with Flecker, Eliot, Hulme, and the Sitwells, he did not conceive of life or literature in any of the accepted categories. Though he was initially appointed as an instructor in Spanish, and primarily lectured in French, he never let departmental barriers confine his interests. He set up courses in subjects that interested him, taught Portuguese on his own initiative to historians who wanted to deal with Brazilian economic documents in the original, grimly built up his own library when the university's proved inadequate. He recognizes that today he would be known as a *comparatiste*, rather than as the student of a single discipline; in the twenties such categories were unknown, and to his colleagues it must have seemed as if a pheasant had suddenly alighted amidst the domestic fowl. 'The symbolist movement,' as Collin observed acidly in *The White Savannahs*, 'was only a rumour in Ontario' (*WS* 15).

Nevertheless, Collin was to teach at Western for the rest of his professional career, through his marriage in 1928 to an Ontario-born daughter of the manse, the birth of two sons, and a busy academic life culminating in election to the Royal Society of Canada in 1950. During this time his interests moved from the study of French literature to a deep preoccupation with contemporary English-Canadian poetry, through a period of withdrawal from that subject which led to an intense study of Cardinal Newman, and finally, by 1941, to a prolonged commitment to French-Canadian literature. Indeed, his major achievement after *The White Savannahs* is the commentary on French-Canadian writing which he contributed to the *University of Toronto Quarterly*'s 'Letters in Canada' for sixteen years from 1941 to 1956. He retired in 1959.

Collin's chosen form has been the scholarly essay or review. But between 1930 and 1936 he produced three books. One was an undistinguished chapbook of late Georgian lyrics, *Monserrat and Other Poems*, which Ryerson issued in 1930. The second, more considerable, was a master's thesis in French literature written for Western in 1925 and published in New York in 1933. *Clockmaker of Souls* was a study of the *fantaisiste* poet and prose-writer Paul-Jean Toulet (1867-1920). The French mentality of Collin's writing in *The White Savannahs*, partly obscured there by his heavy emphasis on myth, emerges with great clarity in his study of Toulet. The book is divided into two parts, 'life' and 'works,' and though the critical writing of the second part is appreciative, it is the 'life' which sparkles, drawing its form as it does from the *Causeries* of Saint-Beuve. Collin builds up almost novelistically a picture of the central motivating experiences of his subject's life, as he was later to do with Lampman, Pickthall, and Marie Le Franc. Toulet was a man of exotic and imperfectly disciplined personal habits, who produced works of exquisite purity in a late Parnassian mode, in which an exploration of the senses provided the bridge between two worlds viewed with glittering irony. One of Toulet's worlds was the metropolitan one of the conventional *fin de siècle* literary gallant. He inherited the other from his creole parents, who came from Mauritius. After a brief visit to that haunting island, Toulet spent much of his life in the French provinces, in Béarn and eventually at Guéthary. His literary landscape, though cosmopolitan, was thus permeated with the colonial and provincial, with the scent of tropic islands and the winds of the Pyrenees. Collin's view of him, at once sensuously appreciative and coolly discriminating, encompasses both the urgent tropical mysteries that are suggested by Toulet's drug addiction, and the contrasting formal rigour of his art. He seems to have recognized in Toulet a figure balanced like himself between conflicting kinds of experience. Between this book and his later article on Grove there is the thinnest of threads, but it is a genuine one, and it runs right through *The White Savannahs.*

His work on Toulet was still ahead, however, when Collin arrived in London in the autumn of 1923, and fell victim to the 'Europe-sickness' which dogged his first years there. At first he tried to cure himself by travelling back to Europe every summer. But slowly he began to search out the sources of creativity in his new country. Literature was only in part what people studied; primarily it was what people *did*, and his first question on encountering the Canadian academic life of the early twenties was 'where are the poets?' Searching for congenial spirits, he began to develop a circle of friends and students who wanted, as he did, to read the most recent and exciting work, which he was innocently confident was being done in Canada, as elsewhere.

Collin in fact had arrived in Canada at what from the vantage point of today seems to have been a critical juncture in the history of English-Canadian literature. E.J. Pratt's *Newfoundland Verse* had been published in 1923. The *McGill Fortnightly Review* was shortly to be founded, the early stories of Raymond Knister were being published, and Morley Callaghan would soon make his first appearance. A gathering reaction to the poetry of the past was beginning to develop, and especially to nineteenth-century Canadian poetry. As S.I. Hayakawa, then an undergraduate in Montreal, wrote with distaste: 'The bulk of poems written in Canada may be classified under four heads. They are, Victorian, Neo-Victorian, Quasi-Victorian, and Pseudo-Victorian.'[17] Though the late-colonial literary establishment was taking stock of its achievements in a series of pious and backward-looking literary histories which appeared between 1920 and 1930, a new kind of writing was already struggling for a foothold, and the Montrealers were to be its heralds.

As his Europe-sickness began to heal, Collin's sense of the innate dynamism of literature began to reassert itself. Infatuated with the art of poetry and the process of creation, he went in search of its Canadian manifestations. By the late twenties he was using every opportunity – chance personal contacts, travel to academic meetings, the summer marking of matriculation papers in Toronto – to hunt for the young moderns. Dorothy Livesay, newly graduated from university, was running a coffee shop on St George Street in Toronto. She remembers that he searched her out when a colleague mentioned her poetry to him, and how flattered she was at twenty by the keenness of his interest in the work she was just beginning to publish. It was not long before he encountered Pratt, who was to remain his friend for many years though they were temperamentally ill-assorted; Collin counted himself lucky to have survived a couple of the famous stag parties without losing too much at poker. Grove he was to meet in the mid-thirties just after *The White Savannahs* was finished. A friendship with Evelyn Albright of the university's English department led him to the work of Marjorie Pickthall, whom she had known. And most important, he discovered the *Canadian Forum*, where by 1929 the poems of Pratt and A.J.M. Smith were being joined by those of Leo Kennedy, Dorothy Livesay, and A.M. Klein. One day in 1930 or 1931 Collin walked into the office of J. Francis White, then editor of the *Forum*, and badgered him into giving him Leo Kennedy's address. When he went camping with his bride on the south shore of the St Lawrence that summer, he phoned Kennedy, and at last made contact through him with the poets he had begun to regard as the most serious and challenging Canada had so far produced.

In a forthcoming memoir, Leon Edel, once one of the 'McGill group,' describes the still-Victorian world of Montreal in the 1920s, and the birth of the little literary group that helped to 'torpedo sentimental verse and make the presence of Eliot, Pound, Joyce, James, the early writings of Bloomsbury, known at least to a small literary minority.' Edel attributes much in their rebellion to the influence of Smith and Scott:

> Both had in them a quality of discreet rebellion: they could not tolerate sham; they were verbal "activists" — but not impoverished, as the contemporary ones are, who only know four-letter words. And they didn't have to blow up buildings. They simply wrote shattering verse. They deflated. They debunked. They expressed themselves in a manner proper to their time.[18]

The rejection of Canadian poetry by this brilliant and skeptical little coterie was complete, and it was more than the normal refusal of the original young to have anything to do with their elders. It was the repudiation of a highly specialized colonial society whose fruits, harvested in the peaceful summers before the War, had been anxiously preserved as a medicine against change. The 'McGill Group' offered instead an aggressive cosmopolitanism, exemplified at its most extreme in Kennedy's statement that Canadian literature should mean 'books from Canada which will definitely be recognized by Europe and the United States.'[19] This cosmopolitanism was strangely untested, as a hidden implication in the title of their anthology, *New Provinces*, suggests; though Scott had sojourned in Oxford, he did not hear of the moderns until he returned home, and

Smith had yet to make the pilgrimage to H.J.C. Grierson at Edinburgh which was to confirm his view of the importance of the seventeenth-century metaphysical poets to a young modern. The worldliness of the McGill Group was the product more than anyone then or now is ready to admit of the very cultural assumptions it was intended to criticize. Certainly to a reader today Kennedy's remark seems more colonial in mentality than the patriotic excesses of the hacks of the Canadian Authors' Association whom he delighted to attack.

By 1930 the group of writers which had grown up around the *McGill Fortnightly Review* and its successor *The Canadian Mercury* had begun to disperse, and it is difficult to estimate the character of Collin's relationship with the remnant he was so happy to discover in Montreal, though all of them still living speak of him with warm affection. Isolated in London, he could not take a full part in literary life in Montreal or anywhere else, and it was only Leo Kennedy with whom he had any regular contact, perhaps because they shared a common interest in *The Golden Bough*. He was close enough to the group, however, to have a detailed familiarity with their poetry in manuscript before it was published, and Frank Scott records his gratitude to Collin for carefully saving papers of his, the loss of which would have made it impossible for him to include many early poems in *Overture*, published in 1945. Poring through such papers in the living rooms of his new friends, Collin recognized in the Montreal poets the energizing austerity which a taste bred on Hulme would appreciate. But his greatest rapture came when he realized that here, as among the poets he had left behind in Europe, there was present the shadowy structure of 'the Myth': of Adonis, Christ, and the blessed cycle of 'life-death-life.' Whatever the source of his response, it is clear that with unerring taste he had singled out – without idiomatic knowledge of the Canadian scene and almost entirely on the basis of unpublished poems – the most promising poets then publishing in Canada.

In the years after his marriage and his discovery of the Montreal poets, Collin plunged into a fury of creative activity. His own book of poems appeared in 1930, and in that year and the next he published three articles in *The Sewanee Review* discussing T.E. Hulme and T.S. Eliot's poetry and criticism. *Clockmaker of Souls* was being readied for the press as well. *The White Savannahs* originated in an article he published on Dorothy Livesay in the *Canadian Forum* in 1931. It was the opening essay in Canadian Writers of Today, a series which Collin suggested the editors organize. Eventually extended to cover Canadian Writers of the Past, this important group of pieces exemplified the practical consequences of the new criticism which A.J.M. Smith had already announced the new era required. Collin's article on Livesay was followed in 1932 by a long essay on Marjorie Pickthall for the newly founded *University of Toronto Quarterly*, another on Leo Kennedy for the October 1933 issue of the *Canadian Forum*, and a discussion of Archibald Lampman for the *UTQ* in 1934.

The project of making a book out of these fugitive pieces coalesced as they were being written, at the same time as Collin and Pratt were helping Leo Kennedy with the promotion of his book of verse *The Shrouding* (1933) and plans were being laid by Scott, Smith, and Pratt for the modernist anthology *New Provinces* (1936). The essay on Dorothy Livesay contains both the earliest of Collin's Canadian writing in this period, having been published in 1931, and the most recent, for it was still being revised as late as December 1935. But the book was basically completed by the spring of 1934, and in July of that year Hugh Eayrs of Macmillan sent a draft to E.J. Pratt for a preliminary reading with the admonition 'mark you, Neddie, this is important.'[20] *The White Savannahs* finally appeared in June 1936, a month or two after *New Provinces*, which had sped more rapidly through the press, and the two volumes in their spring-green paper jackets formed a companion pair in the eyes of the reviewers who were to deal with them during the winter following. No one, in the optimism of that summer of publication, with the great Book Fair of autumn 1936 to circulate news of their work, realized that these bright shoots of the new poetry might face a wintry death indeed in the bookstores, but so they did, though they were both historic volumes.

Collin did not then and does not now consider *The White Savannahs* an organic whole. He gave it a simple historical framework by placing the essays on Lampman and Pickthall first, and they form a pair in which the central problems preoccupying the critic are established through a concrete study of two poets. The chapters on Pratt and Le Franc were written as a hinge between the essays on the earlier poets and those on the moderns. The one on Marie Le Franc is of special interest despite the tenuousness, now apparent, of its subject's connection with Canadian literature as we know it. Against the failures of Lampman and Pickthall Collin exhibits a writer who in his terms does succeed, and his analysis of her achievement leads to the most nearly theoretical discussion in the book, which the chapters on Pratt and Livesay expand and demonstrate in separate ways. The related discussion of the four Montreal poets which concludes the book emerges from the passage on past and present that begins the chapter on Livesay, and moves firmly toward a completion afforded by the assumptions of the final essay on Kennedy. These interrelationships evolved from Collin's overlapping preoccupations rather than from a set of clear aims, and it is symptomatic that the significance of the title *The White Savannahs* is left to assert itself until the last page of the book, though it has been implicit from its opening words.[21]

The progress of Collin's learning as he wrote these pieces was essentially exploratory. In part it was determined by his European literary experience, by the work he had already done on Toulet, by his personal contacts with Pratt, Livesay, and Kennedy, by the pages of unpublished manuscript he was reading. In part it was determined by his real ignorance of the immediate past of Canadian literature. He admits that when writing about Lampman, he had read little of the poetry of other members of the Confederation group; the only study of a Canadian poet he had uncovered was Cappon's book on Bliss Carman. Yet he did what he could, searching old files of *The Globe* to read 'At the Mermaid Inn,' the literary column in which Lampman participated, as he was likewise to comb *The Jewish Standard* for modern poems by A.M. Klein. As a consequence of this curious mixture of strengths and limitations, *The White Savannahs* is not a principled modernist tract but an excited report by a brilliant and only partially informed mind about the current state of affairs at the creative frontier of a new literature.

Collin's method in a single essay — unsystematic by the standards of a critic like E.K. Brown — is peculiarly suited to convey this concrete, immediate reaction. His prose style mixes shrewd humour with a *fin de siècle* grace which occasionally becomes too sweet, it has the shot-silk elegance of fine talk, rather than the sturdy weave of argumentative prose. Each essay constitutes a 'field reaction' to the impress of the artist being scrutinized, and among Collin's contemporaries only the Sorbonne-trained Dorothy Livesay seems to have recognized in their seeming randomness the signs of an essentially French critical method. One or two chapters take a roughly chronological approach, but essentially each piece is structured around the implications of the image suggested in its title. Working from poem to poem, through allusions and hidden interconnections, explicating and commenting on the text and clarifying his central image, Collin recreates the internal imaginative experience of the poet under study. He is not always successful. The method will not do with Pratt; faced with that saurian weight and authority, Collin is reduced to description and quotation. And in studying Smith, he may have been mistaken in identifying the poet's central experience. Sometimes he succeeds only in calling more attention to the approach than to the poem; his manoeuvres in preparation for a study of Scott's 'Frost in Autumn' carry him rapidly over poems by Verlaine, Dowson, Yeats, Sitwell, and Eliot before he returns to his analysis, and the result is too showy. More frequently, however, the method works as it should, and we find ourselves not only possessed of the poet's psyche, but with a critique of it as well.

Yet a confident critical method is not all. Throughout *The White Savannahs* there is a struggle between the frame of the work and the essays that compose it that is caused by the buried nature of its central argument. The book is neither systematic nor comprehensive; the imperfection of the historical pattern shows this, not merely in the scanty treatment of nineteenth-century

Canadian poetry, but in the omission of important moderns like Callaghan, Knister, and Finch. The quality of the essays is erratic, and we begin to weary of the unvarying use of Collin's two simple critical terms, 'myth' and 'metaphysical.' We are justified in asking if Collin seeks to induce in us any generalizations at all. Collin put the problem in his own way —and perhaps, given his idiosyncrasies, it is the best way for us — in his review of Brown. 'What kind of experience,' he asked, 'does his criticism create for us?'[22] If we answer 'a visionary one' we will have to face yet another of the paradoxes of the book, for again and again Collin returns to one form or another of the statement that the poet facing his age is facing his only vital subject. Though Collin is symbolist-trained and entranced with form, he is passionately committed to man's life in poetry and poetry's life in man. This removes him from the abstractness and privacy of the extreme symbolist position and places him firmly in the midst of the ongoing life of poetry.

In facing his own age and his own subject Collin's buried argument considers three kinds of problem. The first is the question of the meanings which 'nature' can have for a poet. The second involves the origins of style and authority in writing. The third considers the way in which man can renew himself in the contemporary desert. All of these points of departure are established in the first two essays. In both Lampman and Pickthall Collin sees a retreat from the problem of nature. Lampman lacked the spiritual authority to set his own power over against that of the cosmic order as Darwinian thought so intimidatingly presented it to his age. His history is one of successive retreats into the summer woods. Though in his own criticism Lampman sought 'the human' as the touchstone of poetry, he was unable to give utterance to the human when he wrote himself. He had redefined nature in its most limited and least threatening form, and was content merely with 'the illustration of nature, the Mighty Mother, in finished, beautiful verse, the slow recitation of its wild flowers, as Saints' names in a litany' (*WS* 34-5). Pickthall comes closer to confronting nature as cosmic order, to articulating 'the Myth,' but she lacks strength of voice to support her strength of eye; 'such language,' writes Collin at one point, 'has no emotional core; and having none, the lines are gossamer' (*WS* 66). Though her work struggles with the experience of the natural, it persistently retreats into dream. Other factors enter into the failures of these two poets. Lampman, partly by circumstance, partly by his own will, was desperately isolated, 'like a solitary and exotic plant which finds itself removed from all its kind, he pined for literary copulation' (*WS* 33). Pickthall's case was just as tragic, for she was locked in her womanhood as in a prison. In the search for authentic utterance, Collin finds that neither poet was able to do what he regards as most important in poetry, to 'live by his own power' (*WS* 68). Pickthall — potentially a real poet by Collin's definition — is seen without illusion as an earnest, maidenly imitator of 'Fiona MacLeod' and William Morris; as for Lampman, 'he thought he was a young Greek when he was only an echo ... of Matthew Arnold' (*WS* 22).

Up to this point, *The White Savannahs* presents a winter landscape of unfulfilled promise and incomplete achievement. In 'Eve in the Bush' Collin turns to Marie Le Franc. Her work, then as now, seems to have a weaker connection with the main body of Canadian literature than that of the other writers he treats. Yet it is in his essay on her that Collin's central critical values emerge most forcibly: his sympathetic interest in myth, his urgent response to the primitive and non-rational elements in Le

Franc – 'the presence of the God' – and his ability to link these in a theory of art and a further theory of civilization. 'It is a world of wonderful and mysterious transformations that Marie Le Franc seeks,' he writes. 'Marjorie Pickthall's imagination only intensified the reality of her loss; the divinity of her dreams escaped her. Reality failed Marie Le Franc, but her subconscious makes light of that reality and passionately holds her gods' (*WS* 105-6). It is out of this that she develops that independence and authority which Collin values so highly in poetry:

> In moments of illumination she possesses that which Marjorie Pickthall contemplates in dreams; and the voice of her lyricism comes from within. She has therefore an isolated identity as a stylist which Marjorie Pickthall has not. (*WS* 106)

But the achievement of such independence is not all that Collin is looking for; he seeks also some sense of its place in human experience:

> Her primitivism is not a revolt against traditional morality so much as a psychic *procédé* for retaining something precious which has been lost. Something has been, and disappeared, and must be given another form in order to be retained. (*WS* 106)

Lampman and Pickthall, then, fall short of a creative position which Le Franc ideally exemplifies: to pass beyond the limitations of mere history into the great rhythm of life-death-life which gives shape to poetry as to all other experience.

These notions are present in a puzzled and incomplete fashion in Collin's chapter on E.J. Pratt, 'Pleiocene Heroics.' Despite perceptive moments, it is one of the least interesting chapters in the book. It seems to have escaped the critic that Pratt might represent the first example in English-Canadian literature of the ideal creative process as it is seen in Le Franc. Through some temperamental problem, Collin cannot get under the skin of Pratt, nor get beyond his parts to the sum. The combination of epic scale and conceptual power holds no aesthetic excitement for him, and although he recognizes Pratt's merits generously — the exactness of his language, his capacity to be grandiose without being gross — neither here nor in his later reviews of *The Titanic* and *Towards the Last Spike* does he show that he understands them. His best writing is done when he can enter into a poet, and he cannot enter into Pratt.

Yet Pratt remains an important turning point in the history of Canadian poetry, and one on which the rest of the book turns. Pratt's importance for Collin lies in his rejection of the effete aesthetic of his predecessors, and in the manifest strength of his grip on life. In the first part of *The White Savannahs* we had presented to us two poets who wrote about nature but could not write about the natural. In the second part we consider 'the natural' as it had been redefined by Collin's young contemporaries. 'We are again on the plane of the human; we have to adjust our eyes and minds to a real world of living and mechanical forces' (*WS* 148). It is Pratt's poetry that first signals the presence of this larger definition of 'natural' and marks the 'renewal of contact with an ethical centre' (*WS* 148).

In succeeding chapters Collin studies with the same seriousness five young poets whose work had just begun to appear. They are separated from the past of Canadian poetry by their rejection of it, by their direct preoccupation with human values, and by the historical position of their art, which draws directly on the metaphysical strain in modern poetry. Paradoxically, whereas the 'white savannahs' of provincial, nineteenth-century Ontario produced a poetry effulgently romantic, the more richly developed social scene of twentieth-century urban man leads to clarity and depersonalization in poetry, and to a concentrated and austere power. Collin attributes this development only in part to the direct influence of the metaphysical poets and their heirs, because he recognizes a similarity between the conditions of experience in the seventeenth-century and the twentieth:

> The poets after Mr Eliot have spent their leisure, not in picnics, but in city streets and homes and factories, keeping their senses open to every new manner of feeling possible to men and women of the twentieth century. ... Their poems, which reflect the spirit of our time, are alert, tense, elusive, intellectual, erudite, dogmatic, sparkling with a new and difficult beauty. (*WS* 149-50)

But though his young poets share a common milieu, Collin is at pains to recognize the independence of their confrontations with art and experience. As he writes of Smith's apprenticeship to Yeats:

> But Smith could not follow Yeats over all those strange frontiers in search of beauty without breaking his ties to his generation. The Judwalis are as nothing to him. His problem is the eternal problem confronting a sensitive mind: to find significant expression for emotions set up by contact with the sophistries, the tacit beliefs, all the impurities that make an age what it is. (*WS* 239)

It is in this spirit that he traces in Dorothy Livesay the evolution from imagist to committed socialist, observes in Scott the 'subtle contrast of ephemeral gestures with absolute principles' and celebrates Klein's radical blending of seemingly distinct heritages. In the same spirit he leaves Eliot behind as a standard when his critical tact shows that Eliot cannot lead poets forced to face the human condition in a wilderness of factories. Just as the poet must constantly remake poetry, so the critic must constantly remake criticism.

Each of the essays on the four Montreal poets has at its centre the image of a single figure who seems to embody the character of the poet being scrutinized: Scott the pilgrim, Klein the troubadour, Smith the ascetic, Kennedy the mythmaker. These images are not merely fanciful, but reveal a critical perceptiveness that in every case except one stands the test of time. Collin's troubadour image for Klein is unexpected, somehow ornate. Yet it catches the ornateness peculiar to Klein. And it is strictly accurate, for Collin knew as a student of Romance languages what Klein had discovered toying with mediaeval themes in his early verse, that the troubadours are connected with beginnings of serious literary language in the modern vernaculars which succeeded to the heritage of Latin. The theme emerges in another form in Klein's *The Second Scroll*, where the hero's quest is not only for his Uncle Melech, but also for 'the eldorado discovery: a completely underivative poet ... who was his own wealth.'[23] If we set aside the controversial instance of Kennedy, we find that Collin's critical perceptiveness fails only once, when he strains to see in Smith an essentially religious austerity where the poet may really only have been ironically playing with his poetic options.

Another level of coherence is present in the way in which each of the essays on the Montrealers — and the preliminary one on Livesay as well — revolves around the topic of rebirth. Each poet in some sense seeks a living art. The artist of the post-war period 'instead of reaping sterility in isolation ... wants to live in communion with society and draw out of its struggles, problems, and collective myths power and vision for the creation of new epics' (*WS* 172). In Scott this appears as an essentially sexual conflict between the forces of rational skepticism and the lure of an Edenic vision. In Klein it is an outright commitment to life over death drawn from the Jewish historical experience of the search for a reborn land. In Smith it is the birth – at dreadful cost – of a particular and very exacting kind of poetic intelligence. Each poet is presented in a state of discovery: Livesay finds her 'new found land,' Scott his mission to strive after justice, Klein begins to grasp that 'as a contrast to the No-Land of exile, sterile and hopeless, there is a land where the calendar is blended with the natural life of the people' (*WS* 221), Smith begins his training in spiritual adventure.

Collin's excitement is greatest in the chapter 'This Man of April,' which considers the poetry of Leo Kennedy, with which Collin felt then, and still feels, a deep rapport. It is useless to consider whether Collin's assessment of Kennedy is just or not; he and Prett shared an enthusiasm for Kennedy's poetry which is hard to understand today even when we remember that Kennedy developed little beyond the poems Collin knew and thus we lack the inescapable perspective thrust on us in considering the other poets by the distinction which all eventually achieved.

In Kennedy, Collin felt that he had found a true original, who represented the ideal condition of poetry in a new land. Kennedy, he wrote, 'feels life intensely enough to be able to nourish his own language without recourse at every turn to the old masters' (*WS* 268). Kennedy's recourse is not to the superficial manner of the old masters, but to the central myth of life-death-life which animates them both. Though Kennedy in his early verse wrote primarily about death, his chosen theme is resurrection, the re-capture of life from death. Writes Collin: 'one way of relieving the agony of life's irony, of cheating death, is to make it give forth life, to fertilize the desert, make flowers grow out of sand and rock. Wherever death possesses the land Kennedy grows tulips and hyacinths, bloodroot and trilliums; immaculate tokens of new life' (*WS* 278). In a sarcastic glance backwards at the end of the book, Collin asks, 'Why was Lampman, who leaned upon the mighty Mother, so insensible to the flow of sap in his own body? Because he disassociated Man from Nature. Anthropology, the study of man and his beliefs, could not absorb a poet whose sole delight is to get away into the bush' (*WS* 274). We may not share Collin's view of Kennedy as a Canadian Henry Vaughan, but the need for nature and humanity to renew their being, which he seeks as his ultimate value, needs no apology.

The White Savannahs draws no conclusions about poetry as it stood when Collin worked on it in the heat of his enthusiasm from 1930 to 1935, and it would perhaps be unfair to the spirit of the original to extract from its pages more in the way of synthesis than we have already done. Nevertheless, one or two points are clear. First, Collin is not a cosmopolitan in the fatigued sense in which that term is frequently used today. True, he con-fronts the 'national problem' in Canadian poetry by asserting the continuity of myth in man's literary experience no matter where it takes place. But he has at the same time the idea (descended from Madame de Staël) that a society left to itself should in the course of events produce an adequate and expressive literature. As a consequence, he asserts the independent origins of style in the poet's confrontation with his situation. Eliot is the model for his young poets not because he affords an absolute ideal, but because he is a historical condition, and where they must leave behind his leadership, Collin carefully notes the new directions they take.

Second, his conception of myth is fundamentally modernist. Unlike that of Frye, who has perhaps the most unified sensibility in contemporary criticism, Collin believes, with Mircea Eliade, that the gods created men and then departed. His interpretation of the resulting despair and fragmentation of man's world is fundamentally optimistic, however, and myth is conceived not as the continuous restatement of the way things always *are*, so much as a strategy for recapturing the way things once *were* but can never be again without this act of recreation.

Third, there is the problem of the merit of *The White Savannahs* itself. Like several others over a long generation in Canadian literature – Grove, Pratt, Birney – Collin began late: he was over forty when *The White Savannahs* was published. Yet the book is a youthful and inexperienced one. The heat of Collin's response to poetry prevents him from reflecting on his own motives, purifying his theory of inconsistencies, and reconsidering erratic judgements. Nevertheless, this sense of immediacy is the book's greatest strength. It places Collin squarely between two types of Canadian criticism. At one extreme is the work of the strictly historical critic as practised by Carl Klinck, Collin's contemporary at Western Ontario. At the other is the elaborate system-building of Northrop Frye. Between them is Collin, resolving all difficulties by the continuous practice of the critic's 'art of reading.' For such an art to flourish, the critic must have a profound belief in the life of literature. It is this that has unified Collin's whole career, and it is in this that his greatest importance lies for the still hesitant, doubting world of Canadian literature.

Despite its distinction, *The White Savannahs* was not a success. Like *New Provinces*, it sold in pathetically small numbers, and Collin and others were certainly discouraged by its failure. By the late 1930s he had turned from English-Canadian poetry to study the psychology of faith as it is represented in Cardinal Newman's *Grammar of Assent*. He continued to read and review contemporary poetry, but this writing lacks the animation of his earlier essays, for his real development was occurring in quite another area. Corresponding about Newman with A.S.P. Woodhouse, he was invited to take on the responsibility of reviewing French-Canadian letters annually for the *University of Toronto Quarterly*. This he did for sixteen years, from 1941 to 1956, and the result was his most mature and characteristic work. Collin's critical spontaneity was ideally suited to the wholesale reviewing of works as they appeared, and his yearly notices were remarkable for the freshness, wit, and ease with which he met in endless succession the novels, poems, dramas, theological works, and theses which issued from the presses of French Canada. Whereas other reviewers for 'Letters in Canada' treated specific genres, Collin dealt by himself with a whole literature, and moving more than he had ever done into the historical conditions under which literature was evolving, he attempted to set each year's account within a larger social and philosophical framework. For nearly two decades he was almost the only channel through which information about writing in French Canada flowed to literate English

Canadians. At the beginning, he was chronicling the old Quebec, with its Dominican journals and its liturgical drama. One of the last books he reviewed was on the Asbestos strike, *La grève de l'amiante*, edited by Pierre Elliott Trudeau. The temperate and utterly unprejudiced perspective he gave to the growth of the Quiet Revolution marks his yearly reports on the changing culture of Quebec as a singular document of Canadian criticism.

Since his retirement in 1959, Collin has published almost nothing, though he has continued to work. Not long ago he returned to Western to speak to a large group of students about his life in criticism. He spends his time reading broadly (Gaston Bachelard and Mircea Eliade are current favourites), and working as the spirit moves him on unfinished essays or the wide and shady garden that surrounds his small house above the Thames just outside London. His old friend Robert Weaver drops in occasionally, and a former student, Alice Munro, recently came to see him. He still reads Gabrielle Roy, and has recently begun to read Margaret Laurence. But the Canadian writings he knows best are those of his friends of the thirties. In his intellectual garden, the study of Cardinal Newman was succeeded by that of French-Canadian literature, and that in its turn by other preoccupations, of which one of the most persistent is the enigma of his old friend Frederick Philip Grove. Though his only article on Grove is hampered by its acceptance of Grove's own fiction about his life, it is nevertheless a fine and durable piece of writing, sensitive to the meaning of Grove's exile, and full of respect for the novelist's struggle with the problem of artistic form. Reading it, one finds that Collin's personal approach to his subjects has here been distilled in its purest form: an egoless, perfect sympathy that reveals more of Grove than any mere document could do. This self-effacement would remind one of the wry epigraph from Toulet which appears in *Clockmaker of Souls: 'la critique, c'est les os du gibier'* — were it not that these bones speak.

Acknowledgements

I am grateful to a number of people for help of varying kinds in preparing this introduction, but most of all to Edwin and Louise Collin for their kindness in answering importunate questions over a period of nearly a year, and to Douglas Lochhead for his patience while I assembled the answers. Useful pieces of information were provided by many others, some of whom may be surprised at my thanking them for scraps which later proved most important; among them are: James Reaney, Robert Weaver, A.J.M. Smith, Frank Scott, Dorothy Livesay, Francess Halpenny, Milton Wilson, Patricia Gallivan, Sandra Djwa, and Norman Houghton. Macmillan of Canada kindly allowed me to read letters and documents in possession of the company.

NOTES

1 Until the projected critical text of Lampman was recently undertaken, there were about 12,500 lines of his verse in print; Lampman's editor has uncovered more than 6000 which still remain unpublished. See Bruce Nesbitt, 'Lampmania: Alcyone and the Search for Merope,' in *Editing Canadian Texts* (Toronto: Hakkert 1975) 33-48.

2 A.J.M. Smith, ed., *Masks of Poetry* (Toronto: McClelland and Stewart, New Canadian Library, 1960), 60

3 Desmond Pacey, *Essays in Canadian Criticism 1938-1968* (Toronto: Ryerson Press 1969) 46

4 This review also touched on Lampman's posthumously published *At the Long Sault*, and is included here as Appendix A.

5 Appendix A 299

6 Louis Dudek and Michael Gnarowski, eds., *The Making of Modern Poetry in Canada* (Toronto: Ryerson Press 1967) 231

7 In a paper given during the panel discussion 'Literature, Politics and Society,' joint meeting of the Association of Canadian University Teachers of English and the Humanities Association of Canada, Toronto, 30 May 1974

8 Reprinted here as Appendix B. The article was originally written in English but now exists only in Guy Sylvestre's translation.

9 W.E. Collin, *The White Savannahs* (Toronto: Macmillan 1936) 113-14. Further references will appear in the text as *WS* with the relevant page number.

10 W.E. Collin, 'T.S. Eliot,' *Sewanee Review* 39 (1931) 24

11 From a posthumous publication of Hulme's, quoted by Collin, *WS* 150

12 T.E. Hulme, *Speculations* (London: Kegan Paul, Trench, Trubner, and Company 1924) 71

13 Hulme, *Speculations* 117

14 W.E. Collin, 'Beyond Humanism,' *Sewanee Review* 38 (1930) 335

15 W.E. Collin, reviewing Ronald Hambleton's *Object and Event*, in *Canadian Poetry Magazine* XVII 1 (Autumn 1953) 36

16 Appendix B 309

17 Quoted by Leo Kennedy in 'The Future of Canadian Literature,' in Dudek and Gnarowski, *The Making of Modern Poetry in Canada* 36

19 Leo Kennedy, 'The Future of Canadian Literature' 35
20 Letter of 13 July 1934 from Hugh Eayrs' secretary to E.J. Pratt. Files of Macmillan of Canada, Toronto
21 The title *The White Savannahs* emerged by some metamorphic process from a line in Francis Thompson's 'The Hound of Heaven,' 'the long savannahs of the blue.'
22 Appendix A 296
23 A.M. Klein, *The Second Scroll*, first published 1951 (Toronto: McClelland and Stewart, New Canadian Library 1961) 82

Bibliography

WRITINGS OF W.E. COLLIN

A *Books*

Clockmaker of Souls: A Study of Paul-Jean Toulet New York:
Claude Kendall 1933

Monserrat and Other Poems (Ryerson Poetry Chap book 45)
Toronto: Ryerson Press 1930

The White Savannahs Toronto: Macmillan 1936

B *Articles*

'The Active Principle in the Thought of D.H. Lawrence,' *Canadian
Bookman* XX 5 (December 1938-January 1939) 17-21

'André Langevin and the Problem of Suffering,' *Tamarack Review*
10 (Winter 1959) 77-92

'Archibald Lampman,' *University of Toronto Quarterly* IV
(1934-5) 103-20

'Arthur Smith,' *Gants du Ciel* 11 (printemps 1946) 47-60

'Beyond Humanism: Some Notes on T.E. Hulme,' *Sewanee
Review* XXXVIII (1930) 332-9

'Canadian Poetry in French,' in Alex Preminger, ed., *Princeton
Encyclopaedia of Poetry and Poetics* Princeton, NJ: Princeton
University Press 1965

'Canadian Writers Today: Dorothy Livesay,' *Canadian Forum* XII
(1931-2) 137-40

'Cardinal Newman and Recent French Thought,' *Transactions of
the Royal Society of Canada*, 3rd ser., 31 (1937) (Sec. 2, 33-43)

'Four Montreal Poets,' *Gazette Literary Supplement* University of
Western Ontario, 20 December 1935
'French-Canadian Letters' annually in *University of Toronto
Quarterly* 1941-56
'French Canadian Literature,' *Collier's Encyclopaedia* New York:
Collier 1950
'French Canadian Literature,' *Encyclopaedia Britannica* Chicago
1952
'French Canadian Literature,' *New International Year Book* New
York: Funk and Wagnalls 1956, 1957
'French Canadian Literature Enters a New Era,' *Books Abroad*
XXIX (1955) 275-9
'La Littérature canadienne-française vue par un lecteur de
l'Ontario,' *Le Devoir* 28 November 1959
'La Tragique Ironie de Frederick Philip Grove,' *Gants du Ciel* 10
(hiver 1946) 28-40
'Leo Kennedy and the Resurrection of Canadian Poetry,' *Canadian
Forum* XIV (1933-4) 24-7
'The Literary Renascence of 1934 in French Canada,' *Here and
Now* II (June 1949) 7-12
'Literature and the Holy Ghost,' *Gazette Literary Supplement*,
University of Western Ontario, 17 December 1937
'Marjorie Pickthall, 1883-1922,' *University of Toronto Quarterly*
I (1931-2) 352-80
'Newman et Ollé-Laprune,' *Gants du Ciel* 3 (mars 1944) 45-58
'Poetry,' in *Canadian Literature Today*, Canadian Broadcasting
Corporation Publications 6 Toronto: University of Toronto
Press 1938
'The Poetry of a Dissolving Society,' *Canadian Modern Language
Review* XI 2 (Winter 1955) 9-12

'Quebec's Changing Literature,' *Canadian Forum* XXXII (1951-2) 274-6

'Roger Lemelin: The Pursuit of Grandeur,' *Queen's Quarterly* LXI (1954-5) 195-212

'Symbols in English-Canadian Poetry,' *Canadian Modern Language Review* XI 1 (Fall 1954) 7-10

'T.S. Eliot,' *Sewanee Review* XXXIX (1931) 13-24

'T.S. Eliot the Critic,' *Sewanee Review* XXXIX (1931) 419-24

C *Reviews*

(Review of volumes of poetry by A.G. Bailey, R.E. Rashley, LeRoy Smith, Jr, and Ronald Hambleton), *Canadian Poetry Magazine* XVII 1 (Autumn 1953) 32-5

'The Dryad of Nanaimo: Audrey Alexandra Brown,' *New Frontier* II 3 (July-August 1937) 27-8

'Evolution of a Poet: Earth Call by Alan Creighton,' *New Frontier* I 3 (June 1936) 32

(Review of *Poems of Yehoash*, by Isidore Goldstick), *The Canadian Zionist* XX 10 (June 1953) 12

'The Power of Imagery' (review of Dorothy Livesay, *Signpost*), *Canadian Forum* 13 (1932-3) 191-2

(Review of E.J. Pratt, *The Titanic*), *New Frontier* I 1 (April 1936) 28-30

(Review of E.J. Pratt, *Towards the Last Spike*), *Canadian Poetry Magazine* XVI 1 (Autumn 1952) 29-30

(Review of Howard Sergeant, *Tradition in the Making of Modern Poetry*), *Canadian Poetry Magazine* XVI 2 (Christmas 1952) 27-8

'The Stream and the Masters,' (review of E.K. Brown, *On Canadian Poetry* and Archibald Lampman, *At the Long Sault and Other New Poems*), *University of Toronto Quarterly* XIII (1943-4) 221-9

D Translations

(Translations from the Spanish of Rafael Beltran Logrono and Pla y Beltran) *New Frontier* II 1 (May 1937) 13; and 2 (June 1937) 24

'St Denys Garneau's World of Spiritual Communion' (translation of an essay by Guy Sylvestre) *Canadian Poetry Magazine* VI 4 (March 1943) 5-11

SECONDARY SOURCES AND SELECTED REVIEWS

Anonymous (review of *Clockmaker of Souls*), *Saturday Review of Literature* X 5 (19 August 1933) 56

- 'New Canadian Poets Compared with Old' (review of *The White Savannahs*) *Montreal Gazette* 22 August 1936
- (review of *The White Savannahs*), *Toronto Daily Star* Saturday, 1 August 1936

Brown, E.K., (review of *The White Savannahs*), *University of Toronto Quarterly* 'Letters in Canada' VI (1936-7) 340-2

Calmer, Alan, 'A Hope for Canadian Poetry,' *New Frontier* II 1 (October 1936) 28-9

'Cuthbert,' 'Prof. Collin's New Book is Work of Scholarship,' *The Gazette*, University of Western Ontario, 2 October 1936

Edgar, Pelham, 'Literary Criticism in Canada,' *University of Toronto Quarterly* VIII (1938-9) 420-30

Gorman, Herbert, 'The Fastidious Literary Talents of Paul-Jean Toulet,' (review of *Clockmaker of Souls*), *New York Times Book Review* 30 July 1933

Lacroix, Benoît, op, 'W.E. Collin dans "Letters in Canada 1949",' *Revue Dominicaine* 56, t. II (décembre 1950) 268-73

Macdonald, J.F., (review of *The White Savannahs*), *Canadian Forum* XVI (1936-7) 29

Mackay, L.A., (review of *The White Savannahs*), *Saturday Night* XLI 38 (25 July 1936) 6-7

Martin, J. Burns, (review of *The White Savannahs*), *Dalhousie Review* XVI (1936-7) 534-5

Sandwell, B.K., 'Quebec's Renaissance,' *Saturday Night* LXVI 44 (7 August 1951) 6

The White Savannahs

FOR

LOUISE

ACKNOWLEDGMENT

Some of these essays have appeared, in briefer form, in *The University of Toronto Quarterly* and *The Canadian Forum*. The author desires to acknowledge his obligation to the editors for permission to use them again and at the same time to thank the poets in the latter part of the book for allowing him unqualified use of their manuscripts.

CONTENTS

NATURAL LANDSCAPE

A RCHIBALD LAMPMAN passed the years of his manhood in a small city of fifty to sixty thousand souls, the nominal capital of a geographical unit covering a tremendous area but supporting only five million people and, in a political sense, not as old as himself. Ottawa, once sneered at as "a backwoods lumber village transformed into a political cockpit," grew rapidly after Confederation. In enjoyed vice-regal prestige and some gaiety in the season, but it was still artistically and intellectually dull. A Literary and Scientific Society and a Progressive Club were in existence, and there was always the Library of Parliament; but books were hard to come by, and Lampman and his associates, who complained of the prevailing drought, kept themselves informed of the flow of ideas in the outer world by reading the great English and American monthlies and quarterlies.

In Canada, journals of that class did not exist. Several literary magazines were launched and collapsed. One, *The Week,* continued to shine during the whole of the Lampman period. For young writers, yearning for literary expression, there were few outlets. South of the frontier, in the early nineties, there were sixty-five millions of people with but half a dozen or so first-rate magazines, admission to which was, in the circumstances, difficult for a Canadian. Yet it was in the pages of *Scribner's* and the others that Canadian readers might follow the work of their compatriots. If Canadian writers crossed the border, it was not because they were renegades. If they remained in their own country, what was there but obscurity and poverty?

Canada's future was one of the "burning" questions of the time. The young writers, conscious that a Canadian literature was in gestation, felt that annexation by the United States would be tantamount to absorption and utter loss. Yet a colonial status was intolerable, and only an independent people, they believed, could produce a great literature. It came about, then, that they espoused nationalism. They were anxious to establish a local distinctiveness for Canada; and if we review the ideas and emotions current at the time we shall conclude that this distinctiveness could be neither intellectual, nor political, nor religious.

Ontario (since we are concerned with that province in particular) did not produce ideas; she imported them from Europe, where the notion of scientific law had created a new vision in all fields of study except perhaps theology, and where historical method had superseded dogmatic method as a principle of criticism.

The ideas which informed nineteenth-century philosophy were produced in Germany, and most of them, as Taine showed in his essay on Carlyle, can be reduced to a single idea: that of development. The idea was capable of innumerable applications, all in the direction of representing nature as an order of facts and man as a continuation of nature. But each country rethought the ideas it took from Germany and applied them according to its own genius.

The English race, endowed with spiritual insight as well as strong common and moral sense, adjusted itself only slowly, after spiritual tribulation, to a scientific and historical view of the world. Adverse to everything that might endanger practical morality and established dogma, the English theologians simply endeavoured to penetrate the mists of the centuries and see the New Testament characters in the dress they actually wore, as they moved and felt when they lived. The positivists, more concerned with moral and social science than their friends in France, yet with a strong determination to reject standards that were *lawless,* asserted that life and conduct would stand for them "wholly on a basis of law," and that no hypothesis, "however sublime and however affecting," would be accepted if it could not "be stated in terms of the rest of our knowledge." [1] In the eighties and nineties it was generally felt that if natural law, which had already been extended to the social and political world, could only be applied to the spiritual world, then the whole universe of phenomena would appear as one great unity. But the spiritual world seemed to be a thing for ever apart, existing on totally different principles and since intelligent men were possessed of the conviction that they could only give intellectual assent to what came under the reign of law, many in England reluctantly abandoned their early faith who would have cherished it longer if they could. It was for them, to restore certainty and faith, that Henry Drummond enunciated spiritual law in the exact terms of Biology and Physics. The difference between a Christian man and a non-Christian man, said Drummond, is the same as that between a crystal and an organism. The old faith could still be accepted when it was understood that the "difference between the Spiritual man and the Natural man is not a difference of development, but of generation"; that a man cannot rise by any natural development from "morality touched by emotion" (in Matthew Arnold's language) to "morality

---

[1] Frederick Harrison, *A Modern Symposium* in *Nineteenth Century*, vol. i, p. 625. Quoted by Henry Drummond, *Natural Law in the Spiritual World*, p. 24.

touched by Life" (in Drummond's), but by con-
version.

What was true of England was doubly true of
Ontario. The explanation of Ontario's peculiar
reaction to imported ideas is to be sought firstly in
her strictly conservative and orthodox bearing,
which kept her from examining new ideas clinic-
ally, ideas in the domain of religion and ethics
especially; and secondly in her isolation, which
made it easy for her to escape controversy and conflict. The years 1885-1900 in Ontario were re-
markably like the period in which we are now
living. Political integrity fell into the Slough of
Despond, stagnation settled upon the land, the ad-
vance of biological science raised the question of
life's purpose and value and distracted the minds
of serious people by stirring up conflict between
intellectual honesty and cherished faith.[2] Universal law and "higher criticism" combined with
social and economic problems to cast a cloud of
pessimism and depression over Ontario. How
did she face the situation? Her politicians beamed
depression out of existence in their usual buoyant

---

[2] "All nature has thus been transformed before the view of the
present generation in a manner and to an extent that has
never before been possible: and inasmuch as the change which
has taken place has taken place in the direction of naturalism,
and this to the extent of rendering the mechanical interpre-
tion of nature universal, it is no wonder if the religious mind
has suddenly awakened to a new and a terrible force in the
words of its traditional enemy—Where is now thy God?"—
G. J. Romanes, *Darwin, and After Darwin*, 1892 (Chicago,
1910, i, p. 412).

fashion. Wherever "higher criticism" showed its head she throttled it. When the monster of evolution came too near her gates she ran to her own Sir J. W. Dawson who assured her that, "as applied to man, the theory of the struggle for existence and survival of the fittest. . . . is nothing less than the basest and most horrible of superstitions" [*] or to Henry Drummond who calmed her by saying it was a popular scientific term for a process already known and accepted by her under the symbol of redemption. In her fussy excitement she feared for the nobility of man, feared that evolution wholly quenched his "higher" spiritual nature. In such a foment of impotent distraction what could be more restful to fevered body and soul than a summer in Muskoka? Ontario has never produced a great poet because none has had the audacity to look at life and think aloud.

In the minds of Lampman's generation, brought up in the practices of the Christian religion and, at the same time, exposed to positivist scientific doctrine, intellectual conviction clashed with religious faith. What did they make of that state of mind? What action, what kind of artistic expression satisfied them? At this distance it would seem that they welcomed any prophet and any kind of art that promised relief from the pain of thinking and knowing.

---

[*] *The Story of the Earth and Man*, London, 1873, p. 396.

Several well-known literary works fell into the waiting lap of people in this condition. Sir Edwin Arnold's poetic life of Gautama, *The Light of Asia,* took the English-speaking world by storm. Riding on the tide of tributes by leading American journals, the people of this continent opened their hearts to Asia's gracious effluence. *The New York Daily Tribune* grasped the author by the hand as a "genuine prophet of the soul." O. W. Holmes began his article in *The International Review* with a remarkable paragraph which dallied with the picture of two Christs, and intensified the glamour of the poem. No words could have been better calculated to win the favour of simple-hearted Christians whose faith had never been rooted in a deep knowledge of Christ. A year or two later Arnold's fictions were scathingly exposed[4] and popular curiosity directed to trustworthy records; the reception given to his writings had attained such "magnificent"[5] and provocative proportions. Ontario suffered no ill-effects from reading the book. She may have felt a quake in her Christian foundations, but it left no permanent fissure; none of her citizens became Buddhist. By 1892 Lampman could describe the author as "one of the most elaborate poetical frauds that ever

---

[4] W. C. Wilkinson, *Edwin Arnold as Poetizer and as Paganizer,* New York, 1884.
[5] Sir Edwin's word.

worked up a reputation by palaver and puffery"; [6]
—an outburst not dictated solely by a literary and
critical humour.　"There is no true sense in which
a man can say, He that hath Buddha hath Life." [7]

Fitzgerald's translation of Omar Khayyam,
which had come into the world very silently a
quarter of a century before, sprang suddenly into
favour in 1885 and maintained an immense popularity throughout the whole period.　One way to
get rid of the *Mécanique Céleste* was to dissolve
it in wine.

Sabatier's *Life of Saint Francis of Assisi,* after
creating a stir in the literary and religious circles
of Europe, crowned by the Académie Française,
sold rapidly on this continent in an English translation.　Philosophical monism prepared the
ground for the seeds of universal brotherhood.
The Franciscan spirit warmed the gentle hearts of
poets in Ontario, the Maritimes, the Eastern States,
in Mexico, who knows where? [8]

It is interesting to note that Frazer's *The Golden
Bough,* in which many poets of our time have
found intellectual relief for their wasting or
withered faith in Christianity, was published in
1890 and, although it was hailed as a "profound

---

[6] *The Globe,* Nov. 12.
[7] Henry Drummond, *op. cit.* p. 83.
[8] For instance, Lampman, Carman, Sidney Lanier, Amado
Nervo.

and epoch-making work" [9] and eulogized by scholars, it made no impression on poets in Ontario, as far as I know. Tylor and Spencer in England and Lewis H. Morgan[10] nearer home in Rochester, New York, had made Anthropology fascinating. If Ontario poets, familiar as they were with *Genesis,* read those men, they could have no religious scruples about accepting the doctrine of the unity of origin of mankind. They were more than ready to accept philosophic monism in a sublimated form redolent of wild nature and fragrant with sanctity. Wordsworth, who was still venerated, and the divine summer woods disposed their hearts to embrace trees and grass, even the distant stars. But how could they embrace Frazer, even the "epoch-making" *Golden Bough?* It was "epoch-making" inasmuch as it presented a vast repertory of illustrations from a new view-point; the dangerous view-point of religion. Frazer was the first English scholar to make clear to the minds of anthropologists the importance of vegetation gods in the history of religion. But what significance could vegetation gods have for poets who feared for Christ? I am not sure that the poets of Ontario read Frazer. If they did I imagine they were hostile; for the same reason that pious Christians were hostile to Sir Edwin Arnold. The resemblance between heathen and Christian

---

[9] Grant Allen, *Catullus: The Attis,* London, 1892.
[10] *Ancient Civilization,* New York, 1884.

practices would appear so suggestive and discon-
certing as to make them repudiate the book. To
associate it, in any form of art, with their mood
would be blasphemy. To espouse it in any way
would be to court trouble with the Inquisitors;
and no matter what temperature or blood-pres-
sure or wasting religious fever oppressed them the
last thing they would voluntarily court was trouble
of that kind. Then again, in that acquiescent state
of mind, which appears to be permanent, all they
dared to take was anodynes. Frazer would excite
them to think, and he would bring their noses too
close to the roots of their religious practices; as
Sir Edwin Arnold brought them altogether too
close to Buddha. Frazer's picture of the unity of
origin of religions was not for them.

Not only was Archibald Lampman born in
Ontario; he was born attached to an Anglican
church in Ontario. The boy who was to be the
poet, grew up under the authority of spiritual,
not natural law. But outside the walls of home,
scientists and critics were challenging that authority, and although Lampman's spiritual intuitions
were not likely to be repressed altogether, his fer-
vour was diverted from the Hebraism of his
fathers. When he was grown up and trained in
the classics, he not unnaturally fell under the
authority of Matthew Arnold, a Natural man, said
Drummond, not a Spiritual man; a Humanist.

What could a poet do? He might read what he

liked. There was no harm, if he happened to be summering in Muskoka, in feeling tired of action and swearing to live in the hollow Lotus-land "careless of mankind." No harm, coming home in the sleigh as the Northern Lights shot their midnight arrows into the sky, in murmuring the words of the Persian Omar:

> "We are no other than a moving row
> Of Magic Shadow-shapes that come and go
> Round with the Sun-illumin'd Lantern held
> In Midnight by the Master of the Show."

No harm in reading Swinburne's pagan ballads. Yet it was not possible for a poet to arise in Ontario and publicly intone hymns to the lotus, the grape, or Our Lady of Pain. What could a poet write about? There were the Greeks. Add Emerson's Oversoul; then imitations of other accepted poets like Browning, Tennyson, Keats; lastly, patriotic or historical subjects. The shocks and adjustments occasioned in the sensibility of a poet as he faced his age, the only vital subject, and one which would have given us a different and important kind of romanticism? Frankly no.

Patriotism was changing its complexion. It had meant loyalty to Britain; but in the sons of colonists, with a belief in independence, the idea of loyalty was changing into reverence for the Canadian soil. This was a departure. It opened

a way to what there is of uniqueness in the Canadian
poets of the Lampman period : not ideas, not mysticism, not dialectic, but the smell of the Canadian
soil.   Lampman spent some of his boyhood at
Lakefield.   No boy would ever forget the flavour
of that delightful countryside; it would penetrate
his body to the bone.

Lampman's sensibility was Nordic. [11] If we
are accustomed to the love-lyrics of the warm lands
of Spanish America we shall miss them here.
From beginning to end he felt the northness of
Canada.   This was one reason why he read Long-
fellow and William Morris.   Morris made Nordic epic literature known to England.   Besides,
he was a master goaded by the impulse to create
beauty; he knew colour effects not as a poet only
but as a craftsman who works with dyes.   No
matter how ineffectual Lampman thought Morris
as a poet, he should not have ignored that; since
his own "tastes and inclinations were guided by
the pure love of beauty." [12]

One is bound to write "band of blue," "garland
of lilies," "girdle as red as blood," [13] after reading
Pre-Raphaelite poetry.   But there were some
traits in that art that were beyond Lampman's
frontier.   The tone of the literature of the period

---

[11] He named Whitman "the venerable old Scald."
[12] *The Globe*, Sept. 3, 1892.
[13] "The Little Handmaiden," 1886.

was realistic, so that poetic anthropomorphism and symbolism (the symbolist movement was only a rumour in Ontario) were out of fashion. And the love passion, so conspicuously absent in Lampman's poetry, may have dried up under the austere respectability of Ontario and the polite humanism of Matthew Arnold. Yet I feel that it was a question of power as well as fashion or attitude with Lampman. For example, he changed his opinion of Shelley radically. He discovered, as others before and since, that Shelley lacked something which, for want of a better word, he called "the human." [14] Perhaps. But "the human" was lip-homage to Arnold. If he had been true to himself he would have admitted that he could not endure the blaze of Shelley's imaginative splendour any longer.

It is evident that he admired the natural and direct method in landscape painting; the direct, simple style. He caught Rossetti's idea of making sonnets for pictures; he clung to novel and pretty descriptions of place or scene. As soon as he got to Ottawa he wrote: "This is a place not of 'wind and flowers, full of sweet trees and colours of glad grass,' but a place of chill fierce colds, full of rheumatism and damned snowstorms." Such language may indicate a volte-face from Swin-

---

[14] *The Globe*, Mar. 5, 1892.

burne and dream pictures towards naturalism, but the new picture from *Poems and Ballads* stuck with him. Nine years later it comes out again, this time in its original setting: "Now it is that in the long afternoons we dream of some place of wind and flowers,

'Full of sweet trees and colour of glad grass.' "

There was something memorable, at any rate, in Swinburne. Words and the sweet sound of words! J. E. Collins, for whom Lampman had a genuine affection, wrote in 1884:[15] "About a thousand silly young men in this country repeat the following line till they grow drunken and inspired:

'And his heart grew sad, that was glad, for his
    sweet song's sake,'

and, inspired, they go away and endeavour to write in the same strain." I take it that Collins had heard the line about a thousand times and was quoting from memory:

"And men sit sad that were glad for their sweet
    song's sake,"

which is a jingle from Swinburne. [16]
    Collins was exaggerating, but there is ample

---

[15] *The Week*, Aug. 28.
[16] "In Memory of Barry Cornwall."

proof that Canadian poets were loath to try their
own wings. But that is not to be wondered at.
Youth is everywhere prone to "form itself on one
or two private admirations."[17] It cannot remain
youthful and keep our attention. One of a critic's
duties, the easiest and probably the dullest, is to
remove those "private admirations" before passing on to more delicate and more satisfying questions of style and power.

Lampman's appropriation of another poet's
pictures and the gentle merging of them into the
work in progress is very obvious in his "months."
Keats' imagery, in which he could find Pre-
Raphaelite fancy and gem-like colours applied to
a perfectly healthy landscape, was never far
behind. Especially in the earlier poems of
Among the Millet, 1888, Lampman is under his
influence. The weird narrative of "The Monk"
is charged with Keatsian atmospherics and with
fragments of realism which indicate the way
Lampman is to go. But before he attains the pure
objectivity of the sonnets, he has a lot of super-
fluous adjectives and romantic clap-trap to get rid
of: sobbings, poison, and melodramatic *bour-
soufflure*; and the old romantic hero who *goes* but
does not *know*:

> "Whither I go I know not, and the light
>   Is faint before, and rest is hard to win."

---

[17] T. S. Eliot, *The Sacred Wood*.

Of this decadent baggage Lampman will keep, even in his most realistic pictures, certain effects of vagueness: "austere" beauty; in his landscape there is often something "afar off," something "dusky," "gray"; and how often he says *many a* this and *many a* that!

There is a statement about beauty and truth which the world will not let die. If Keats had been writing prose, said Lampman, "he might have added that goodness is another synonym for both truth and beauty. The love of beauty is the love of truth and goodness." [18] That proves how securely Lampman was held by the weighty morality of Arnold. Lampman added goodness to Keats, as Arnold added virtue and character.

Nothing is gained, in a literary study, by insisting that Lampman believed in goodness, unless that belief is operative in his work; but it is within our purpose to examine how far he believed in Matthew Arnold.

Arnold's *Essays* shone in Ontario "like the Tables of the Law on Sinai." [19] Not a critic but blandly parroted the inspired formulas. Poetry was "a criticism of life" and literature must conform to Arnoldian standards of "sweetness and light." None, I venture to say, was more thoroughly penetrated by the new revelation

---

[18] *The Globe*, Aug. 6, 1892.
[19] Gautier; of Hugo's *Préface de Cromwell.*

than Lampman; to the point that old allegiances
were forsworn. All that was irksome in the
rather rigid and stern Christianity in which he
was reared made it easy for him to represent
Arnold as a saviour. "From Maine to Florida,
and back again, all America Hebraises." Arnold
was right. "Now, and for us, it is a time to
Hellenise." And those who had been overexposed
to Hebraism, that is, to a discipline which pays
"exclusive attention to the moral side of our
nature, to conscience, and to doing rather than
knowing," followed where Arnold Hellenised.
Arnold resolved Lampman's mental and moral
difficulties, showed him a way out of confusion,
led him away from natural law and that process
of development within the law which we call
Evolution; from the scientific spirit of the age,
to the quiet waters of Greek life and art which
would calm his passion and fortify his mind
against the crassness of provincial existence.
Feeling himself alone and hopelessly rut-bound
in Canada, Lampman dreamed of sailing-ships
and southern ports, of delightful adventures with
boon companions among the sunny Isles of
Greece. [20]

"It is pleasant to remember," one disciple [21]
has written, "what Matthew Arnold did for some

---

[20] "An Athenian Reverie."
[21] Philip Littell in *The New Republic*, Jan. 2, 1915.

of us, who were young in the last century's eighties. He bettered our enjoyment of books. He made us feel, rather intimately, the presence or the absence of the grand style, natural magic, fluidity and sweet ease, the lyrical cry. He gave us the illusion that we too were incapable of confusing elegance and nobleness, of mistaking *simplesse* for *simplicité*. With what confidence we used to distinguish, in those early days, between the best and the not quite so good!"

When Lampman wrote about books in "At the Mermaid Inn"—a column which he, together with D. C. Scott and W. W. Campbell, contributed weekly to *The Globe* during 1892—he wrote with just that confidence. What could be more like Arnold's manner than this estimate of Robert Bridges' poetry?

> "The essence of his verse is that unexcited pleasure in life which is the more lasting because it is contemplation, and is based upon the eternal truths and upon nothing shifty or compromising. So we get back, as it were, to the springs of poetry, and see the beauty at its source where the water is clear and flows limpidly with a small, pure stream." [22]

What confidence could be firmer than that which is based upon "the eternal truths," those

---

[22] *The Globe*, Nov. 26, 1892.

"veritates aeternae," as Descartes called them,
which have come down from Aristotle through the
Renaissance to govern our lives to this day?

He had one favourite "touchstone": he judged
writers and their work by the presence or absence
of something which he called "the human." As
we have already remarked, Arnold made it easy
for him to deny Shelley. Rossetti was not a great
poet because he had not "the masterly ability to
enter into every variety of life." Tolstoy was for
him a "wonderful man, the greatest after Shakespeare in his vast and subtle knowledge of the
human heart." "It lacks the warm human sense,"
he wrote of a book by Barry Pain. Of Stevenson's work he wrote: "It is very clear, strong,
subtle, picturesque, but it has not the fine breath
of life." What he saw in Christ was evidently
what Arnold saw, "mildness and sweet reasonable-
ness."

> "So long as the figure of Jesus Christ through
> every change in the fashion of faith shall stand
> as the representative of whatever there is in
> human nature of pure and patient, and pitiful
> and divine, the recurrence of His day shall pro-
> duce a certain tender heart-awakening in every
> one who has not become so callous as to be no
> longer human." [23]

"The human" was a convenient "touchstone"

---

[23] *Ibid.,* Dec. 24, 1892.

for a critic; but his belief in the fine breath of life and the warm human impulses, however charming a companion it may have made him, did not govern his attitude to life. He thought he was a young Greek when he was only an echo of the familiar phraseology of Matthew Arnold. The Greeks faced life: Lampman turned his back on humanity. "The greatest poets have been men of affairs before they were poets," he wrote—and went off into the woods. Arnold taught—no doubt Lampman thought it a hard saying—that poetry is a criticism of life, that a poet becomes provincial if he is not in contact with the main stream of human life. Yet, strange irony! a disciple who follows that master finds himself on the hills, out of the current of human life altogether. Arnold's lofty and expansive serenity inspired Lampman to fancy a house built upon a hill where his mind would be "blown clear as by the free wind of heaven," where he could indulge in "that unexcited pleasure in life which is the more lasting because it is contemplation, and is based upon the eternal truths and upon nothing shifty or compromising." Arnold's "high seriousness" set the tone for his dogmatic prose, for sermonizing such as this:

"It is not the brilliancy, the versatility, the fecundity or the ingenuity of a poet that makes him 'great'; it is the plane upon which his imagination moves, the height from which he looks down, the magnitude of his ideas. The largeness of vision is often accompanied by extreme simplicity in the literary faculty. . . . Arnold is not so triumphantly the poet as Tennyson, nor is he so various or so clever as Browning, but he looks from a grander height than either, his imagination has its natural abode in a diviner atmosphere." [24]

But what sensations can a poet have who attempts "to survey the extent of life" from a hilltop? What vision of an "actual moving world of delightfully animated people"? What call is there to open one's heart to "warm human impulses" in a fire-ranger's tower? Lampman himself, writing about the same time, reveals his retiring disposition. "It is only in solitude and seclusion," he writes, "that the fruit of a man's genius can be fully and wholesomely developed . . . the coarse contact with the popular touch . . . cannot be otherwise than utterly destructive of that silent and patient concentration which is the secret of the great in art." [25] There we hear the real Lampman, in words that picture the artist in his tower; a figure of speech which defines an anti-humanistic vision of life. To the æsthete,—and Lampman had something of Mari-

---

[24] *Ibid.*, June 25, 1892.
[25] *Ibid.*, July 23, 1892.

us in him,—coarse contact with the popular touch, grossness, lack of taste, the mechanical routine of city life could only bring disgust. He was not a strong man. It is probable that he could not forget his body even if he wished. Rheumatic fever, from which he suffered as a boy, must have unfitted him for the services, for active political life; it makes its victim sensitive, makes his blood tingle under the skin at the slightest provocation. The life that Arnold looked forward to, serene and equable, with time left over from the routine activities of the common day, was the kind of life most congenial to Lampman. In Lampman's case, however, the routine activities were not to be ignored, he had to live by them; they pressed in upon him with all the more rigour since he wanted to brush them aside. A greater poet, taunted by circumstances such as these, [26] might have written a masterpiece; but there is no work of Lampman's to which we can apply that word. There was some active element in his nature which made him shrink from passionate utterance; a constitutional disposition to reverie, some controlling force which had come into his life as a result of his training, some "inner check" which said no to the expression of personal experience. He hated

---

[26] T. S. Eliot is to the point in his late remarks on Arnold: "though he speaks to us of discipline, it is the discipline of culture, not the discipline of suffering." *The Use of Poetry and the Use of Criticism*, 1933.

routine. Why not mock it and create a new genre in Canadian literature? It is a testimony to his mind's poise that when other poets were writing patriotic verse he felt that the times were ripe for satire. Yet he was not the poet to write satire: because of the emotional discipline referred to and, it must be admitted, because he was not sufficiently intimate with life in the city, not sufficiently chafed by coarse contact with the popular touch. Only once did he try it: in "The City of the End of Things."

Ottawa corresponded to Arnold's definition of provincial. It could not claim to be the centre of anything except legislative authority. Ideas were stagnant there. After ten years of going and coming along its streets, seared with its gyrating and snoring, Lampman felt it to be the "end" of all things, the haunt of Philistines and Mother Earth's prodigal sons; under its walls and towers he was a slave chained to the wheels of "hideous routine."

The city and its towers, from his first acquaintance with it in 1883, had been a pretty pictorial accessory in his poems:

"Yon city glimmering in its misty shroud."

"The slender misty city towers."

"The bell-tongued city with its glorious towers."

"Cupola and pointed tower,
　　Darken into solid blue."

But in 1892 it comes into the foreground:

"Canst thou not rest, O City,
　　That liest so wide and fair;
Shall never an hour bring pity,
　　No end be found for care?"

Then in 1894 it takes on vast and infernal proportions and becomes a nightmare city builded
in the abysses of a northern Tartarus.

"And only fire and night hold sway;
The beat, the thunder and the hiss
Cease not, and change not, night nor day.
And moving at unheard commands,
The abysses and vast fires between,
Flit figures that with clanking hands
Obey a hideous routine;
They are not flesh, they are not bone,
They see not with the human eye,
And from their iron lips is blown
A dreadful and monotonous cry."

Iron towers and eternal fires might lead us to
think of Milton and Dante, but those poets offer
us no clue to the contemporaneity of the poem.
The city is an epitome of a mechanical universe
which rolls round without purpose, heart or
mind, grinding out life and death mercilessly and
for ever. Such an universe was the nightmare of

the nineteenth century; and it continues, in the form of a tentacular man-eating machine, to harass the twentieth.

Matthew Arnold gave the epithet of "physician of the iron age" to Goethe and regarded Wordsworth as a ministering angel who

> "Had fallen—on this iron age
> Of doubts, disputes, distractions, fears.
> He found us when the age had bound
> Our souls in its benumbing round;
> He spoke, and loosed our hearts in tears.
> He laid us as we lay at birth
> On the cool flowery lap of earth,
>
> *   *   *
>
>   there was shed
> On spirits that had long been dead,
> Spirits dried up and closely furl'd,
> The freshness of the early world." [27]

"The iron age" and "the benumbing round" must have been familiar words to a disciple of Arnold; yet Lampman's iron foundry or doom city from which sweetness and light have departed, where the trinity of powers are masters of men who are only ghosts of robots, stolid as idols, hissing through their iron lips as they clank the treadmill, seems to have a nearer and more definite reference. Something more spectacular than Arnold's words induced him to write the

---

[27] "Memorial Verses, April, 1850."

poem. I am persuaded that "The City of the End of Things" [28] was composed by a poet who had read "The City of Dreadful Night." [29]

The two poems differ enormously in importance and power. Thomson's masterpiece is an elaborated composition throbbing with strange depths of feeling in all its episodes; but that is not all: the tortured thoughts are quick, they have been born into visible life, have taken on flesh and bone so that they grip us. This is the result of a special kind of vision, peculiar to artists who can see their anguished thoughts as creatures alive and rampant. Baudelaire's vision was of that order; Nerval's too. A good example of this kind of imagination is the German engraver, Albrecht Dürer, to whom Baudelaire and Thomson went as students to a master. In Nerval's well-known lines,

"Ma seule *étoile* est morte,—et mon luth constellé
Porte le *Soleil noir* de la *Mélancolie*,"

the *sun* appears *black* as in Dürer's *Melencolia*. The mental anguish and cerebral overwork that wore Thomson's faculties, his *melencolia*, engendered apocalyptic visions which took on recog-

---

[28] *The Atlantic Monthly*, Mar., 1894.
[29] First appeared in 1874. In 1892 an American edition was published by Mosher at Portland, Maine.

nizable forms as they spun themselves about
motifs from Richter and Dürer; but the substance
of them was his London experience. What is
important is that Thomson's anguish engendered
drama; and his poem has power. Lampman's
poem is not drama. His city was predestined to
quick annihilation because it was not built on
earth. If any human should go near it

"His soul would shrivel and its shell
    Go rattling like an empty nut."

An excellent simile! By ridding his city of every
human trait he defeated his purpose, which was
to rouse us against "inhuman" routine. We
cannot pity "inhuman" and ghostly mechanism.
Lampman's city might have been the City of Dis;
but he saw it from a distance on a black night in
a dream. His poem needs the vivification of
illustration from actual life. It is built about
a general idea, not with living experience, and
relies, for its power and effect, upon fugitive
sensory vibrations set up by stupendous and hair-
raising adjectives. At the end a gigantic, grim
Idiot—Dürer's figure is a brooding lady, and
Thomson's an impenetrable Sphinx—sits gazing
out across the silent desolation into the lightless
north. "Where there is no vision the people shall
perish."

Lampman's disgust was more potent when it

expressed itself directly. "How utterly destitute
of all light and charm are the intellectual conditions of our people and the institutions of our
public life! How barren! How barbarous!" [30]
Like a voice among dry bones he wails: "We
believe neither in God, humanity, nor self." [31]

When the religious beliefs that had warmed
men's hearts were shaken, when there was no resounding call to great deeds of statecraft or battle,
when politics were rotten with boodling and gerry-
mandering, where could he turn for that "earthly
human heartiness" and "neighbourly warmth of
touch," that cultured companionship he hankered
for? To Chaucer's merry England? To Greece?
To poetry? Out of corruption into art's perfection; disdain sublimated into Parnassian sonnets.
Out of the city into solitude and dreams; away
from the "strange disease of modern life" to lie
in the "cool flowery lap of earth" and have "the
freshness of the early world" drizzle upon him
like manna from the skies! At this juncture he
needed no masters. Had there been no Arnold, no
Wordsworth, he still would have followed his
bent.

From his own pen we are sufficiently informed
of his disposition:

"If you are like me you will spend most of the

[30] *The Globe,* Feb. 20, 1892.
[31] Sonnet on "Chaucer."

long quiet winter evenings with your feet disposed upon an opposite chair, a long-stemmed
pipe between your teeth and some entertaining
book of travels placed comfortably against your
knee." [32]

"Out on a country road, walking in a quiet and
silent downfall of snow, when distances are
veiled and hidden and my mind seems wrapped
about and softly thrown in upon itself by a
smooth and caressing influence, I become immersed in . . . depth and intensity of reflection." [33]

Tobacco, books of travel and country walks
induced a condition of reverie which became
chronic: the word itself, or its cognates, occurs
on most of the pages of *Among the Millet* (1888),
and *Lyrics of Earth* (1895). The condition, however, changes from actual reverie to a mere use
of the word. We have the effect of it in "An
Athenian Reverie," a long poem full of the joy
of human converse, comradeship and travel. Nowhere else in Lampman do we meet with such
characterization. What are "open" eyes or "liquid" eyes compared to that merry girl's eyes
which were

"Full of the dancing fire of wanton Corinth"?

Who is speaking these lines?

---

[32] *The Globe*, Feb. 6, 1892.
[33] *Ibid.*

"To me is ever present
The outer world with its untravelled paths,
The wanderer's dream, the itch to see new things.

*   *   *

A single tie could never bind me fast,
For life, this joyous, busy, ever-changing life,
Is only dear to me with liberty,
With space of earth for feet to travel in
And space of mind for thought."

Tennyson's Ulysses? A young dreamer tethered
to a plot in Ontario, who had never been out of
it except in books and dreams, who yearned for
freedom and life, who yearned. "How full life
is, how rich!" he wrote. "How dull life is, how
poor!" he felt. No. The poise attained through
multifarious activities among men in many places
was a dream. Greek friends, the happy adventures
of Grecian youth: the daydreams of a sensitive
student. This unique poem is a poet's yearning
realized as substantial joy. One would hardly
suspect that it was composed by the same man
who wrote that "the poet attaches himself to no
dream. He endeavours to see life simply as it
is, and to estimate everything at its true value in
relation to the universal and the infinite."[84] Sublime irony! The more we read Lampman the
more we pity the fate of a cultured and sensitive
mind, the more we feel that he was cheated out

---

[84] *Ibid.*, Apr. 2, 1892.

of life. When his course was nearly run, as he
looked back over his real experiences, he wished
he had seen more of life in his twenties; more
cities and countries. Like a solitary and exotic
plant which finds itself removed from all its kind,
he pined for literary copulation. "The human
mind is like a plant, it blossoms in order to be
fertilized, and to bear seed it must come into contact with the mental dispersion of ideas." [35] It is
his continual complaint that "the Canadian lit-
térateur must depend solely upon himself and
nature. He is almost without the exhilaration of
lively and frequent literary intercourse . . . that
force and variety of stimulus which counts for so
much in the fructification of ideas." "At the
Mermaid Inn" was a rather sorry attempt to create
a centre for the dissemination of ideas. Lampman, I believe, took it very seriously. He expressed his views on books, on cremation, on the
woman question: one or two of the descriptive [36]
and critical [37] passages are compositions of a high
order. But that was not what he meant by literary
intercourse. Consequently ideas languished and
died out. Convinced, then, that he "must depend
solely upon himself and nature" he strolled off
into the country and found complete serenity only

---

[35] *Ibid.*, Aug. 27, 1892.
[36] *Ibid.*, Feb. 20; Sept. 3; Dec. 24, 1892.
[37] *Ibid.*, Sept. 10.

when the city was completely forgotten.[38] We
have D. C. Scott's testimony that "the only existence he coveted was that of a bushman, to be completely hidden in the heart of the woods." [39] He
was a *promeneur solitaire;* not haunted by hallucinations, it is true, nor yet gifted with the imaginative power of Jean-Jacques. The country was
his love, his life, his adventure. "Just to see and
hear." His definition of life is now:

> "To lie at length and watch the swallows pass,
> As blithe and restful as this quiet grass."

> "Blue, blue was the heaven above me,
> And the earth green at my feet;
> 'O Life! O Life!' I kept saying,
> And the very word seemed sweet."

Calm soul of all things. He has come to that.
Calm, peace, perfect peace amid this world of
strife. No disharmony in his mind, one with nature, not separate from it but close to it, on the
same level as nature:[40] then naturalistic art is possible. Then Lampman can proceed to the illustration of nature, the Mighty Mother, in finished,

---

[38] "And nature will seem a perfect companion to the Rousseauist
in direct proportion as she is uncontaminated by the presence
of man." Babbitt, *Rousseau and Romanticism,* p. 279.

[39] *The Poems of Archibald Lampman,* edited with a Memoir by
Duncan Campbell Scott, Toronto, 1900, p. xix.

[40] "Rousseau's great discovery was revery; and revery is just
this imaginative melting of man into outer nature." Babbitt,
op. cit., p. 269.

beautiful verse; the slow recitation of its wild
flowers, as Saints' names in a litany.[41]

In his earlier mood, and to a certain distance
out of the city, he noticed the country folk at
their labours:

"Up the steep slope the horses stamp and strain,
   Urged on by hoarse-tongued drivers—cheeks
      ablaze."

"A little old brown woman on her knees
   Searches the deep hot grass for strawberries."

Later, and farther from the city, he stops and
with deliberate purpose he forces his eye to register the details that compose the scene. He must
be careful to keep the precision of the details as
he works them up into a perfect picture. Watch
him before the canvas of a sonnet pencilled in
for a sunset. Mountains to the left, hay-carts on
the river beach, the incoming tide and the opposite
shore of the St. Lawrence are there under his eye.
He submits himself to the landscape; his identity
merges into it.

"Broad shadows fall. On all the mountain side
   The scythe-swept fields are silent. Slowly home
   By the long beach the high-piled hay carts come,
   Splashing the pale salt shallows. Over wide
   Fawn-coloured wastes of mud the slipping tide,

---

[41] *The Globe*, May 14, 1892.

Round the dun rocks and wattled fisheries,
Creeps murmuring in. And now by twos and
    threes,
O'er the slow spreading pools with clamorous
    chide,
Belated crows from strip to strip take flight.
Soon will the first star shine; yet ere the night
Reach onward to the pale-green distances,
The sun's last shaft beyond the gray sea-floor
Still dreams upon the Kamouraska shore,
And the long line of golden villages."

As a contrast to this depersonalized landscape and impersonal pentameter line, turn to look at it again through the temperament of his friend D. C. Scott who is there with him. Scott's art is not purely naturalistic, he is separated from nature by an intermediary. Here he feels the landscape through "A Psalm of Life."

"Far and faintly far to southward
    Like an hamlet dim of dreams,
White the line of Kamouraska
    In the mirage floats and gleams." [42]

When poets feel landscape through their emotions (Verlaine, for example, and the earlier Yeats), or through their intellect (some of the new poets), we no longer have naturalistic art. But to return to the pure contours of Lampman's sonnet. The objects have taken time to exist, have elongated

---

[42] "At Murray Bay." *The Week*, vol. ix, 1891-2.

themselves, as they actually do, in the penumbra; the rhymes too: "fisheries," "distances," "villages." The work has been done for its own sake, for the joy of making alive. Yet "silent," "dreams," are a poet's words, not a painter's. The work is not absolutely plastic and impassive; an intangible quietness and repose and warmth linger over the lines and colours. If we feel those things it is that Lampman has made us feel them by his personal and distinctive use of language. He makes us see things in nature directly. There he was Greek. He had a visual imagination. He wrote:

"The curly horns of ribbèd icicles."

and "frozen pine forests, plumed and bonnetted with snow." Because he felt that there was poetic power in objects seen in clear light he dispelled the mists in which commonplaces slumber complacently, he made new combinations of images, and selected words for their aura of high visibility. He was usually so close to nature that metaphors and similes, the harmonics of vision, only infrequently lured his eye: when he was in a state of reverie.

". . . a few cloud-like flakes of foliage that seem to have drifted off from its stem and to lie afloat upon the inaccessible air."

"Far up beyond its silent top my thoughts take

jocund flight, bathing themselves like birds in
the radiant ether." [43]

But the harmony and joy which he felt when he
was close to nature are communicated in passages
of almost pure description. He loved nature from
boyhood and described it as faithfully as he loved
it. But his work falls short of greatness. Had he
known life as well as he knew flowers! He pretended to judge writers by their knowledge of the
human heart and literary works by their power to
create a living world of living people. If we
come to his own work with those same criteria,
what power, what knowledge do we find? "The
human" is singularly absent. And we are forced
to conclude that his "humanism" was literary,
specious; a state of mind, not an active principle
of life. He was inclined to reverie: so was Rousseau. He was a dreamer: as Arnold his master
was before him. What work of art did he fashion
out of his dream? That is the question. Lampman disappoints us. He had, undoubtedly, intellectual resources which he never used; he never
called on them to grapple with monsters; he slid
down the path of least resistance: he sought comfort in nature. Nature was his stay. Not religion, not science, not companionship, not love, not
life, but a boy-like delight in fields and woods.
It is no use lamenting that he followed Arnold's

_____
[43] *The Globe*, Feb. 20, 1892.

example instead of profiting by it. He could do
no other. To a literary humanist with a natural
desire for woodland delights, Arnold's example
was nicely adequate. It is impossible to consider
either poet's work as a "criticism of life." All the
inferences that we can glean from Lampman's
work lead us to conclude that life in his time was
an endless whirl, people pessimistic, intellectual
conditions barbarous and, in a narrower sense, that
the men of his calling were charmed by Matthew
Arnold and the clap-trap connected with cosmic
consciousness. But the temper of the age was not
assimilated experientially into the texture of his
poetry. He criticized the barrenness and barbar-
ity and philistinism of Ontario largely by looking
away. Even to criticize is not enough. The pessimism distilled upon man by the notion that he is
subject wholly to natural law, and the terror which
possessed poets such as Thomson as they stood confronted by a vision of perpetually revolving machinery, did not scourge Lampman; because he
had an easy way of escape. Cosmic consciousness
reveals itself in his poetry as sympathy with trees
and flowers. Between himself and the world of
men there was his dream. That caused whatever
disharmony there was in his life and work. But
nothing came between him and his love of nature.
He knew where he could find joy. It was well:

for his imagination was not of that order which pictures gloomy thoughts as rampant beasts, and conjures drama out of an anguished heart.

DREAM-GARDENS

NOW we can hear the thunder of the surges. A rocky coast with long sands below; sea-poppies and wild thyme. A wild swan is perpetually calling up the spring. That piercing, indignant wail is a curlew for ever "seeking the long lift of the sea." They are not so much birds as voices that are calling us to romance and love. There are swallows, too; and moths when twilight falls. The trees give us a creepy feeling, we suspect them of having eyes and souls. If we walk among them we come upon a clearing, a sacred place where the old wisdom was practised; a Druid may just have left. A monastery has been built there. Monks and lay brothers live there now. The oak trees change to olive trees as we walk. We come to a clump of them; a long-robed figure is slowly wending his way through the copse—the radiant figure of Christ. And when the soft marine breezes blow out all the spices of Anatolian gardens we see Love crucified, and our hearts inwardly grieve, for ever stricken by that passion. Geography is no longer an exact science in this land of symbols. Is it Iona, Brittany, Palestine, Arabia? Soil, air, light, flora, fauna are insubstantial things: veils, voices, yearnings, dreams: the geography of a heart.

How did Marjorie Pickthall come to possess this land?

She was born a woman. She moved in an aura of feminine sanctions; for the people who had anything to do with her life were women: at home with her mother and aunt; as a girl at St. Mildred's Church School, Toronto; as a young lady at Bishop Strachan's School; and after—.

She read what she could devour, she swallowed all that her father could tell her about the North Country, but she did not have a direct knowledge of varieties of people which a great writer can present to us instinct with life, nor of places and events which, described by a great writer, convey an impression of definite actuality and conviction.

In the late nineties, when Marjorie was in her teens, Kipling was a best-seller, and *The Jungle Book* was at the head of all his books. Little Toomai of the Elephants has fascinated every young reader. She undoubtedly remembered "Quiquern," too, when she wrote her first stories. "How long," thought Two-Ears, the little Indian boy in Marjorie's story,[1] "shall I be dependent upon women for my very dinner?" Two-Ears and Geronimo are both Indian boys who are determined to break away from discipline and make their manhood prevail. Here we have also the first inkling of a conflict which will occupy her

---

[1] *The Globe*, Nov. 11, 1899.

later: the conflict arising when an imported religion is grafted upon a native stock. In this order
of phenomena, Yeats and Macleod are coming to
exercise an authority over her.

Nature and fortune predisposed her to vision-
ariness. She was a very shy girl. Had she been
born a decade or so later when hardly any form
of activity was regarded as the exclusive preserve
of the male she might have lost some of her reserve. But as it was, the life of adventure for
which she yearned all her days was denied her.

"To me," she wrote two years before her
death, "the trying part is being a woman at all.
I've come to the ultimate conclusion that I'm a
misfit of the worst kind. In spite of a superficial femininity—emotion with a foreknowledge
of impermanence, a daring mind with only the
tongue as an outlet, a greed for experience plus a
slavery to convention—what the deuce are you to
make of that?—as a woman? As a man, you
could go ahead and stir things up *fine*." [2]

She felt like a spirit in a tower on the brink
of a tall cliff listening perpetually "to the soft
winds full of voices, night and day, but she cannot follow, for she has no wings."

It was wanderers like Kipling and Stevenson,
and Celts like Yeats and Macleod, who sang to
her "the song of the calling voices, the mystery

[2] Lorne Pierce, *Marjorie Pickthall: A Book of Remembrance*,
Toronto, 1925.

of the road, the vision behind the unattained hill, the star of all quests that lights the following feet." [8] The loneliness which gnawed silently into her heart is epitomized in Macleod's line, which she copied in her notebook: "My heart is a lonely hunter that hunts on a lonely hill"—while her body was shut in. She loved the *Song of Songs* not only, we may divine, for its poetic beauty but, as other poets and mystics have loved it, because it passionately chanted her most secret and insatiable hunger. Whatever permanent and perhaps unsatisfactory results that hunger may have had in other ways, it found some relief by passing out of her heart into her work in the form of emotional symbols.

Her shyness of the world, her fear of the full light of day find perfect expression in a poem which she wrote at seventeen: "Dawn." Each of the stanzas of nine and eleven lines begins with a group of three lines of five feet and continues with lines of three and five feet as though she had deliberately fashioned her poem on the principles laid down in Verlaine's "Art poétique." It is a miracle of rhythmic feeling, whispering melody and intangible nuances: "opals, cobweb-strung," sea-pearls veiled in "pearlier mist," "shadows lingering dim," "half-seen beauties," "airy tremors." It is not a picture that Lampman or any human eye would see. It is not visible; it is emotion clinging to trembling things; it is the poem of trembling adolescent femininity. Quietly as a faun she comes to the forest pool "where fragrant lilies are," and where the world is "hushed, as if the miracle of morn were trembling in its dream." Every line is softened by the muted emotion in her voice exulting in the birth of beauty, tremulously clinging to the happiness she fears is doomed, pleading: O keep . . . keep all things hushed in promise "too sweet to be fulfilled."

At twenty her favourite books are the *Song of Songs, Job, The White Company, The Jungle Books,* Keats' Poems, *Heroes and Hero Worship.*[4] She had an uncanny talent for imitating the literature she liked. "Death of April"[5] runs easily along Keatsian lines:

> "sweet April lies
> With hair outstretched upon the daisied sod."

"And throstle voices, borne upon the breeze."

The language of *Solomon's Song* is her native air; her poems are, as it were, ozonized by all that Oriental and Jacobite lyricism: some owe their life to it.

At this time she is about to explore the fas-

[4] *The Canadian Bookman*, May, 1922.
[5] *Ibid.*

cinating domain of folklore which "has always
been very much to her taste." "Shortly," she
writes in 1904, "I expect to go in for a course of
Norse, Irish and American folklore." [6] Her
reading of Indian legends served as a basis for
the stories [7] she wrote for *The Globe* in 1905 and
1907.

She saw the old Celtic world through Yeats and
Macleod as, at a later date, about 1911, she saw
the Norse sagas in the "strange, gay, stiff word-
embroideries" [8] of William Morris.

Yeats' shorter poems are "simply lovely."
Some of her own lyrics at this time ("Wander-
lied," "My Father he was a Fisherman," "Duna")
are flavoured with a wistful Irish idiom.
"Armorel" [9] is "Mr. Yeats' favourite." No wonder. It is so like his "Stolen Child." There is
moonlight in it and bats, and elfin voices, and
"Gates o' dream are held ajar." There is a
garden in it, and Mary-lilies, and a white moth.
The Celtic call is there at its loudest. "The
Immortal," composed of the melancholy last ooz-
ings of pretty things that pass away yet perpetuate
"that immortal which we call Beauty," [10] is the

---

[6] *Ibid.*

[7] Based on John Maclean's *The Indians, their Manners and Cus-
toms*, Toronto, 1899.

[8] *The Canadian Courier*, Oct. 21, 1911.

[9] *Armorel*, Walter Besant's romance of the Scilly Isles, may
have suggested this title.

[10] Macleod.

Celtic, twilight counterpart to "Dawn." "Kerry" deals with purely Celtic emotions which she has not deeply felt; yet the music is as sweet as Yeats', and sweeter than Masefield's "Sorrow of My- dath."

Since Masefield's first sea-ballads are still steeped in the music of Yeats, Marjorie Pickthall easily slipped into Masefield who, she writes, "always seems nearer to me as a writer than any- one else." [11] He who wrote "D'Avalos' Prayer," "The Dead Knight," "A Wanderer's Song" and "Vagabond" would recognize his own vintage in "Pieter Marinus," "The Tramper's Grave," "The Rover" and "Ebb-Tide"; even after the piquancy has been dulled by the addition of elfin voices and the special word "fain."

Compared to Masefield's genuine pictures of the sea, the sea as Dauber would paint it, Miss Pickthall's might be hung in a nursery. Here are some:

"The tides go up and the tides go down."

"In vain the long-ridged swell shall raise the keel."

"No more our prow shall leap above the foam."

"Gods! how the keel cut seaward through the blue
When the long galley raced the roving stars!"

---

[11] Pierce.

"Out of the winds' and the waves' riot,
Out of the loud foam."

There is no storm at sea in her pictures, no
picture of men in ships battling with mountainous
waves, no glory of battle, no cry of conquest, but
soft, unexciting pictures, and the old trick of
wringing the sentiment out of "last" and "no
more." But the swing of the old sea-chanties is
there, and the interior rhymes and endings of an
old Irish song:

"And a dawn will *break* when my soul shall *wake*
    and call from the isles to me—
'Come gather me *up* like a silver *cup* from the
    heart of the swaying sea,
Like wave-washed *gold* from a wreck of *old,*
    and hide me safe in your breast.' "

The call from the isles or to the isles of the
west is mournful and clear:

"No more the winds shall call us to the west."

"Drowned like a shell in the tides that swell
    by the dim sweet isles o' the west."

"O, there I'd lie and watch the sails go shining
    to the west."

Miss Pickthall chose mariners, as she chose
certain landsmen, not to picture the sea, certainly

not to picture it buffeting men and ships, but to
show how strongly man is attached to nature. All
her heroes are bound to wild nature by a spell.
They are like that wild swan which, as he passed
the sea witch's tower,

>   "Was laggard through her loveliness."

Ole Varenne [12] had no kin but the trees and the
wild birds. He carried with him "the glamour
of wandering, the gipsy charm that draws the
heart of youth." To the author, he was one of
those "wild swans calling up the spring."

The scene shifts, names change, but the symbol
of the "wild swans" remains almost constant,
linking up her emotional being with the wild life
of Canada. It is a definitely Canadian symbol,
as in Brittany the wild duck. The "call" is perhaps most diffused in Macleod.

>   "When the day darkens,
>   When dusk grows light,
>   When the dew is falling,
>   When silence dreams. . .
>   I hear a wind
>   Calling, calling,
>   By day and by night."

is representative of his lullabies.

The Celt does not describe nature in "the

---

[12] *The Inevitable Hour, The Canadian Courier,* Sept. 7, 1907.

faithful way," as Matthew Arnold puts it, not as Lampman describes it. He looks at it with ecstacy. "(Corona) stared into the silver moonlight, doubtful a little, a little afraid." So Miss Pickthall wrote in 1910. [13] "A while ago she had known of nothing there but the frost-mist and the little wind of the high pasture, which even in summer kept the cows cool. Now it seemed she saw wings, shadowy faces, white feet that were never still." That is Celtic vision. That is the way Macleod looks at the world. Once she heard Macleod, she was in the Isles. What she saw there, saw with his eyes, hallucinated eyes, she confided to readers of "The Shadow on the Dial": [14]

> "People said that Evan was fey, and that when he went to drink at a pool *a face* looked over his shoulder *that no other christened soul could see.* 'And that is a very true thing,' said little Evan, 'for it is *white feet among the foam* and *a following shadow* in the thick of the heather, and *the eyes of beauty* in the stars at night, and *the lips of her* in the curve of a flower.' "

Celtic writers are hyper-romantic, they dissociate attributes and qualities from the objects to which they belong and look upon them as persons

---

[13] *The Globe*, Feb. 12.
[14] A page she contributed monthly to *The Canadian Courier* during 1911. The italics are mine.

—in order to create mystery. White feet, a face, eyes, lips are not flotsam, they are mermaids. Macleod commits the arch-atrocity when he says "it is Loveliness I seek, not lovely things"; as though Loveliness were a girl that one could find and pick up in one's arms. But no; she is a *white vision*, a *haunting voice,* or that *Dim face of Beauty haunting all the world.* But let us pass under the veil of "strangeness and mystery" with little Evan:

"So Evan followed the gleam and the vision of the face and the travelling feet, and he found [it] at the break of the cliff, where the grass and the bracken broke down into running sand, and a young birch tree held the earth with its roots in a close warm hollow, and underneath was an inlet of the loch and a constant crying of birds. For a pool lay in the hollow, and Evan stopped to drink, and it was as if the twilight had dropped. But it was only the blowing abroad of *her dark hair;* and again it was as if it were a twilight full of stars, but it was only the *light of her eyes* as she stooped above him. And Evan gazed into the pool, and saw that his dream had form and spirit, and was held with the vision and thought of that only, so that *he did not even think to turn round and look at the reality, but was content with the shadow* in the clear water and the stars that sank into his soul." [15]

---

[15] *The Canadian Courier,* Feb. 18, 1911.

To Evan and to all his kin, Beauty is a young
dove calling "Evan, Evan Rathmhor!"

What Miss Pickthall did in *Evan Rathmhor*
after reading Fiona Macleod, she did in *The
Gleading of Ygunde*[16] after reading William
Morris.

Macleod called some of his tales "legendary
moralities"; probably after Laforgue, whose
moralités légendaires are old tales tricked out in
a Laforgue jacket. Certainly the old tales would
have difficulty in recognizing themselves after
passing through Macleod. Marjorie Pickthall
performs the same sort of magic in *Ayvad and
Turkanna,*[17] *The Tears of Helen,*[18] and *How the
Hepaticas forgot to bloom.*[19] The second of
these stories follows a distinctively Pickthall formula, which we shall consider later. The first is
the story of Turkanna, a soulless beauty—whom
men have worshipped under many names, under
the name of Lilith and Venus and Helen too, and
Isis—created by Ayvad the Wise by laying a hand-
ful of apricot blossoms upon the snow and breathing upon it. It is the most delicately imagined
of her legendary moralities, composed with the
skill of a miniaturist, woven of "strange, gay,
stiff word-embroideries" which William Morris

[16] *Ibid.,* Oct. 21, 1911.
[17] *Ibid.,* Jan. 21, 1911.
[18] *Ibid.,* Mar. 18, 1911.
[19] *Ibid.,* Apr. 15, 1911.

had taught her, scented with the perfumes of the
East:

> "Upon her feet was fine silver work, and the
> scent of her garments was jasmine and the
> breath of the long white-budded rose that
> grows in khans' gardens. Jewels lay over her
> fine brows like the dew along a briar and veils
> thinner than the mist of spring followed her
> as she went."

"O Master," it ends, "I followed love, and I
found sorrow." Thus her soul was born, and
shone like a drop of dew or rain among the flowers.

The story resembles the passage in the *Mabin-
ogion* about the making of "Flower Aspect."
Yeats would say that Flower Aspect and Turkanna were created by the "natural magic" of the
Celt, which "is but the ancient religion of the
world, the ancient worship of nature and that
troubled ecstacy before her," the certainty that
men had that "fair women could be made out of
flowers, or rise up out of meadow fountains." To
such men life "seemed so little and so fragile and
so brief, that nothing could be more sweet in the
memory than a tale that ended in death and part-
ing, and than a wild and beautiful lamentation." [20]

In Yeats we read of a gleeman "waking forgotten longings" in the hearts of young friars by
singing of Deirdre and the Sons of Usna; [21] of a

---

[20] *Ideas of Good and Evil.*
[21] *The Secret Rose.*

girl whose wits were stolen by the people of the
Shee "while she sat crooning to herself on the
edge of the sea and dreaming of Cleena;" [22] of
foreshadowings, apparitions and transfusions of
souls. The Countess Kathleen, though she has
sworn to pray before the altar until her heart "has
grown to heaven like a tree," can still hear the
cry of the curlew and the horn of Fergus calling,
calling.

All that is in Macleod. But Macleod more
especially sought to express the conflict between
natural and spiritual religion, to give impassioned
utterance to "our deep primeval longing for
earth-kinship with every life in Nature" in revolt
against the Christian ethic of renunciation. Marjorie Pickthall may have had Macleod in mind
when she wrote of those discontented souls who
"fled to the caverns of the hills and the dark
hearthstones of an older race." She who suffered
abrasions from an ill-fitting and imposed ethic
was on the side of those discontented souls. Had
she not created a little rebel of a Geronimo?
Had she not felt that "Amun is gentle and Hathor
the mother is mild;" [28] that the Lord of Israel's
judgment against the gods of Egypt was harsh and
cruel? Had she not seen Moses on Pisgah, after
Joshua had relieved him of the burden of the

[22] *Ibid.*
[28] "A Mother in Egypt."

Lord, looking back to his boyhood days in Egypt
and thinking

"on old forgotten things—
A song within the temple-court, to her,
Isis, the Lady of Love"? [24]

When she turned to the Western World,
there was much in the circumstances attending the
Christianizing of Europe to remind her of Israel's
contact with the gods of Egypt. If the religion
of the Celts was "the ancient religion of the world,
the ancient worship of nature and that troubled
ecstacy before her," then Marjorie Pickthall
wanted nothing with fashionable gods. "Thou
hast conquered, O pale Galilean." But her Joachim and Jasper are there to testify how difficult
a thing it is to stifle the call in a young pagan's
heart. Those lads may have seen some coracles
coming ashore on Iona and, wide-eyed and open-
mouthed, watched Colomba and his monks, even
helped them to build their church and small
wattled huts about a green court. For it was in
surroundings such as these that Joachim and
Jasper listened to Christ's missionaries and
changed their names and became brothers in the
monastery.

"Over the long salt ridges
And the gold sea-poppies between,

---

[24] "Mons Angelorum."

They builded them wild-briar hedges,
A church and a cloistered green.
And when they were done with their praises,
And the tides on the Fore beat slow,
Under the white cliff-daisies
They laid them down in a row.

Porphyry, Paul, and Peter,
Jasper, and Joachim,—
Was the psaltery music sweeter
Than the throat of the thrush to him?

      *   *   *

When the wild swan's shadow passes,
When the ripe fruit falls to the sod,
When the faint moth flies in the grasses
He dreams in the hands of God." [25]

And in dreams the incessant calling monastic discipline could not stop!

"I can hear the wild swan calling
  From the marshes broad and dim,
  'Follow, follow, Joachim.'"

He is brother to that other cloistered gipsy, Jasper, who sings:

"follow, O follow the white spring home."

How many of Macleod's people have "the gloom" upon them? One often had "the light

---

[25] "In a Monastery Garden."

in his eyes . . . it was the sea he was dreaming
of." He tells of a "man who went (from Iona)
to the mainland, but could not see to plough, because the brown fallows became waves that
splashed noisily about him. The same man went
to Canada, and got work in a great warehouse;
but among the bales of merchandise he heard the
singular note of the sandpiper, and every hour
the sea-fowl confused him with their crying." [26]
The same kinship with nature is the theme of Marjorie Pickthall's "Forest Born" and "The Woods-
man in the Foundry." [27]

Anatole France took great delight in torment-
ing religious ascetics by hallucinations of that
sort. His monks have enough of the old Adam
and the old pagan religion in their blood to get
into ludicrous situations, exquisitely amusing to
Gauls and Saxons alike. The Celt, on the other
hand, is serious; he is a rebel and he is sad. Macleod's "Cathal of the Woods," when he falls in love
with the pagan girl, Ardanna, spurns the very
hymns that Colomba had taught him. "They are
idle, foolish songs . . . It is a madness, all that.

[26] *The Divine Adventure.*
[27] "My face against the old earth's face," in "The Shepherd Boy,"
may have to do with the Gaelic rite of mothering, when the
child's brow is laid against the earth to receive its kiss and
its blessing.
The very fear of Nature dying haunts "The Little Fauns to
Proserpine" and "Persephone returning to Hades"—condensed,
of course, around a different race of symbols.

See, it is gone; it is beneath my feet. I am a man now."

Perhaps it was through Macleod, who wrote on Villemarqué's *Barsas Breiz* (Ballads of Brittany), that Marjorie Pickthall was led to read Tom Taylor's translation (1865). Some of her prettiest names are in that book, Breton and French names: Jannedik (little Jean), Jeffik (little Jeff), Mathieu, Franch, Bran, Marchaid. [28] As she brooded on the Golden Legend of Saint Yves of Brittany, those pretty names became dramatis personæ, "suffretous and poor," in the old English of William Caxton, [29] "that ran to him from all sides, followed him, for all that he had was ready to their behoof as their own," even to God's need, whom he recognized in the form or likeness of a poor man holding out his hands towards the steaming soup bowl. But "St. Yves' Poor" bears the unmistakable marks of her own art: the familiar dove, heron, curlew, wild swan, the picturesque detail, the rhythmic cadences of Old Testament

---

[28] She was always scouting for pretty names. The names of the three bells in "Bega" occur in *Hereward the Wake*, chapter xx. "Turkeful" is wrongly rendered because in the American edition of the book, which she probably used, "Turketul" was printed as "Turkeful". See *The Globe*, Toronto, March 12, 1932.

There are other connections between her poems and Villemarqué's ballads. "Song" seems to be based on "The Silver Mirrors." "All the little sighing souls" in "Mary Shepherdess" are obviously "souls in pain."

[29] *The Golden Legend or Lives of the Saints as Englished by William Caxton*, Dent, London, 1900.

poetry, the trance in which is revealed a resplendent vision of Christ's face.

"A thin, white blaze of wings, a face of flame"

are images that Macleod uses to describe rapt vision. The difference is that this "face of flame" is Christ's face—which it never is in Macleod. True, in *The Wayfarer* and *The Fisher of Men* he tells how Christ comes among the islanders in the guise of a strange visitor, "ill-clad and weary, pale, too, with dreaming eyes," who "hath not where to lay his head." But Christ is still an outland god even in those stories, which are quite exceptional in Macleod's work. Much of the beauty of Celtic legend derives from the blending of Christianity with pagan nature-worship but Macleod, wholly dazzled by the glamour of the nature-worship, ignores the other. It is here, then, that Marjorie Pickthall leaves him. She is dazzled by that "face of flame," which is Christ's face.

The Celtic call, as Macleod apprehends it, is a call to Beauty. An old man of the Isles, standing looking seaward with his bonnet in his hand, said to him: "Every morning like this I take my hat off to the beauty of the world." And Marjorie Pickthall's "Prophet" has the "gloom" upon him, his head is "all misty with dreams, and his eyes on fire." Looking out over the valley he sees nature ecstatically, but—here he differs from the Celt—he sees

it as "the strength and beauty of God out-rolled in
a fiery screed." He hardly remembers that there
are common duties to be done: cattle to be fed and
watered. The secret of his rapture and his apparent indifference to his sister's affectionate services
is that he is a man who is already dead to the
world.

There is something terrifying about Prophets,
about Deborah, about Moses, about those who have
seen God. But Christ's face is all gentleness and
love. To dazzle a lover with an intenser passion,
to bring before a bridegroom's adoring eyes the
transcendant beauty of Christ's face! That is a
dramatist's or an artist's touch, a Rossetti touch,
very daring. And then what do the winds of the
dawn say? Not

"Follow, follow, Joachim"

but

"Follow, follow
Jesus Bar-Joseph, the carpenter's son." [80]

That was a tense moment in the house at Cana.
And the change in the poet is significant: she has
come through a surrender to the wonder of the
world to a surrender to the wonder of love. Yet

---

[80] "The Bridegroom of Cana."

it is a poet's surrender, not a lover's: couched in the
pretty imagery of poetry:

"Love, I am fain for thy glowing grace
 As the pool for the star, as the rain for the rill.
 Turn to me, trust to me, mirror me
 As the star in the pool, as the cloud in the sea.
 Love, I looked awhile in His face
 And was still.

 The shaft of the dawn strikes clear and sharp;
 Hush, my harp.
 Hush, my harp, for the day is begun,
 And the lifting, shimmering flight of the swallow
 Breaks in a curve on the brink of morn,
 Over the sycamores, over the corn.
 Cling to me, cleave to me, prison me
 As the mote in the flame, as the shell in the sea,
 For the winds of the dawn say, 'Follow, follow
 Jesus Bar-Joseph, the carpenter's son.' "

The symbols have not changed, but the symbolism.
Singularly enough—yet not so strange since she
usually transfers her feelings to a male—it is
the bridegroom who is speaking. Partly on that
account, and partly because the feeling is over-
done with pretty pictures, the poem expresses an
artistic but not a passionately human experience.
You remember the Rossetti poem. Mary Mag-
dalene has left a festal procession to go to the house
of Simon the Pharisee where she knows Christ
is. Her lover is pleading with her to go to the

banquet-house.   She puts him away, she puts all
her old lovers away.

"Oh loose me! See'st thou not my Bridegroom's face
    That draws me to Him?   For His feet my kiss,
    My hair, my tears He craves to-day:—and oh!
    What words can tell what other day and place
    Shall see me clasp those blood-stained feet of His?
    He needs me, calls me, loves me: let me go!"

There's no mistaking the sincerity of that cry.   Nor
the love-cry from the heart of Julian of Norwich:
"I saw Him, and sought Him, I had Him and I
wanted Him."

   At Cana the bridegroom's love is mystic love, if
you will:

> "Love, I looked awhile in His face
> And was *still*."

However it be, the call is to love now, not to beauty.
Yet Love escaped him; as actual tangible reality
eludes us in our dreams.   And that same elusiveness
pervades the very language of these love lyrics.
Place "The Gardener's Boy" beside its model and
you will see what happens to imagery when it passes
through the mind of a dreamer.

   "All day I have fed on lilied thoughts of her."

Now Solomon, if I may use that name for the author
of the *Song,* would not have sung those words.
"Feed among the lilies," yes.   But not "fed on

lilied thoughts." Instead of "she is quick," Solomon sang: "My beloved is like a roe or a young
hart."

"her garments make a lovely stir,
Like the wind going in an almond tree"

is Hebrew in its beauty and precision. So is

"When the palm shadow barred the juniper."

But "when evening grows" lacks the neat contour
of a visible image. How the sense of reality conveyed by

"She shall feed among the lilies where I am"

vaporizes when it has to wear a poetic appendage
such as

"Learning their silver names!"

The word "silver" is disastrous, and she is fond
of it. It has not one individual and inalienable
mission. It illustrates her tendency: to pass from
simile, which conveys a single and clear image, to
metaphor, which troubles the water so that the
unique and crystal impression is lost. The last
stanza leaves the model. It is visualized as drama
and ends with a splendid line because the poet felt
the emotion.
  Elsewhere she writes:

"And the *grey feet of the silence* with a *silver
dream* are shod,"

which is pure Macleod. The effect of metaphor
within metaphor is to destroy the reader's conviction that the emotion is sincere.

"Mine are the *wings of silence*
Folded in *silver sleep* before my face"

equates

"All the *glooms* were *rosed* with wings."

"Lovely things" have gone, and fragile "loveliness"
fills the air with wraiths of the departed. Such
language has no emotional core; and having none,
the lines are gossamer.

At times she surprises us, after the manner of the
Pre-Raphaelites, with an assortment of curious
details:

"I have left a basket of dates
   In the cool dark room under the vine,
Some curds set out in two little crimson plates
   And a flask of amber wine."

"Drowsing Joseph nodded near."

"You have carved Our Lady's hair in Indian
braids."

which create an impression of reality.

The metric of much of her poetry is decided by
the rhythm, the cadence of the phrase, not by her
emotion. The lines sing in her head, many of
them pretty close to the parallelism which scholars
have found to be characteristic of primitive "oral"
literature, and if we put any stock by the theories
of Marcel Jousse we may cite the following samples of the poet's most individual style:

"I have dwelt with the little fox,
      with the owl and the gerfalcon
I have made my nest."

"The thunder has been my cymbals,
And the night-wind   my sweet music."

"The great fair king that fought with us so well,
The great fair king that faced our hosts and
      fell."

And triple-termed anaphora:

"Now the sweet stream turns bitter with our tears,
Now dies the star we followed in the west,
Now are we sad and ill at ease with years,
Lord, we would rest."

Undoubtedly it is a very primitive music of lamentation. But it is hardly necessary to invoke a theory
of composition here. This metric is found where-
ever a poet has been nurtured on the Bible. A poet,
busy with biblical themes, does not ponder over

Deborah's Song, the Psalms, the Book of Job, and the prologue to the Gospel of Saint John with impunity. That is not denying the rhetorical effect of the lines, their insinuating power to move us by their plaintive, iterated sadness. But the purpose that parallelism served in oral literature can hardly be said to exist any longer, and instead of being the poet's instinctive manner of expression, her imitation simply indicates that she wished to induce the full flavour of her text. "In a Monastery Garden," for example, is an original poem because she is working with emotions she has really felt and with things she has seen; the diction is controlled, not merely reminiscent. Only at such moments does an artist live by his own power.

Concurrently with the poems we have been considering, Marjorie Pickthall was producing stories at a rapid rate. In the wake of her master-adventurers she concocted stories of men's adventures in regions more or less remote from prosaic Toronto; derivatives of a yearning to slip the noose of the conventions and set her sails for "those fair countries far away" where she could "stir things up *fine.*"

Not so far away were French Canada and the Canadian Northland, but she had a magic carpet on which she could go in search of rubber and strange Mexican gods, hover around a Japanese garden, or follow the mirage across the deserts of the East and South.

Some of her stories are marred by a too liberal
dose of the sensational, some by meretricious sentiment, some again are perfect. The most significant of them are those in which love is calling.
The dramatic force in stories of the type of *The
Voice and the Shadow, The Interlude, The Lost
Orchard* and *The Seventh Dream* is love's call to
happiness. Wild nature, woods or desert symbolize happiness; the accompanying mirage or
dream occasion disillusionment; a gun or sword
(an arrow in *The Wood-Carver's Wife*) represent
the ever-present menace of death to love. And
when love is killed?—"Pity not the dead; but
rather the living, who find earth desolate and the
ways of it strange because one face is gone from it
forever, one voice stilled, one shadow fallen."
What can a bereaved lover do? Retire to the
valley of loveliness or to a convent or fall upon a
sword, as they do apparently in Japan.

Two stories will illustrate how sorrow is caused
by mistaking the dream for the reality.

The boy François had a picture given him by a
grown-up who said it was painted near Taormina
in Sicily.

"François used to sit watching it in the twilight,
and he used to lie at night and watch it in the
moonlight . . . And he always wondered where
the stone-walled path led, and longed to go and
find out . . . There came a time, briefer than

the movement of a dream, when it seemed that
he and the picture changed places; that the
picture had the reality of life . . . And it
seemed to him that every day at sunsetting the
wind woke and cried to the hills, 'Has she
come?' . . . At length she came, slowly by the
walled path, and as she came she veiled her face
in her long hair and wept that the city was
fallen and many slain for her sake . . .

But in the dark, the dumb life that was the
life of the child felt that her hands were near,
and rent him from his place and laid him
against her lips, though he was but a poor weed;
and that she wept above him for the sake of days
that were past and men that would come no
more.   And in those tears he felt his dumb life
change and pass, and there was nothing but
the moon moving slowly across the window and
the dark picture upon the wall.

François knew that he had seen Leuce and
felt the tears of Helen.   But it was only the
dream of a child." [31]

That is subjective art as practised by a master like
Anatole France, and I feel that the dream has a
meaning.

The Seventh Dream is the story of Freeth Duncan, a young architect, whose dream made "reality
unreal and life loneliness."   On the table in his office he kept a toy garden in a carved wooden tray
containing willow trees, a pool, a gray heron and

---

[31] *The Tears of Helen.*

a clump of peonies, which some Japanese artist
had contrived out of a pint of sand, some coloured
stones and a few toy trees. Duncan would work
till he could not see and then drop into a chair
and stare at his garden. As he slept the wall went
down and he found himself inside the garden. The
little lady who is love's martyr brought a silken
bundle with her each time, containing objects
of jade, and laid it at Duncan's feet and went away.
She had not spoken, but she had given all she had
to him and, kneeling, was ready to give her life
for love, which dark reality, she knew in her
woman's heart, constantly threatened to filch from
her.

When Marjorie Pickthall brings us into a real
garden—as she often does, for a garden or orchard
or wood is a symbol of happiness—we feel that
she knows the ground intimately.

> "The oaks were furred with warm green moss
> to their very twigs, they felt alive when the hand
> was laid on them. The thorns were so silvered
> with lichen that they looked as though their
> bloom should be of frost, not flowers. The hol-
> lies were black and low to the ground, and the
> whole wood was bound together in a net of the
> bare brown stems and suckers of clematis and
> honeysuckle. It was a strange little ancient
> place, an enchanted forest in miniature." [82]

We read the passage with delight, as though we

---

[82] *Little Hearts*, Methuen, 1915.

were seeing those trees and plants with our eyes. Yet it is hard for her to keep the intimate reality. When Flaubert has directed our attention to one thing after another in a long series, he closes his paragraph with some commonplace picture which binds us securely to the earth. But, as the last words of the quotation indicate, this prose periodically breaks away from its mast and soars into the ether of an ancient enchantment. Marjorie Pickthall will strive in vain, against her own life-current, to bind her fancies to earth. She sees fairies where eyes, at best, see rainbows.

A crisis came into her life with her mother's death in 1910, when she found herself loosed from her moorings and adrift. She discontinued writing, and for a while assisted in the library of Victoria College in Toronto, then in 1912 went to stay with relatives in England. No matter where she went now she would be confronted with a world of real things. She was faced with the necessity of earning her own living, and the obvious way, since her health was not robust, was by writing. For six summers she lived in a cottage on the Wiltshire Downs and literally wrote herself to death. Her output increased to feverish heights in 1919-1920. "Just think of it," she says, "a novel, a play and sixteen stories between September and April! That's an unheard of production, you know! Simply crazy." It betokens not only a well-stored mind but a knowledge of the craft and a gift of fluent expression.

The play was *The Wood-Carver's Wife* and—we have Dr. Pierce's word for it—"in some respects it stood higher in her own estimation than almost anything else she had written." In what respects? It is a drama which aspires to poetry and it has the shortcomings of a hybrid form. We are not persuaded that Jean talked like that; that language is Marjorie Pickthall's. Although she chose for her scene a picturesque craft which flourished, and still flourishes, in Quebec, the dramatic interest is independent of the craft: it results from the clash of two passions. A wood-carver has willed to make his wood incarnate with a perfect resemblance of a human form. The ideal Mary in its perfect expression is there set up before his mind's eye. In front of him is his wife and model, Dorette, who is in love with a young nobleman and has no interest in the carving. But Jean's artistic conscience makes everything bend before its ideal.

"You are hard,"

Dorette reproaches him.

"You love your cold woods more than loveliness
Of look and touch."

And that artistic conscience retorts with the implication: "Yes, but imagine yourself elevated to a shrine prepared for you in the Church!"

"They'll see you there between the candle flames
A hundred years. The lads will worship you
And maids with innocent eyes will wonder at you.
Your beauty will lift many souls to God."

    "They will hail you mystic rose,
The tower of ivory, the golden house,
Sea-star and vase of honour."

So he taunts and martyrs Dorette till he has her sitting with her dead lover's sword across her knees looking down upon it with eyes "the barren houses of despair," like those of Mary looking down upon the dead Christ. Under his hand the cedar wood, after the ultimate gashes of his tools, becomes the ideal reality. And if Jean, the perfect craftsman, is a symbol, so are they all, all symbols. Dorette has no desire to be a wooden Madonna in a shrine. She craves a human love and, like the others we have been discussing, she has heard love's call to the forest. Her lover pleads:

    "When will you to the forest,
My dear wild dove? I saw red lilies there
Burning in sun-bleached grass, and gentians spread
Beside a little pool, less blue than he,
The great kingfisher poised on the dead bough.
Black squirrels chirred against the quarrelling jays,
There came a flight of emerald hummingbirds,
While through the wind-swayed walls of reed and
    vine
Laced the quick dragonflies. Sweet, will you
    come?"

Dorette's cry echoes the Bridegroom's at Cana:

"O Mother (Mary), hold me fast against his voice."

And the voice continues:

> "In those deep woods
> I found white flowers beside a little stream
> With three waxed petals round a core of gold.
> I would have brought them to you, but I thought
> To crown you with them there."

That were a fitting apotheosis, when Love should crown her with trilliums, white tokens of spring's bursting joy, beside a blue pool of happiness in the Canadian woods. But we are not surprised that she is afraid of the shadows in the forest, afraid of Shagonas' knife, afraid of the thought of blood. They are Aphrodite's intuitions that her Adonis will be slain in the forest, and that those white flowers will change to red anemones.

This piece of work stood high in her estimation because it is the drama of her own soul. The time-distance from the subjects is sufficient to permit her to lend them her own idiom, which is exquisitely imaged; but since they all speak as poets, the author could not be satisfied with them as real persons. In the next two or three years, according as her art progresses toward reality, which means coming into the present out of the past, to convey the illusion of reality, it will have to modify chiefly its idiom.

Before leaving England for Canada again she wrote some stanzas in which all the powers that her art commanded thronged to the surface of her lyrical being and fused into a poem of impassioned beauty: "Palome."

"Dearest of all, lean nearer, kiss me now.
*   *   *
I am Love's weakest, worthless, lost, unwise.
*   *   *
'Rise up, my love, my fair one, come away,
My love, my dove, my sister, undefiled.'
I rose, I followed, but my friend was fled."

Love, as we have seen before, merges into Christ and love's loss into His everlasting Passion.

"To-day we were with Love in Paradise.
*   *   *
Yea, it is finished, yea, it is enough.
*   *   *
Into thy hands, immortal Love."

No poem in our anthology throbs with such passionate grief sorrowing over love crucified and irretrievably lost. From those immortal accents of love and grief she could not escape.

Marjorie Pickthall spent the last two years of her life in British Columbia, a land of sunshine and romance. Her health was failing her but she managed to write some stories and began another

novel.[33] It was the beginning of her work on
purely Canadian themes, toward "the birth of Canadian legend, the making of the white man's
myth"; for she believed that, besides its other natural resources, Canada possessed abundant literature in the ore. The scene was laid in the region
of the Pacific coast and in recent times and de-
manded realistic treatment. "Upon this latest
story," says Dr. Pierce, "she fastened her highest
hopes." She felt that she could master her problem. She knew what it meant. It meant

> "*Hold it down* to curt matter-of-fact detail,
> as opposed to poetic description."

It meant

> "*Can* the fantastic." [34]

It meant denying herself the use of some of her
gifts: poetry of melodious phrasing and romantic
imagery and, to some extent, the thrill of fantastic
adventure. On the other hand, she would exercise
her gift of careful observation of nature-detail
which would serve as accessory: a gift she always
used magnificently. The demands made upon a
modern novelist include also a close knowledge of
men and women of conflicting character, so that
his art may reflect their varied feelings and

---

[33] *The Beaten Man.*
[34] Dr. Pierce; quoting from her scribbling book.

thoughts in language which they use ordinarily; their reactions in general to their environment as well as their actions in given circumstances. The Pacific coast had just enough romanesque elements in it—the virgin forest, pioneer life, "longing, sacrifice, the sense of fate," sieges and escapes, with the Orientals thrown in—to keep her imagination charged. As the plan stands, the book would have contained a fair amount of fantastic adventure, but of the finished work we cannot judge. To hold it down to matter-of-fact human reality was an almost impossible achievement for an artist of her genius, which revolted against the sovereignty of present fact and reacted to stories of "old, unhappy, far-off things."

She looked at nature, then at her own heart. Her troubled ecstacy before nature passed into the ecstacy of passion and so into the drama of frustrated love. In the sense that it bodies forth those emotions, her poetry is pure experience. For those were the emotions that wore her heart. They were her reality. Since *The Song of Solomon* is an ecstatic yearning for love as for earth's fragrant spices and most luscious fruits, it is not strange that her poetry constantly trembles with the accents of that most familiar and unexcelled love-song. Yet all that possessed her senses and mind, things in nature and what she absorbed by reading, was so thoroughly assimilated into her emotional and imaginative experience that when it passed out into her poetry it was dissociated from all legend; it was warmed and tinted when it left her pen, for her feminine heart had yearned over it and thrown around it the festoons of a poet's symbolism. Whence the delight and the pathos which we feel in her work. The power thus to transmute emotion into poetic reality was her great gift. Her imagination was as keen as her physical vision, but it could only be nourished by a great variety of experience. She possessed exquisite artistic sensibility. Had she been gifted with as resourceful a social instinct her fame and fortune would have been immense.

EVE IN THE BUSH

MONT TREMBLANT, of Indian legend, is the highest peak in the Laurentian Mountains. Emerging from its firry garment the monster raises its bald forehead three thousand feet above the shimmering waters of the lake. The country, which is speckled with lakes lying in cups or curling round the spurs of the mountains, is a favourite resort of city people and tourists in the summer, of hunters in the fall and skiers in winter. The temporary occupation by visitors and sportsmen is only one aspect of life in the hills; there is a fixed population. Settlers migrated from south of the St. Lawrence, felled timber, built shacks, sowed the clearings, grew vegetables and tobacco—apples if they could—and forced the niggard earth to nourish their numerous progeny. It is a story of courage, labour and privation. Common necessities like soap and candles were made at home. The mother baked her bread and knitted stockings, underwear and bedding against the cold and rheumatism—for the lakes bring nightly mists down upon them and the temperature is extreme. The old peasant society of the French-Canadian *habitants,* their struggle for mere existence, their tense and heroic fortitude which would inspire any regional novelist do not, however, con-

83

cern this author whose Paradise is the solitude of the
virgin forests that drape Mont Tremblant and the
lake, still unravished by man's mechanics, his
pseudo-beliefs and hypocritical manners, his purple and yellow books, his reverence for stocks,
automobiles, newspapers and cushions.   O for the
rhythm of elemental life common to wind, water
and trees!

"O for a lodge in some vast wilderness!"

Why? In what sense is she a "stricken deer"?[1]
    Marie Le Franc, who was born at Sarzeau in
Brittany on October 4, 1879, is descended from
fishermen and salt-makers of a small island in the
Gulf of Morbihan, humble people who loved to
read the books which were left in her great-
grandmother's granary by monks who fled from the
Terror to that island a century and more ago.
Between the knees of her grandmother she learned
to read the Latin words of a missal and often got
raps on her knuckles with large knitting needles
for playing with the clasps.   But her grand-father
gave her a pocket-compass which fascinated her
more than words in a book: she "looked at the
page of the sea for whole hours without any desire
to turn over."   In the early morning, at dawn, her
father used to leave the house, which clung like a
mussel to the rock, go down to his boat and push

---

[1] Cowper, "The Task."

off to sea with all the familiar tackle around him. She sees him still, continuing his ghostly voyage that will last for ever. "There was always either in reality or imagination a flock of wild ducks on the point of an island. Some days he looked as though he were returning from a distant cruise after passing his time chasing them . . . I suspect that the game gave him the illusion of crossing the seas. It enlarged his Morbihan, put a wild feather in the beak of every rock, gave to the wind a challenging cackle." [2]

The illusion she speaks of enlarged her horizon too; the flock of wild ducks is her image, her symbol of escape into the unknown. But the first twenty odd years of her life were passed on the lonely south coast of Brittany, famed for its menhirs and haunted, every rock and bay, by the souls of the dead, *les trépassés*; the same Brittany that Renan described in his lyrical prayer to the blue-eyed goddess when, moved with contrition on the Acropolis, he remembered that he "was born of barbarian parents among the good and virtuous Cimmerians who live on the shores of a sombre sea bristling with rocks, always lashed by storms." [3] The solid mass of the rocks and the geometry of the sea—circle, centre, periphery, depth and surface—permeated her being as a child and temper the fibre of all her writing. Walking over the rocks,

---

[2] *Inventaire*, Paris, 1930, p. 231.
[3] *Souvenirs d'Enfance et de Jeunesse.*

along the dune, or sailing upon the sea, the spirit
of those things entered into her.   She is possessed,
and the spirit can not be exorcised.

At eight years of age she dreamed of engaging
herself as servant to an old man with a wooden leg
because it was said that "love-apples" grew in his
garden. [4]   It was a pretty name, new to her ear,
and the fruit—or flower—round and red on a short
green bush, seen from a distance, unexplained,
mysterious, was enough to enchant an imaginative
child.

She was still a child of eight or ten when one
night—the first time she ventured alone so far from
her grandmother's where she was spending a vacation—she met on the sea-shore a young man dressed
in the white uniform of a Colonial Infantry
Officer. [5]   He was an unexpected apparition in
that neighbourhood, different from the fishermen
and shepherds whose earthy hands she would have
hated to feel upon her.   As she listened to him she
read her first love-story.   Life separated them.
The "Colonial" died at Dakar in his twenty-sixth
year: her first love, the symbol of lost love, the
symbol which shoots like an elusive shuttle in and
out of all her books.

The illusion of the wild ducks, perhaps a sentimental desire to see the colonies, prompted her,
after leaving the Normal School at Vannes, to

[4] *Inventaire*, p. 138.
[5] All this is told at length in *Enfance Celtique*, a book of
souvenirs d'enfance.

apply for a post, though without success, in a far-off French possession: Madagascar or Indo-China.

For a few years she resigned herself to teaching school, but she could not remain hawsered inescapably to Morbihan. In January 1906 she sailed for Canada without a cent, without any practical knowledge of English and without any warm clothing. It is apparent, too, that the wild duck chase was an opportunity for something else, for satisfying her desire to write. On the morning of her arrival in Montreal she placed some articles with the editor of a French journal. She reported for a newspaper for a time and realized that reporting necessitated a knowledge of English. It was a simple matter to arrange, she would exchange French lessons for English—and in what picturesque surroundings!—tobogganing down the mountain as her pupil recited the verb *glisser . . . je glisse . . . nous glissons.* Since then she has been a permanent resident of this country, occupying various teaching posts and living, part of the year near the St. Lawrence, and part in the Laurentian Mountains. As for the sentimental adventure of living in Canada, it brought about a repetition of the experience with the Colonial Infantry Officer but accompanied, this time, by different emotional complexes: the lover in this case did not die, he went north on business. The experience may be at the root of her iterated desire to shut herself up in a cenobite's cell on the top of the world, in a monastery amid the snow.

Her first poems are vibrant with disappointment, with lamentations we are accustomed to hear from poets who have loved and lost.

"Les mots que vous n'avez pas dits.
 Ah! si vos mains m'aimaient."

The words you did not speak! Who was he, this Man of the North who did not dare to love her, who hardly ventured more than to kneel before her and place his head on her knees?

"His warm heart was enclosed in a cold zone in which it beat more strongly.

He was wearing the fur coat which she did not like, which was so opulent, so brutal . . . she turned down the collar. He cast it off with the same deliberation as formerly, lowered his warm face towards this lifted face.

He was going to take her in his arms, feel this body abandon itself with such elasticity, such tenderness, such passion to his embrace.

But . . .

He sat down at her side. He lit another cigarette. He began to talk of his affairs. He had gone round the world several times since. Eve saw a succession of hotels, stations, restaurants. There were telephone calls in the air, taxi calls at the door, jazz orchestras.

There were, on shining table-cloths, costly

flowers which exhaled a stale and syrupy hot-
house odour, there were cards on green baize,
soda-water syphons, bottles of whisky. There
were two anxious shoulders stooping over a tele-
graph apparatus under a glass bell in which a
tape was unwinding, giving the latest Stock Exchange news . . .
There was an atmosphere of agitation, of
waste of effort and time, of business appointments, of excursions undertaken because of a
need of change, of feminine intrigues . . ." [6]

That is probably the best description of him.
How had they separated?

"There had been no scene. Strong characters
don't make scenes. He announced to her over
the telephone that he had just been commis-
sioned by the Government to make a tour of in-
spection of the Fur-Trading posts strung out
along the Arctic Circle. The project, which
had been under way for some time, had just been
decided upon. He hadn't spoken about it before, since he wasn't sure about it . . . But now
. . . The trip would last at least a year . . .
The sporting and adventurous side of his nature
was calling him . . . And from the point of
view of business . . ." [7]

The words he did not speak are a torture. Eve, in
the story, feels his head on her lap, and those feminine intrigues cause her pangs of jealousy. The

[6] *Grand-Louis le Revenant*, Paris, 1930, pp. 173-5.
[7] *Grand-Louis l'Innocent*, Paris, 1927, p. 108.

telephone is "still warm with a voice she has loved"; but the separation is a river between them.

Such "idées fixes" may cause neuroses in any woman, may dog any woman to write. In the Grand-Louis books they spark like fire-flies in the dark, because they are apprehended through a peculiarly ghostly medium, through Breton beliefs concerning the fate of human souls after death. Very probably the sorrow which she had to suffer consequent upon the death of two brothers in the war brought to the surface of her consciousness all that was Breton in her nature.

> "J'ai vu ton visage, mon frère,
> A travers une vitre, un soir;
> Tu t'étais levé de la guerre
> Pour venir en rêve me voir.
>
> *   *   *
>
> Tu ne pouvais me faire signe,
> Je t'interrogeais sans effroi,
> Mais quand je compris l'intersigne,
> Jusqu'au fond de mes os, j'eus froid." [3]

Intersigne, the Breton word for presentiment or omen! What happens to our beloved dead? They are still sailing their boats, continuing their quest. In Brittany, she has written,

> "they believe in ghosts. They believe in reincarnation. If a child dies, the mother gives the

---

[3] *Les Voix de Misère et d'Allegresse,* Paris, 1923.

same name to the child born after him, with
the conviction that the soul of the dead inhabits
the body of the new-born child.

In winter especially, all this land is the domain
of phantoms which float in the scarves of mist
and wind.   At nightfall, straying animals are
sacred.   They know that fishermen return to
earth clothed in the skins of animals, to expiate
their sins.   A sheep bleating in the moonlight on
a hillock near an abandoned mill is the defunct
miller who used to cheat on the sackfuls of flour
. . . And a soul in pain resides in that animal,
half-dog, half-wolf, with fiery eyes and its
tongue hanging out, that one meets at night at the
cross-roads." [9]

Those same Breton beliefs are ingrained in her
psyche; and are most potently operative, naturally,
in moments of crisis.   They inform and illuminate
the pages of her work where emotional experience
is interpreted in terms of a belief in the transfusion
of souls.

That belief is common among primitive peoples,
for whom the personal soul or spirit is "a thin un-
substantial human image, in its nature a sort of
vapour, film or shadow; the cause of life and
thought in the individual it animates." [10]   Primitive peoples believe also that the soul can leave
the body of a sleeping person and visit the regions
where the body it belongs to has been already, and

[9] *Grand-Louis l'Innocent*, pp. 105-6.
[10] E. B. Tylor, *Primitive Culture*, 1871, i, p. 387.

that a soul can leave one body and take up residence in another. What more ingenuous theories could we desire to explain the structure of *Grand-Louis l'Innocent* and *Grand-Louis le Revenant?* [11] The animistic theory of vitality, regarding the function of life as caused by the soul, has, fortified by recent theories of the subconscious, determined the style and structure of *Inventaire,* the most difficult because the most psychic of her books, the book which is herself, her subconscious, her *moi.*

One windy night of September 1924, Marie Le Franc was in a shop in Port-Navalo, Brittany, when she observed a tall fellow, a half-wit, point to a box of nails on the counter and, without speaking a word, make the shopkeeper understand that he wanted some nails. It was amusing to see him command the haughty *bourgeoise* with a nonchalant gesture. That night—she was leaving for Canada the next day—Marie Le Franc composed in her head and in all its details the story of Grand-Louis. In four or five weeks the manuscript was completed and in the hands of a Paris publisher. The silent, lanky vagabond was the figure about which some notions, held in solution, spontaneously crystallized.

---

[11] The two books named after Grand-Louis were one manuscript. The first part, *Grand-Louis l'Innocent,* described as ridiculous by its first reader, was written in October 1924 and published in Montreal in 1925. The manuscript obtained the *Prix national de Littérature,* Paris, the same year.

In the story, Eve is sitting at her table with the
sheet of paper in front of her covered with scrawls
and erasures. Outside a storm is lashing the walls
of her cottage which is particularly exposed to its
fury on the high coast of Brittany. Her fancy is
mischievous. She tries to put the black Breton
storm out of mind by picturing the white "jungle"
of snowy Canada where she has been living. She
had known a man in that country who was always
preoccupied with stocks, who 'phoned one day to
say he was leaving the city to go north on business.
The telephone is warm with his voice. But he has
gone. In this mood of reverie she is ready to welcome the apparition of a lanky fisherman at the
door. She sees in him the Man of the North come
back to her. Reading further in the story we learn
that the gaunt fellow is the dream-man, the supernatural man, the phantom-man, a reincarnation.
"Seeing him stride over the *lande,* one thought of
the Breton belief in souls in pain returning to
earth." He is the Man of the North who has returned to earth to expiate a sin. What sin? Are
the Grand-Louis books—like Nerval's *Aurélia,* for
example—to be explained as a distracted quest of
redemption? What is this mysterious sin? Is it
the sin of leaving Eve? Now that his soul inhabits
the body of a witless fisherman, can she possess it
and never let it go? "Ève, il est l'heure." [12] There

---

[12] Cf. Gérard de Nerval, *Aurélia*: "Que ce soit donc un hymen
véritable où l'époux s'abandonne en disant: 'C'est l'heure.'"

is some connection broken inside the man. He lost his memory in the war. He has to be taught his letters. Eve teaches him, feeds him, shelters him, mothers him. Kneeling he turns his child-like face to her maternal face; their supernatural glances mingle. His eyes are the eyes of a vision-ary, an *illuminé*; his head the head of a Christ with a halo around it; he is a household god; he is the eternal Man. Louis may be the Canadian, he may be Saint Guénolé of Brittany. He has many avatars. But the process of apotheosis is an illus-tration of her great need—which is to possess a soul and establish it in a glorified body so that love shall be immortal and eternal. One of her most subtle yet instinctively personal expressions describes rov-ing, an abstract idea, as though it were an immortal soul choosing man for its successive domiciles. [13]

In the second part of the story, *Grand-Louis le Revenant,* Eve and Louis are drowned. They have quit their earthly dust and passed into a spirit state, not ceasing, on that account, to hold our curiosity since they are the substance of human experience; primitive or civilized we cannot help imagining what form we take, body and soul, in the life beyond. In her treatment of Eve and Louis as spirits or souls Marie Le Franc has all the resources of Breton beliefs at her command. Two silver silhouettes visit the places where they used to live: the Breton *lande,* Montreal, the Laurentian

[13] *Hélier Fils des Bois,* p. 16.

lakes. They talk with the people they knew when they were alive—and vanish from human sight at the chapter's end. The *lande* is crowded with such ghosts. Among them is Tristan Corbière, dead many a bright year; Alain René Lesage, too, dead these three hundred years, still haunting the house which bears the plaque to his memory. What are they doing, these ghosts? We learn that they found earth too narrow for their dreams and life too short for the realization of them; they are continuing their quest in this annex of infinite possibilities. Here, on this rational plane where we live, our reason decrees that things have a beginning and an end; they have an historical moment and pass away. Yet death it cannot understand. Yeats [14] says there is a "world-wide belief that the dead dream back, for a certain time, through the more personal thoughts and deeds of life." And this visionary, Marie Le Franc, believes that we, being dead, shall journey on in quest of love through successive deaths and resurrections for ever and ever. Love shall be tracked through all his avatars, but he shall not escape.

A very pathetic passage in this second part describes a conclave of lost souls aboard a liner. *They had not met in love, they would meet in regret.* What does it matter now? It is too late! Gérard de Nerval might have been among those ghosts for his is the pathetic cry: *It is too late!*

---

[14] *The Dreaming of the Bones.*

She is lost! [15]   One of them sat down beside her, lit
a cigarette, tried to explain:

" 'Eve, you remember a certain afternoon when it
    had been raining . . . '
    'What does it matter now? '
    'And at Paris, you remember? '
    The tall ghost despairingly let his eyes weigh
    on Eve . . .
    'What does it matter now? ' "

Then he went through the old gestures, took his
watch out of the little pocket at his waist, got up
brusquely and vanished to a business appointment.
But when Eve visits again the apartment where
she used to live in Montreal, it is the old story of the
telephone.   She listens for a call, a long-distance
call.   He will never come.   Agony and a sense
of frustration overshadow her passion in a society
the watchword of which is business.   But desire
shall not fail.   Eve, with her Louis, shall continue to follow it through successive deaths and
resurrections.   And so they pass out into the white
jungle of the snow-storm.

   As we read these books we are often reminded
of Gérard de Nerval, the tragedy of whose life
was brought about by a dream love which drove
him mad.   Reincarnation, the survival of souls
and the possibility of communicating with them,
are rooted beliefs which send out strange tendrils

----

[15] *Aurélia.*

through all his stories. The death of his boyhood love did not end his ardent pursuit of her. His desire to retain Aurélia caused him to see her divine form in those of other women: in Isis, Saléma, the Queen of Sheba, and in Mary. It caused him to escape to the land of souls where it brought the ghost of his beloved visibly before his eyes. Where is the abode of souls? Nerval, like Marie Le Franc, was hallucinated by the theory of a spiritual after-life and the possible return of souls in the form they had on earth. The circumstances of his early life brought him into contact with the writings of the eighteenth-century illuminists and their doctrine of metempsychosis. Marie Le Franc, however, in order to lay hold of a doctrine which would interpret her psychic experience, had no need to go to the East or even to study illuminist literature; she had only to trust to the instincts of her race. Her best books may be regarded as surrealist fictions. Even her cult of nature is surrealist. What distinguishes her from other Rousseauists is her will to apotheosize natural man. She glorifies the Canadian Bushman.

Hélier Fils des Bois is a romance of the Bush. The people in it are masks that dramatize the author's elementalist view of wild nature and her scorn of the rational social world. She adorns Julienne with all the intellectualist graces that modern academies can bestow, in order that intellectualist theories can be dramatically eschewed. She presents Renaut in the apparel of a punctilious attaché, so that the flimsy tinsel of social etiquette can be blown to the winds.

Soon after Julienne takes to the woods, in the vicinity of Lac Tremblant, where she has decided to spend a summer after much strenuous schooling, she burns her books. As she lies stretched out in a hammock—the horizontal is the receptive plane—new impressions take possession of her. She feels that a breath of air laden with resinous odours is worth an "impression d'art." At first she did not understand the language of nature, but she discovered that it was not necessary to understand. She felt her heart beat, and that was enough. "The voluptuousness of being in contact with things with one's flesh, skin, surface, and to let one's mind sleep. That was Julienne's new experience."

As she progresses in the *vita nuova* she experiences a mystic identification with nature. "In the murmuring water she heard the eddying of her own blood." Then by logical inference, since Hélier, son of the Bush, is the embodiment of natural life, "to think of him was to tune her heart to the rhythm of the great free life." It is in moments of intuitive insight, in moments when she feels a rhythmic accord between herself and Hélier, that she is astonished how small a place Renaut occupies. That is just the point. Renaut is the common rational consciousness, busy over the multitudinous little arrangements of social existence which the author passionately spurns.

Renaut had a ready quiver of impromptu speeches, compliments and answers to questions. After a ceremony he had a short summary of the discussion to hand to newspaper men. He knew how to introduce speakers of international repute to the élite audiences of big cities. At a ball given by the Governor of the Province he appeared as a Spanish Infante of the Golden Age. On a summer evening he recited Ronsard under the trees of his garden and at night, after his social engagements, he read a page of Montaigne "for pleasure and for his health's sake, as he regularly took his shower." He had a summer cottage near to where Julienne was living and when he happened to be there they frequently spent some hours together. It was understood that Julienne would return with him to the city when her vacation was over, but as the moment approached and she was about to leave Lac Tremblant she wished to take him to the top of La Palisade. Despite her knowledge of the woods, which she got from Hélier and of which she was proud, they lost the trail, began to walk round in circles and eventually realized that they would have to pass the night in the forest. As Renaut was cutting some ferns to pile up under a dog-wood bush for a bed he accidentally cut his finger which Julienne bandaged with her handkerchief. It had begun to rain, her dress was wet and she was trembling with the extreme night cold of those mountains. Holding his hand in hers for a moment she said: "Ah! lucky there are two of us." He looked surprised and remarked sententiously:

"Whether there is one or two, the danger is the same. I see realities."

Now that *I see realities* is the epitome of the common consciousness. This man who kept his Montaigne by him as he would a mirror in which to contemplate his surface *grandeur* and recited Ronsard under the trees in his garden sees *realities,* sees them with the eye of a trained *mondain.* The author's intention is to reduce that ornament of Spanish pomp and chivalry to common dust. She attains her object by crushing Renaut when he is out of his native element and when he is most concerned with preserving his important skin.

" 'Renaut, you were asleep . . .'
'My dear girl, of course I was asleep.
There's nothing better to do . . .'

*   *   *

'Has it sleeves in it, your golf jacket?'
'Of course it has. Why do you ask? You are shivering. My conscience, what can I do? . . .
Would you like my sweater?'

*   *   *

'No, no, Renaut.'
'Ah!' he sighed, 'what a wretched business.
My head is frozen. You, you have a hat to

protect you . . . I was never so miserable, even at the war.' "

Needless to say Renaut Saint-Cyr, of tender memory, was no more. He had become a stranger to her, chiefly because he had not taken off his jacket and given it to her. A shallow man, she thought. Never had she felt herself so alone.

It was Hélier who found them. The author conspires with the forest to throw Julienne into Hélier's arms. Hélier is a husky fellow who lives by carrying supplies and mail to summer cottages and by shooting game. He knows how to build a cabin, how to manage a canoe, he knows the woods. He is indefatigable. He is the Huron definition of a man.[16] He is the uncultured mind, the antithesis of the mind that sees *realities,* the antithesis of Renaut and of Julienne as she was before coming to Lac Tremblant.

In the remarkable last chapter of the book Julienne is wading through wild berry bushes toward him ostensibly to say good-bye but attracted, as Ruth to Boaz, not knowing what God wanted with her. He was standing near his cabin, his eye

---

[16] Adario, a Huron Indian, whom a sentimental traveller held up as a model to the civilized Parisians, defined a man in precisely these terms: "First of all he must be able to travel on foot, hunt, fish, shoot an arrow or fire a gun, manage a canoe and fight. He must know the woods, be indefatigable, live on little when need be. He must be able to build cabins and canoes, do, in a word, all that a Huron does. That's what I call a man." —Baron de Lahontan, *Dialogues Curieux,* Chinard edition, Baltimore, 1931, p. 200.

steadfastly fixed on a distant object, calm and mo-
tionless like a navigator looking over the waves of
the forest. What were *realities* to him? He was a
"form of the landscape. There were rocks, trees,
sky, water, and then there was Hélier, all linked
together forming part of the same whole." But he
was most like a tree; his blood was the colour of
sap. "His immobility resembled the inertia of a
tree, which is suggestive of life"—the vertical in
contrast with the horizontal. "There he stood like
a tree that has had its branches broken off by the
storm, erect, sombre, dense, distinct." Not Pascal's
thinking reed, but a staring poplar, "cast in the
immobility of a pose." Thought is movement:
Hélier is inertia. Renaut is intentionally Ameri-
canized, he symbolizes modern social activity:
Hélier is a symbol of life, erect, undying, a concept
of eternity within the flux, a form of the World-
Spirit. "He looked into time rather than into
space": time conceived as an image of eternity, the
life of Being. Looking at the forest and at him,
Julienne could not think that either would ever
cease to be. He is obviously related to Yeats'
heroes, to Finn, for instance, of whom Yeats says:
"It is doubtful that he dies at all, and certain that
he comes again in some other shape." He is
"hardly so much an individual man, as a portion
of universal nature." [17]   Hélier "would push him-

---

[17] Introduction to Lady Gregory's *Gods and Fighting Men*,
Murray, 1904.

self into the earth like a root, he would merge with
the forest like a sprig. Death would cover him
slowly with darkness, lassitude, rest, with a humus
of peace. He would be taken into the great
rhythm, into supreme content. He would be another voice, a sigh added to others, a murmur." It
is a pagan conception of death, like Rupert Brooke's
and Mme de Noailles'; in its more animistic expression not unlike D. H. Lawrence's. "Perhaps
when he was annihilated in the bosom of the forest
it would teach him the secret of man. He would
learn from underneath, from the gods of the
lakes, to understand him. For the lakes remained cold, deep, distant from man. He would
create the spiritual link, he would weave the net of
love." Lawrence believed in the hidden mystery
of the world, he believed in the lords of the under-
world and was distressed by that feeling of aliena-
tion. Hélier, son of the Bush, was a myth, designed to answer the needs of the author. He was
"guide, boatman, spirit of the waters, god of the
forests. He was a fantastic creation of the forest,
a hero of northern legend, man-child, man-god, a
large face split with a great laugh, physical joy,
desires, appetites"; a reincarnated Pan. "Perhaps love with him was a need of the same order."
As Julienne approached, a mystic pale green light,
spread over the bushes, gave her the turning sensation or vertigo experienced by mystics in all ages.
She was in the presence of a god. A few paces

from him she realized that he could see her as
clearly as though she were naked. The forest had
power to transform her, for she had brought with
her "the pus of sick civilizations . . . the dis-
equilibrium between heart and head." Now she
could not place herself again in time. Her past
was an episode, Renaut an incident. And when
Hélier saw her, his notions of time and space
slipped from him too. What he had been staring
at was "the distant desire, the infinite aspirations
which lately had secretly mined their way into
him." Is it not a sweet name for the eternal *libido?*
Does not "the distant desire" give us the key to the
obstetrical myth which is the core of *Inventaire?*
"For the first time the forest no longer represented
contentment." For the first time he felt that he
was not self-sufficient. The great mystery was
pulsing in his body. He closed his arms around
Julienne and pressed her gently against his breast,
as once he had caressed a stricken deer.

Thus we are drawn up through all the ascending
degrees of mystic experience—to what?—to the
union of two bodies. The timelessness of Hélier,
of his surroundings and his oneness with them, and
all that smacks of a theory of being, is an elementalist's description of eternal man in the eternal garden and a means towards divesting passion of
properties which belong to the lower life of time
and space and reason. When we get beyond Montaigne we confront those instincts which souls like

Pascal and Newman wrestled with honestly but which the so-called *honnête homme* repressed because he had no true satisfaction to give them. The first principle of Marie Le Franc's inner life is a deep hunger for an abiding love, and before she can satisfy it she has to jilt the *honnête homme*, desert the ranks of reason and custom and fly beyond the pale of "censor mechanism." From the standpoint of ordinary social ethics it is preposterous for Julienne to repudiate a brilliant career with the Infante Renaut in favour of a primitive existence in the forest with Hélier. The author is content that we should feel that. It is unreasonable for a novelist to transplant a couple from Breton soil to the frozen shores of James Bay. [18] But it is a world beyond the world of rational philosophy, it is a world of wonderful and mysterious transformations that Marie Le Franc seeks. She cultivates the horizontal pose of passive receptivity, expecting sudden revelations from a non-rational plane of reality, from her subconscious.

From the first she has been seeking otherness. She has created that otherness with the aid of animism and her subconscious. Marjorie Pickthall's imagination only intensified the reality of her loss; the divinity of her dreams escaped her. Reality failed Marie Le Franc, but her subconscious makes light of that reality and passionately

---

[18] *Le Poste sur la Dune*, Paris, 1928.

holds her gods. In moments of illumination she possesses that which Marjorie Pickthall contemplates in dreams; and the voice of her lyricism comes from within. She has therefore an isolated identity as a stylist which Marjorie Pickthall has not. The business man and the attaché, two incarnations of the civilized man who failed her, are replaced by Louis and Hélier. Her primitivism is not a revolt against traditional morality so much as a psychic *procédé* for retaining something precious which has been lost. Something has been, and disappeared, and must be given another form in order to be retained. Her ethic has its *raison d'être* in a psychic need.

The new science of the subconscious gives a fashionable philosophical air to her psychic outlook on the world which resembles George Sand's only on the surface. Instead of "the chains of society," we read of "repressions." The taciturn Breton who leaves his native dune for James Bay is going to begin a life in harmony with things. "All the lyricism of a repressed nature which had lost its voice in the presence of humans would express itself in contact with things." The doctrine of repressed nature being inarticulate in the presence of humans is an application of the doctrine of the subconscious regarding the repression of instincts by the will; the inarticulateness of the ego during our conscious waking life. On the shores of James Bay the Breton will escape the repression

of the common consciousness; his instinctive life
will encounter no check.

In the speech of an author who has never lost
her childhood impressions of sailing on the Gulf
of Morbihan, the notions of liquid, surface, depth
and circle gain an added metaphorical and sym-
bolical sense when they subserve a belief in the subconscious.

"Why am I a depth below a surface?"

"He explores the successive and vague depths
of himself."

"It was necessary to descend into the interior
kingdom."

"I dive into the vast ignorance of my ancestors."

—and in that way escape the repressions of the
rational world. *Inventaire* is the story of such
dives. If Fénelon were alive and she went to
him—as she might to a psycho-analyst—he would
teach her precisely to cultivate that *instinct du fond.*
In the uncharted depths of her subconscious she
discovers her real life; she dives, however, not for
the salvation of her soul but for reasons more sub-
lunary and æsthetic. She cultivates those states
of consciousness during which her ego, her subconscious self, is given an opportunity to reveal

itself. Reality, her own truth, comes to her in
solitude and in dreams into which she enters, as into
a mysterious land, with a sensation of vertigo and
disorientation.   All those of her race have known
solitude.   When they arrive at solitude, "they take
up again their personal way of thinking."   She
herself came to Canada and discovered a vast land
of solitude, to which she chants a hymn of praise
and to which she brings her people, for there they
can establish contact with rock, water, air, and feel
the rhythm of elemental nature pulsing in their
blood.   Like a country seen in dreams, it is spa-
cious and unconfined. Night, of course, is propi-
tious to revelations of subconscious phenomena:

"We shall, night and I, be shut up in the fortress
of work."

—after the manner of Saint-Pol-Roux, another
hermit of the Breton dune, who worked when he
was asleep.

"We shall come up again to reality with our
faces wet with nocturnal waves."

She is grateful to her memory for what it retains
of nocturnal revelations.   But sometimes it lets
them slip.

"Have you brought nothing from the depths—
no visions?"

The subconscious is not altogether, in her conception, a reservoir of sleeping memories and instinctive desires but a spring, a well, a fountain of life. Even if we ignore the sex preoccupations of psycho-analysts, the fact that revelations come forth without our being able to foretell the nature of them easily accounts for the obstetric imagery often used by Marie Le Franc:

"The obscure attaches us to itself by an umbilical cord."

Délivrance, déchirures, sperme, matrice, frequent in *Inventaire,* belong to the same order of words as *ombilical.* The revelations may be apprehended as literary inspiration, which is born in the ordinary way:

"It gnaws from within out. It takes its time. Nothing will make it burst open before the time, even if we cry out that it is overwhelming us, that it is stifling us, that it is too much for us. We cannot get relief. We cannot even describe it, foretell its sex, or the colour of its eyes. There is nothing to do but wait, in one's inferiority, till the delivery." [19]

Inventaire is her *Manifeste du Surréalisme*; and André Breton's imagination would be taxed to bring forth such a dense collection of reveries

---

[19] *Inventaire,* p. 217.

crowded with so many surrealist images, "connections exquisite of distant worlds," [20] as Edward Young said of our human composition, subtle analogies hooked up over long distances of sense to try our wit:

"The cemetery prolongs the house."

"Will is a door that opens and shuts."

"The face came forward, detached from the body."

"I am in time as on a beach."

The surrealists believe in pure dictation and free association of images. André Breton, the theorist of the group, wrote in his manifesto:

"Dictation of thought, in the absence of all control by the reason, without preoccupation æsthetic or moral . . . Surrealism is founded on a belief in the superior reality of certain forms of association neglected up to now, in the omnipotence of dreams, in the disinterested play of thought." [21]

Marie Le Franc would not subscribe to Breton's definition altogether—for what is the use of writ-

---

[20] "From diff'rent natures marvellously mix'd, *Connection* exquisite of distant worlds!" . . . *Night* I.
[21] *Manifeste du Surréalisme*, Paris, 1924, p. 42.

ing if the *préoccupation esthétique* does not come first?—yet the chapter entitled "Le Plus Précieux" in *Inventaire* is a sermon on the text: "Have the audacity to transcribe everything from dictation." With the coming of morning, society exercises its authority again; day-time, during which we are the playthings of our minds and memories, is a "phenomenon of interference."[22] To cut out interference and establish ideal conditions for the continuous reception of wonderful, mystic revelations a surrealist writer would join night to night: "L'écriture est une longue nuit."[23]

The surrealist theory of spontaneous composition is revolutionary in the country of Flaubert and Corneille where everything takes place in plain daylight and with the consent of reason. But it is in perfect accord with Marie Le Franc's vision of a non-rational world. She lives in an aura of reality very different from Flaubert's. When we read of Julienne and Renaut watching the Aurora Borealis, do we wonder why the visible spectacle escapes us? It is because we are treated to so little description; the author disappears so suddenly below surface reality into the ocean of her subconscious and we do not *see*, we *feel a reaction*. Her account of French Canada, *Au Pays Canadien-Français*, is, for the same reason, of no service to tourists or the Immigration Authorities. During

---

[22] André Breton, *op. cit.*
[23] *Inventaire*, p. 206.

a trip up the Saguenay, the colossal banks of the
river left a vivid impression on her memory, but
what we have in her account of the trip is a dream
rather than a description of the gigantic walls:

> "They crush our feeble memories. They place
> their two hard bars in our soul and make it elon-
> gate itself to their measure, dress itself to their
> perpendicularity and weight. We are no longer
> in the domain of the human. We lose our voices
> and the power of expression. Our stature is re-
> duced to an infinitesimal scale. We stand
> clutching the gunwales of the boat all the time
> the trip lasts, without thinking that we might
> move, laugh, or pass a remark over our shoulder
> to a companion. I do not know who were the
> sailors on this phantom-boat. One's eyes are
> nothing more than openings through which the
> soul avidly absorbs the spectacle. We feel it
> flow into us, we store it in the depth of our being.
> We are haunted by the fear of losing a small
> portion of it. We enlarge ourselves to contain it
> all, throw ourselves forward to meet it." [24]

Three hundred years ago Samuel de Champlain
made a voyage of discovery up that identical river
and this is what he wrote:

> "Meanwhile I was able to visit certain parts
> of the river Saguenay, which is a fine river, and
> of incredible depth, as much as 150 and 200
> fathoms. Some fifty leagues from the mouth

---

[24] *Au Pays Canadien-Français,* pp. 114-5.

of the harbour, as already stated, there is a great waterfall, which descends from a considerable height and with great impetuosity. There are some islands in this river which are very barren, being nothing but rocks, covered with small spruce and heath. It is half a league wide in places, and a quarter of a league at its mouth, where there is such a strong current that at three-quarter tide running into the river, it is still running out. All the land I saw there was nothing but mountains and rocky promontories, for the most part covered with spruce and birch, a very disagreeable country on both sides of the river; in short a real wilderness uninhabited by animals and birds; for on going hunting in the places which seemed to me the most agreeable, I found only quite small birds, such as swallows, and some river birds, which come there in summer. Beyond these there are none, by reason of the excessive cold which prevails." [25]

It was not that mysterious kingdom of Saguenay which the Indians had described to a still hopeful Cartier as a new Cipango abounding in gold and silver, cloves, nutmegs and pepper but a "very barren . . . very disagreeable country." So it appeared, so it was in fact, to a colonizer. The dream of cloves, nutmegs and pepper vanished at a touch of reality and nothing remained but the unpleasant fact. Yet even a barren, useless and forbidding land can be absorbed into one's soul and issue forth

---

[25] *Les Voyages*, Book ii, 1608-12; translated by John Squair, The Champlain Society, Toronto, 1925.

again metamorphosed into a memorable picture of psychic experience; for the passenger who is æsthetic rather than practical the landscape is interesting and valuable for itself, it has self-value. Champlain was an explorer, a navigator in space and time; soundings and facts in a world of sense were of first importance to him. His mind was a surface mind; his prose, a report of findings. Now the excursion up the Saguenay was more than a journey of exploration for Marie Le Franc. The vision became a prodigious power that overcame all resistance. The monster took her by force. She gloried in her surrender. There is nothing of that experience in Champlain. Only the elementary functions of his mind come into play: his words are rectilinear, units of one dimensional power only. In terms borrowed from Claudel and Bremond,[26] Champlain was subservient to his *Animus,* as Marie Le Franc is to her *Anima*: her deep, psychic self. All her writing, however, is not homogeneous. To be at all times subservient to her *Anima* implies a bondage which is sometimes oppressive: to the point where she feels that her only salvation is to become rational and write with surface clarity. One can distinguish two manners, as with Nerval, and for the same reason: the surrealistic we have spoken of, and a descriptive, travelogue style. But a plain style of reporting, of which we have samples in *Le Poste sur la Dune* and *Dans l'Île,* is not na-

---

[26] Henri Bremond, *Prière et Poésie,* Paris, 1926.

tive to her and is soon eclipsed in the refulgence of her instinctive art which illumines the cold northern heavens of her romances with flashes from the depths of subconscious experience and primitive beliefs. Even an unwilling student, having no love for heroes who are portions of universal nature and do not die but become gods, could not read very far in *Inventaire,* the Grand-Louis books and *Hélier Fils des Bois* without marvelling at the spectacular brilliance of this psychic and animistic prose. As to its moral significance, it is this: Confident of the reality of love Marie Le Franc tramples upon and transcends the mediocre realities of social life. Her whole effort is to break through the axiomatic confines of ordinary social consciousness, to possess "some boundless contiguity of space," to enlarge reality, not—if we rightly understand her intention—to deny or evade it, but to rebuild it on essential and primordial truth, on the immutable foundation of the human heart against which society, closeted in cities, surface-polished, club-ridden, enfeebled in its emotional life, tongue-coated with pseudo-scientific gibberish, will always boom in vain.

PLEIOCENE HEROICS

L ET us accoutre our bodies and dispose our
minds for this armageddon. Ere the anchor
be weighed and the cables slipped from the bollards
may the good abbot of Saint-Denis bless our ensign
and commend us to God's mercy, for we are destined
to encounter perilous adventure on the high seas.

Lampman did not know the sea; Marjorie Pickthall only superficially. Marie Le Franc, descended from fishermen, grew up on the coast; the geometry of the sea fixed her notion of planes and sten-
cilled her prose, though it did not wholly fashion
it. She was neither fisher nor hunter. Dr. E. J.
Pratt will give us something we have not experienced before.

Throughout his early years in Newfoundland
where he was born, the Atlantic rolled and roared
about him, hugged him in its mighty grip, sent its
spirit coursing through his man's body, tempered
his nerves for chivalrous adventure, accustomed
his digestion to gargantuan revelry, till his imagination could only be nourished by the titanic and
heroic. From his earliest published verse, from his
shorter epic of sealing off the Labrador [1] to his last
important works, *The Roosevelt and the Antinoe* [2]

---

[1] *Newfoundland Verse*, Toronto, 1923.
[2] New York, 1930.

and *The Titanic*,[3] he has been absorbed in the heroic. The complexion of his imagination is heroic, always engaged in epic battle, always young. Only an imagination that has that quality of fresh young life can reel in such spontaneous revelry as *The Witches' Brew*.[4] Some imaginations remain young; Rabelais's for instance. Now when I say young I do not say youthful. I insist on the distinction between young art, youthful art, and an art which is characteristic of a mature civilization and artists of very complex emotions, because it will help us to keep Pratt apart from other poets, and help us to appreciate the epic qualities of his writing. A writer whose imagination has this complexion will keep us perennially gaping with wonder, even if our heads are white, will stimulate within us, even if we are not lusty drinkers, a magnificent thirst for adventure. This cyclopean cauldron containing the witches' brew which can be sniffed by all the nighthawks of the watery deep and even by the ghosts in Hades, is an unfailing delight. The flavour lasts; it triumphs over time and circumstance. Returning to it like heroes with torn garments and spent bodies, it will invigorate us again. This *chante-fable* makes no demands on us, it simply invites us to a rollicking ecumenical stag party.

Three witches, Lulu, Ardath, and Maryan, hav-

---

[3] Toronto, 1935.
[4] London, 1925.

ing decided to try "the true effect of alcohol upon the cold, aquatic mind," had a huge cauldron forged of copper from the Carolines,

"A thousand cubits in its height,
Its width a thousand breadths as spanned
By the smith's gigantic hand,"

and upon it they poured various brands of sunken liquor spiced with oysters, shrimps, "the kippered hocks of centipedes" and numerous other delicacies. Volcanic fires kept the brew boiling and Lulu churned it with her ladle. Then the smith built a towering palisade around the cauldron and Tom the cat from Zanzibar, who was the bravest warrior of his day, was set on top of it to keep away mammals and all creatures who were not thoroughbred fish. The Shades from Hades, "that dry land," were permitted to witness the revels. There were hordes of

"Scribes with wide phylacteries,
Publicists and Sadducees,
Scholars, saints and Ph. D.'s.

Doctors, auctioneers and bakers,
Dentists, diplomats and fakirs,
Clergymen and undertakers.

Rich men, poor men, fools and sots,
Logicians, tying Shades in knots,
Pagans, Christians, Hottentots,

> Deacons good and bad in spots,
> Farmers with their Wyandots."

Byron, Wolsey, Pepys, Carlyle and others among them expressed their surprise and admiration on seeing the fish change into Troy-like heroes. Their torture must have been intense and their wonder inexpressible as they watched Tom the cat emptying the flagons as fast as Lulu brought them. This was the last spectacular event for, after draining the hundredth, he took a flying leap and careered around the ocean hounding out all his enemies. He returned next morning after littering the water with many victims but, as he found the cauldron dry and the fish dead or paralysed,

> "He sharply turned, began a lonely
> Voyage pregnant of immortal raids
> And epic plunder";

and in the water

> "Appeared a phosphorescent trail
> That headed for the Irish Sea."

The two poems which Dr. Pratt bracketed and published as *Titans* [5] are epics of gigantic slaughter. First "The Cachalot," Prince of a line of Olympians, mighty rulers of the sea for a thousand years, whose race-history is starred with marvel-

---

[5] London, 1926.

lous exploits against men and fish. In his prime
this sperm whale was a hundred feet long,

> "And every foot of that would run
> From fifteen hundred to a ton."

And, as the poet says,

> "He was more wonderful within.
> His iron ribs and spinal joists
> Enclosed the sepulchre of a maw.
> The bellows of his lungs might sail
> A herring skiff—such was the gale
> Along the wind-pipe; and so large
> The lymph-flow of his active liver,
> One might believe a fair-sized barge
> Could navigate along the river."

After gobbling up a kraken for breakfast the monster proceeded to the equator to sleep a siesta.
Whalers found him lying on the swell between the
Cocos and Seychelles and spent the tropic afternoon trying to master him.

> " 'Two hundred barrels to a quart,'
> Gamaliel whispered to Old Wart.

> 'A bull, by gad, the biggest one
> I've ever seen,' said Wart, 'I'll bet'ee,
> He'll measure up a hundred ton,
> And a thousand gallons of spermaceti.'

'Clew up your gab!'
   'Let go that mast!
There'll be row enough when you get him fast.'

'Don't ship the oars!'
    'Now, easy, steady;
You'll gally him with your bloody noise.' "

The harpooners standing ready struck with their blades which "penetrated to the gut."

"The hemp ran through the leaden chock,
 Making the casing searing hot;
The second oarsman snatched and shot
 The piggin like a shuttlecock."

You must read it all to appreciate the poet's mastery of full-blooded masculine realism; and as you read you will probably think of *Moby Dick*.

Pratt was brought up with whalers and sailing ships, he is familiar with rigging and tackle and ship's routine; he had only to listen to old salts, as Amyas Leigh listened to Salvation Yeo, to feel the pricks of heroic desire. But why, at the beginning of a true story, does he stop to relate the ancestry of the monster and the prodigious breakfast of kraken, "le kraken qu'on prend pour une île," [*] a fabulous sea-beast said to be seen at different times off the coast of Norway? Because the ancestry and the feast are in the epic tradition and they contribute

---

[*] Gautier.

towards an aggregate impression of the colossal, which he wants. If seamen display their trophies as landlubbers do who hunt big game ashore, then Pratt's men will adorn their cabins with walrus tusks, seal pelts and sword-fish swords and appoint their shore-gardens with polished porticoes, with "the iron ribs and spinal joists" of whales. But it is not the trophies that Pratt is after, it is the fight, the epic thrill. He can effect a catharsis of this emotion by treating two or three classes of epic material: erudite material worked upon capriciously by his imagination (*The Witches' Brew*); that lying within his own physical experience ("The Cachalot," *The Roosevelt and the Antinoe* and *The Titanic*); or a very remote, palæolithic material; all of them, it will be noticed, sanctioned by science and controlled so as to satisfy his demand for reality.

"The Great Feud" is constructed out of palæolithic data. It is a long poem covering forty-two pages, prodigiously sustained, describing the war to extinction between fur and fin "along the stretch of the Blue Lagoon." Long before the birth of Man, at the time of the birth of continents, when

> "Grasses, ferns and milk bulrushes
> Made up the original nursery
> For fauna of the land and sea,"

when species began to originate and blood stirred in fish and made them venture ashore where the

strongest or more fortunate survived heat and pred-
atory lizards and snakes, at the time of the threatened extinction of fish by plantigrades, a turtle
came out of the flats in the Australian zone and
ambled up to where an anthropoidal ape was
lecturing a Parliament of animals on the subject
of revenge, fixing a date and summoning them to
battle with the water animals.   Thereafter a cavalcade of brutes came trooping down from everywhere to the muster in the "Juranian Valley," as
they did—before or later, I am not sure which—
into the ark.

> "Black bucks whose distant ancestry
>   Sprang from the (now) Westphalian hills;
>   Wild boars with hair as stiff as quills,
>   Of Brandenburgian pedigree;
>   Wallachian elks, whose antlers spread
>   A full five feet above the head,
>   Trekked around the Caucasus,
>   Sounding with defiant stare
>   Their gutturals blent with blasphemous
>   Umlauts upon the stricken air;
>   And they were joined near Teheran
>   By camels down from Turkestan,
>   And elands from Trans-Caspian snows,
>   Persian gazelles with harts and roes,
>   Arabian antelopes and masses
>   Of quaggas, zebras and wild asses,"

and many more.   And the war began.   The carni-
vores rushed upon the walruses and dolphins.   To

stem the tide sperm whales came blowing around
the headlands to be attacked by "bulling elephants
from Canton" which plunged into the quicksands
and sank.   On another part of the front a thousand
tigers were fighting sea-cats, on another sword-fish
were decimating antelopes, hippos and bears.   So
the battle went, and hungry ospreys, cormorants
and kestrels gathered in the sky.   But the most
spectacular slayer of the day was a hybrid monster who came out of a dinosaurian mother's egg
hatched by a moa, Tyrannus Rex, who did not
know his ally from his foe and clawed them all.

> "Fish and land animals alike
>   Were objects for his fangs to strike;
>   Elephants and jungle cats
>   Met the same fate as hares and rats."

At last, overwhelmed by numerous odds, he flung
himself into the Austral Sea, "the rolling cradle
of his race."   To end the strife, Jurania shot forth
her fire fifteen thousand feet into the air and del-
uged the world in lava.   Only one fighter escaped
to tell the tale: the female anthropoidal ape.   Or
where should we have been?

When Pratt sat down to write his last important
works, *The Roosevelt and the Antinoe* and *The
Titanic,* he set himself to manipulate epic material
that came within the range of present experience,
material indeed which no age but ours could provide.   In *The Roosevelt and the Antinoe* his will

was to present a slice of heroic life, to depict life
in moments of tense activity; if poetry could not be
bent to that purpose, then poetry could go.   What
mattered was not the rhyme or rhythm—they were
sometimes a nuisance—but the storm, the cry for
help, the blind run to the rescue, the suspense, the
gallantry of seamen pitted against an ocean's fury.
It is not a work to which we turn for anæsthetic
music or metaphysical wit, but a drama of adequate magnitude, purging us of pity and fear
which, in the Aristotelian tradition, is the characteristic of tragedy.   There are pages during which
we are held in a grip of suspense comparable to
that conjured by a great master of tragedy.

A few years ago, early in 1926, the newspapers
on both sides of the Atlantic for a whole week
were full of this magnificent exploit.   During a
terrific January storm a British freighter, the *Antinoe,* in distress on the North Atlantic, sent out a
call for help.   Captain Fried, of the *Roosevelt,*
brought his direction-finder into play in an effort
to locate the freighter.

> *"Where are you, Antinoe?*—The keys kept rap-
> ping."

Messages flashed back and forth:

> *"Tarpaulins ripped.   Another hatch let go.
> Bad list. Grain swelling fast. Seams loosening now.*

*All lifeboats gone from starboard davits. How
Many knots are you making? How far away
Do you reckon you are?*
                    *Ten knots: now eight:
Now ten—top speed allowed by sea.*
                                    *You say
That we sound nearer to you? Cannot wait
Much longer.*
            Twelve.
                    *Find it hard to steer,
Ice-chest has crashed into the steering gear.
Coming."*

When Fried reached the *Antinoe* he manœuvred
his liner and tried every means to rescue her perishing crew. The fog was treacherous, the waves
hungry. He poured oil on the water, slung running loops and cork-grips over the side for drown-
ing men to cling to, let down a lifeboat which
bucked on the swell and flung the crew into the
water where the oil made their fingers slip, got
into their eyes and throats and hampered them for
swimming.

"Heitman, crushed between the ship and boat,
  Slipped from a life-buoy and was seen to float
Senseless away, down by the liner's stern,
Where he was lost under the wave and churn
Of the propeller. Wertanen, who twice
And willingly released his own firm grip
To take within his teeth a rope eye-splice,
Swam fifteen yards to leeward of the ship
To help an exhausted mate, and paid his price
In drifting past the adventure of return."

The *Roosevelt's* bugle sounded a call to prayer. A priest, in cassock, surplice and purple stole, left his cabin, climbed the stairs to the boat deck and, lifting up a crucifix, recited the office for the dead. Fried edged his vessel closer, tried the Lyle gun without avail. Nothing remained but to try the boats again. The fifth lifeboat was ready. Miller, commanding, set out for the *Antinoe* listing dangerously. He brought off a first instalment of her crew but his boat had to be scrapped. For the third time he dared those two hundred yards of yawning ocean and secured his men. They were all saved and brought back to life again by hot milk and coffee and "the red authority of rum."

The *Roosevelt* proceeded to England. When she docked again in New York, Pratt went down to see her. He inspected the ship, bow and stern, boats and tackle, talked with the crew, read the log to register the exact positions and the calls that came through. He located the cabin which the Catholic priest had occupied and then, to fix the movements in his mind, he walked out of that room, up the stairs, through a door, along the floor of the deck to where a davit stood. There, on the spot, he focused his eye to scrutinize the tangible masses that had played a part, bent his mind to grip the living material of the tragedy. I say that is epic method; it produces an art which is robust, young, a narrative near to the event.

The *Titanic* disaster is still recent enough to be

remembered by most of us. This White Star liner
was built to exceed other passenger vessels in size
and to win the blue riband from the *Mauretania*.
She was said to be unsinkable and she sank on her
maiden voyage after colliding with an iceberg.
The poet deals with the experience in such a way
as to bring out the sense of security felt by officers
and passengers alike in a ship designed to meet any
conceivable emergency. That feeling dominates
the poem to the exclusion of other forces which a
dramatic poet might have laid hold of in the tragedy. Pratt sees accumulated masses of things:
passengers trooping down to the dining-room like
an army at the call of a bugle; he sees corridors and
saloons as masses of decorative detail and in the
galley he sees a medley of rich dishes reminding
us of Trimalchio's glorious dinner party:

"Cauldrons of stock, purées and consommés,
　Simmered with peppercorns and marjoram.
　The sea-shore smells from bisque of crab and clam
　Blended with odours from the fricasées.
　Refrigerators hung with a week's toll
　Of the stockyards delivered sides of lamb
　And veal, beef quarters to be roasted whole,
　Hundreds of capons and halibut. A shoal
　Of Blue-Points waited to be served on shell.
　The boards were loaded with pimolas, pails
　Of lobster coral, jars of Béchamel,
　To garnish tiers of rows of chilled timbales
　And aspics. On the shelves were pyramids
　Of truffles, sprigs of thyme and water-cress,

Bay leaf and parsley, savouries to dress
Shad roes and sweetbreads broiling on the grids."

He makes all the episodes live for us in the present:
we are at the launching of the ship, we board her
at Southampton, we ride out to sea with her, we
walk the decks, meet passengers, hear their chatter
about what Smith, the captain, or Phillips, the
wireless operator, said. We even read the messages as they come and go. We watch a demon-
stration in the gymnasium, we play poker at a stag
party, we eat at a table where the talk is punctuated
with a word to the steward and a glance at

"That group of men around the captain's table,
Look at them, count the aggregate—the House
Of Astor, Guggenheim, and Harris, Strauss,
That's Frohman, isn't it? Between them able
To halve the national debt with a cool billion!"

We hear the band "Zip her up." And, as the life-
boats are lowered away, we watch gentlemen salute
departing ladies with "Castilian courtesy." Finally, as survivors, we watch the water climb up
her decks thronged with fourteen hundred souls,
until she sinks. He brings out the feeling by show-
ing us characters and things in action, by building
up a picture of the gigantic proportions of the
ship, her speed, all her gadgets and appointments.
The reader gradually gains complete consciousness of the majesty and miraculous workmanship
of the colossus from the narrative:

"Her sixty thousand tons of sheer flotation,"

from talk among the passengers:

> "I heard Phillips say
> He had the finest outfit on the sea;
> The new Marconi valve; the range by day,
> Five hundred miles, by night a thousand.
> Three sources of power,"

or in a direct way: by watching a group of boys
gathered round a spot

"Upon the rail where a dial registered
  The speed, and waiting each three minutes heard
  The taffrail log bell tallying off a knot."

Dinner on such a ship

> "gave the sense that all was well:
> That touch of ballast in the tanks; the feel
> Of peace from ramparts unassailable,
> Which, added to her seven decks of steel,
> Had constituted the *Titanic* less
> A ship than a Gibraltar under heel."

The calm sea

"And night had placed a lazy lusciousness
  Upon a surfeit of security."

The feeling develops ostentatiously in the poker
game:

"Let's whoop her up.   Double the limit."

Even after the collision some went up on deck but soon returned to their state rooms satisfied that nothing "could harm that huge bulk"; and when commanded to get into the life-boats they

> "stepped inside,
> Convinced the order was not justified."

Even at the end, after the last life-boat had vanished,

> "In spite of her deformity of line,
>   Emergent like a crag out of the sea,
>   She had the semblance of stability."

To offset this accumulated feeling of security there is a running reference to sinister omens: the old salts' talk

> "Of whirling shags around the mizzen peaks";

the apparition seen above the funnel rim as they were leaving Queenstown; the maleficent influence of the Egyptian mummy they have aboard from The Valley of the Kings.   But all omens explode when they meet the solid wall of security erected in the hearts and minds of the people.   *The Californian* was continually warning her of icebergs.

> *"Say, Californian, shut up, keep out,*
>   *You're jamming all my signals with Cape Race."*

That feeling of confidence overrode the most elementary notions of prudence and precaution so that the ship threshed the serene waters of the night like a mighty but unwary marine monster scouting the very idea that any enemy could match her brawn and nerve. When she came up, the iceberg, lying in ambush, had no difficulty in ripping her bows. There was no struggle; she dropped and took

"Her thousand fathoms journey to her grave,"

while "out there in the starlight," coldly looking on,

"Silent, composed, ringed by its icy broods,
The grey shape with the palæolithic face
Was still the master of the longitudes."

Pratt has got out of the material all there was in it of epic value; in opposition to his natural penchant he could not resolve it into a fight between palæolithic leviathans. A dramatic poet, I say, by choosing from the episode a different set of objects or events, would have evoked a different emotion. Where there is no conflict there is no drama. This poem does not move us as *The Roosevelt and the Antinoe* moved us. Implicit confidence in machinery is typical of twentieth-century man but there is something in this tragedy that is alien to a scientific age, an uncalculated thing, an epic vestige the principle of which is fate. *The*

Titanic belongs to the Greek order of tragedy in the sense that it is blind; it is epic rather than dramatic. No traveller who has ever crossed the North Atlantic will be moved to tears when he reads of the death of dollar princes and princesses who, with a tremendous ice-field ahead, felt nothing so much as a granite sense of security in the unsinkableness of their ship. If we could forget the unsinkable mass and the Roman luxury and think of the fragility of human passions that pass like a ship's lights under the eternal stars; if we observed a young couple on their honeymoon leaning on the rail of the doomed ship and heard the girl say, as she raised her eyes defiantly from the ocean: "This is our moment—complete and heavenly. . . . This is our own, forever,'" then our hearts would go out to them in pity. That is not the feeling we have here. And when we reflect, it seems to be that dominant feeling of security that keeps order among the escaping women and robs the Castilian courtesy of some of its spectacular insouciance.

Mr. T. S. Eliot has said that "the only way of expressing emotion in the form of art is by finding an 'objective correlative'; in other words, a set of objects, a situation, a chain of events which shall be the formula of that *particular* emotion; such that when the external facts, which must terminate

---

' Noel Coward, *Cavalcade.*

in sensory experience, are given, the emotion is immediately evoked." [8]   I believe those words define Pratt's art and they will serve my purpose in differentiating between young art, youthful art, and older, complex art. I feel that in Pratt's work the material he uses evokes an equivalent emotion, whereas in youthful art the emotion is not inherent but adventitious, factitiously created by blowing into the material. A dinosaur, a cachalot, a cauldron a thousand cubits high, a muster of all the animals in creation, an iceberg, a modern liner, a tempest on the North Atlantic are intrinsically huge, gigantic; youthful art needs the adjectives. I am aware of the *towering* palisade, I am aware that he uses Gibraltar in a simile, I am aware that he says *gigantic* and *huge*—never out of place— but that is exceptional in Pratt whereas it is the rule in Roy Campbell. Pratt is not likely to mention

"*Gigantic* flowers, *exploding* from the sand"; [9]

that is hyperbole, extravagant, youthful. He would not write:

"Where old Zambesi shakes his hoary locks,"

"And like a mountain, barnacled with stars."

---

[8] *The Sacred Wood*, p. 92.
[9] The Campbell quotations are from *The Flaming Terrapin*, Cape, 1924.

His animals are life-size; they may be gigantic, but the impression of gigantic stature is conveyed in a natural manner, by presenting them against the background of their habitat:

> "a neck whose reach
> Topped the high branches of a beach."

> "his figure set
> Black like a poplar's silhouette
> Against the orb of an inflamed moon."

If they do not impress us by their size, they impress us by their accumulated masses. In the same way the old epic poets built up an impression of princely plunder or knightly slaughter, of the marvellous workmanship of Achilles' shield, Alexander's tent or Darius' chariot, of the supernatural power of Roland's sword. Pratt, like his *trouvère* ancestors before the final combat, calls his champions "from Rio to the Celebes" and covers the field with battalions of mangabees, Tasmanian tigers, emus, elks, and populates the water with tarpons, manatees and ursine-seals in their infinite variety. See them troop past the colours in the Juranian Valley. They appear one after the other in the traditional manner, evoked by a simple and direct narrative which subjects them to mutual carnage and closes the action with the lively exit of the hero.

"White angels rinsed the moonlight from their
  hair"

is a pretty, Aphroditish silhouette;

"Over far Edens waved the golden lights
  Trailing their gorgeous fringes o'er the heights"

is full of cosmic splendour;

"Night is a Captain hustling up his stars"

is poetry. Far be it from me to deny the splendid
beauty of Roy Campbell's poetry; I am saying that
it is not primitive or mediæval epic. How easy it
would have been for Pratt—though his mind is
not so inclined—to say of his lions and buffaloes
and antelopes that they *scampered, stormed up,
careered on the winds, stampeded with a wild
halloo, crashed through brakes and thorns* or
bawled their fell triumph far along the Styx! But
in his case they are as orderly as Cook's tourists;
not swift, neither are they shod with seven league
boots: they *trek* "around the Caucasus" and they
are "*joined* near Teheran by camels *down* from
Turkestan." In comparison, the animals guilty of
trembling, scorning, crashing, scrawling, are fictions of a clever journalist scouring the continents
for the grandiose and terrifying.

What Victor Hugo does with sentiment in

"Oh! qu'un coup de poignard de toi me serait
  doux!"

Campbell does with descriptive narrative in

"Slamming the huge portcullis of his jaws."

And although Pratt's eye is as vigorous as Hugo's and his imagination spirited, his sensory impressions are controlled, his mind has undergone a scholar's discipline, it never runs berserk. I do not say that mental discipline has changed the complexion of his imagination, not that, but simply implemented and kept it in close proximity to things. The metaphysical poets were scholarly men but their poetry is very different from Pratt's. There is a hierarchy of imaginations. Donne, for example, had what we might call a metaphysical imagination; Pratt an epic or heroic imagination. A simple way of appreciating the difference between the art of Pratt and Donne is to consider any of Pratt's rare similes:

"Her seven mooring ropes to break at the stern
And *writhe like anacondas* on the quay,"

"And made the smaller tethered craft *behave
Like frightened harbour ducks,*"

or rarer metaphors, as when he speaks of the iceberg:

"Silent, composed, ringed by its *icy broods.*"

The power that those pictures have upon our minds

is not due to magniloquence or hallucination but to our immediate, unreflecting perception of the fact that, in every case, the comparisons suggested by the two images so brought together are nicely adequate, perfectly just and reasonable, indeed inevitable. Even where his imagination has freest rein, in *The Witches' Brew,* and "The Great Feud," it does not inflate the material his mind provides. It moves gracefully among palæolithic giants; if it seeks their society it is because it sees them in action as brutish but royal dramatis personæ, not frogs imitating cows, not figures of speech or symbols. This poet works with things; his winds and currents are not thoughts or moods. Things have a sovereign identity, seldom given in marriage, seldom enriched or obfuscated by metaphor. That statement reveals at once his art's innate strength and its deficiencies. What occurs in other poets as extended metaphor, humour, curious or surprising combinations, incongruous rhymes, cosmic energy or instinctive *élan vital,* is the primordial stuff of Pratt's poetry, inherent in his zoological and geographic vocables:

"Leguminous leopards full of beans."

"Bashan bull and Cashmir ram,
 The male spring-bok, chamois, gnoo,
 The reid-buck and the kangaroo
 Heading downwards through Siam."

"A white giraffe began to scale
A scraggy monolith of shale."

"Of bison worsted by becunas,
And weasels at the throat of tunas."

It delights us; yet we would go to other writers for subtler, mysterious pleasures that metaphysical and Symbolist poetry afford. In Campbell's poetry, things exist as images, encrusted with florid tracery, aggrandized but metamorphosed; rocks turn to shadowy cities. His art belongs to a later period, of metaphor and symbol, to the Rimbaud period: *The Flaming Terrapin* has certain resemblances to "Le Bateau Ivre." Of the three poets reeling with geographic intoxication, Campbell and Rimbaud are visionaries, Pratt is not. We understand then why they voyage among myths and symbols, why they traffic in Leviathans, Behemoths, sea-serpents and spectres like Adamastor: they have seen what others have only dreamt they saw.

The influence of Rimbaud has been so wide-spread and so various, his "Bateau Ivre" so easily parodied yet so difficult to equal, that I hesitate to speak of it in one breath. Miss Sitwell caught the spirit of his *Illuminations* but she might have chosen another way to honour her mother-in-law or demonstrate her mastery of the mouth-organ, dulcimer or zither. [10]   Osbert's dream [11] of wood-

---

[10] "Fantasia for Mouth-Organ."
[11] "Adventure."

land nights in the tropics, entertained by slim monkeys, bare yellow women, trumpets and gaudy drums, is Rimbaud caricatured by Pierrot in beach pyjamas. But Campbell, in his adventures, follows close on the heels of Rimbaud

"Down unimagined Congos proudly riding,"

through a jungle of lichens, phosphorescent flowers, panthers' eyes, gleaming serpents, cosmic pulsations, green nights and yellow dawns into wild, polar lights, glaciers and pale icebergs. There is exaggeration and magniloquence in Rimbaud; they are youthful and not the intrinsic characteristics of his poem. And Campbell's lines, even in passages where they recall Rimbaud's, have not their complexion. They are flamboyant, fantastic, imaged, exotic, visionary too, but gushing, fluid; they have not the mysterious bouquet and piquancy of a Rimbaud cocktail, his "confiture exquise aux bons poètes." The sea, for Rimbaud who had never seen it, was mystery. The emotions it evoked were mysterious, the visions it engendered were of the nature of hallucinations. I think Rimbaud lives because he found the verbal equivalent for those emotions and visions. Versification is nothing, he can dispense with it, he has found an "objective correlative": the mysterious hallucinated verbal cocktail is the formula of his particular psychic experience. Tested by this criterion much of Hugo and Gautier and much of Campbell, splendid though it be, fails to satisfy us.

Now what Rimbaud miraculously achieved with mysterious emotions and visions Pratt achieves with less complex ones. He is illumined with the heroic: heroic merriment, heroic battle and adventure, the heroism of man and brute. That, I have said, he has put into heroic verse, into muscular lines of objective formulæ with little room for metaphor. That, I have said too, is the complexion of young epic verse. Pratt has rejuvenated our poetry; a Canadian Masefield has enriched its vocabulary. He has reformed it by turning it away from wilted, sentimental flower-gardens, by overcoming its soft femininity, by restoring its pulse with tonic realism and inebriating fun. If a newer generation of poets, reared in a tempest, render homage to Pratt while refusing Lampman and Pickthall, it is because of his heroic imagination and his grip on life.

MY NEW FOUND LAND

TO THE young poets we are about to study, Marie Le Franc, whose native idiom is French, is no more than a name; but Archibald Lampman and Marjorie Pickthall are important titles in the Canadian anthology which was their pottage and which turned their stomachs. Pratt occupies an intermediate position between the older and newer modes of poetic expression in Canada; his poem on an eight-cylinder stream-lined locomotive [1] awakens a response in these young poets who vigorously reject the older writers. Romantic beauty, emotional cadence and well-built rhyme, heritages from a ghostly Tennyson, are not their criteria of poetry, nor can they be satisfied with a copy, however faithful, of the natural landscape. [2] Against that effete æsthetic, I say, we have Pratt's heroic imagination, his grip on life and his epic realism. When we meet Pratt, after Lampman and Marjorie Pickthall and Marie Le Franc, we are again on the plane of the human; we have to adjust our eyes

[1] "The Man and the Machine," *Many Moods*, Toronto, 1932.
[2] Modernism and romanticism clash in these two lines from Stephen Spender's "The Express":

"Wrapped in her music no bird song, no, nor bough
Breaking with honey bud, shall ever equal."

and minds to a real world of living and mechanical forces. Now this renewal of contact with an ethical centre will promote some easily foreseen processes and establish certain attitudes. After a time, as we gradually lose an embarrassing sense of foreignness and isolation, we may identify our destinies with what is human in us and experience a delightful sensation of renewed vigour as a result of communion with our kind; on the other hand, we may feel that humanism cannot satisfy us and turn our backs upon it, strive to purge ourselves of it; and thirdly, we may take up the human cause to the end of making conditions favourable to the flourishing of the spirit and, in our work, interpret the struggle by reference to the eternal problem of human destiny. One of the most striking consequences affecting the nature of the poetry is a process of depersonalization as the ego turns outward and merges into the mass. Poetry which at first reflected mental states and personal attitudes and then flowers again in the tension and heat of our economic life will surprise us by its vigour and novel beauty. But to apprehend the full import of the phenomenon we must look back upon all that these poets have come through; and that jungle includes something that the older writers never met. Before coming into this new environment of marts, factories and counting-houses, these poets, in a special sense, contracted familiarity

with the metaphysical poets; they have undergone a mental and spiritual discipline that will
not be lost: the realism is toned by the austerity
and bareness which we associate with metaphysical wit. Even that margin of difference is
enough to distinguish the realism of Dorothy
Livesay's latest poetry from that of Pratt's;
enough to distinguish the art we are about to study
from the art we have studied up to this point.

Dr. Johnson long ago, and Mr. Eliot fairly
recently, [3] disserted on metaphysical poetry in
essays which are of especial interest to us in this
connection. But to resume in as few words as
possible the character of metaphysical poetry, all
we need to remember is that the poets of Donne's
company eagerly assimilated the new knowledge
so abundant in an age of discovery and that they
"recreated thought into feeling."

To come to our own times: whereas the mis-
called Georgian poets (who continue the romantic tradition of the nineteenth century) pay
regular visits to the English countryside and muse
on Saxon scythes and mattocks, the poets after
Mr. Eliot have spent their leisure, not in picnics,
but in city streets and homes and factories, keeping
their senses open to every new manner of feeling
possible to men and women of the twentieth century. The odd words they use are modern technical and scientific words, Latin rather than Saxon

---

[3] In *Homage to John Dryden*, 1924.

(we shall see why Kennedy is an exception), and if we are still under the spell of the nineteenth century we may feel that they are not poetic words. Their poems, which reflect the spirit of our time, are alert, tense, elusive, intellectual, erudite, dogmatic, sparkling with a new and difficult beauty. Such a sensitive awareness to intellectual stimuli, particularly acute in the cultured American mind, results in a characteristic tone and accent: an aristocratic disdain of the sentimental and dull brain, and a cult of wit, which Mr. Eliot has endeavoured to restore to modern poetry. And since wit consists in bringing together objects which, because of their opposed natures, are not usually associated in our minds, the poets under review originate unusual combinations of elements with a view to creating energy and power. Brevity is still the soul of wit; and the art of a metaphysical poet tends to condensation of thought and phrase, to epigram and ellipse. No matter from what conscious or unconscious source they spring, metaphysical wit, surrealist imagery and Hulme's analogies all have a constant purpose: to produce surprise, to create power, "to enable us to dwell and linger upon a point excited." [*]

Dorothy Livesay was born in Winnipeg and left there at eleven. Some few years ago she

---

[*] T. E. Hulme: "The main function of analogy in poetry is to enable us to dwell and linger upon a point excited." *The Criterion*, July, 1925.

graduated from the University of Toronto where, as in most universities, there are some students who are inspired towards creative literature. What moves them most—outside their own poetry —is poetry which reflects the modern temper. And so this poet set out as a disciple, not of the metaphysical poets of the seventeenth century, but of recent women poets like H. D., Elinor Wylie and Emily Dickinson, the last two of whom knew not Browning or Tennyson but looked to the seventeenth century for their art: to Sir Thomas Browne and John Donne.

Dorothy Livesay's early poetry [5] is contained in a brochure, *Green Pitcher,* 1928, and a volume entitled *Signpost,* 1932. [6] At first her manner is akin to H. D.'s. The repetitions in the poem "Defiance" and the characteristic Imagist trick of referring by analogy to things concrete and solid remind us immediately of H. D.'s "Oread." H. D. makes us feel the oppressive heat in a garden in the same way as Dorothy Livesay makes us feel oppressive gravity. *Green Pitcher* is in the Imagist manner:

> "Gloves
> As ruddy brown
> As oak leaves, fallen."

[5] Her latest and best is beginning to appear in the magazines.
[6] Both published by The Macmillan Company of Canada Limited.

"The terrible animal
Pain
Crouched low."

"Whales are the waves
Bellowing on the shore,
Whales harpooned."

continued too in later poems: in "Sea-Flowers,"
for instance. The poems have the rounded completeness, and the lines the individual and spontaneous rhythm that the Imagists claimed for their
poetry. That is not all.

"I cannot shut out the night—
Nor its sharp clarity."

"The deliberate moon,
The last, unsolved finality of night."

Clarity, deliberate and *finality* affect us with a
feeling of strangeness.

"I dread the sun
For his fierce honesty."

Honesty! These words have a new sound, a
rather odd silver timbre as though they were
foreigners but, in contrast to the Imagist use of
words, they do not refer immediately to some new
object in order to present a new analogy. They
are Latin, not Saxon words, used in an intellectual,

not merely poetic, sense. Dorothy Livesay so
completely repudiates the romantic tradition that
she abhors words which are supposedly poetic.

She has brooded in the same sequestered places
as Emily Dickinson and Elinor Wylie and, in a
manner similar to theirs, her emotion receives its
final sanction in her mind. Narcissus-like, she
sees herself in the limpid mirror of her mind;
each poem is a thought expressed through the
medium of dry, coloured, visual, often feminine
images:

> "I saw my thought a hawk."

> "words
> On little shelves—
> As one touches
> Delicate china?"

> "Take out your sorrow
> Shake it, and iron it,
> And put it on tomorrow."

> "I dreamed that I dwelt in a house
> On the edge of a field
> With a fire for warmth
> And a roof for shield."

> "The thought of you is like a glove
> That I had hidden in a drawer:
> But when I take it out again
> It fits; as close as years before."

The last lines come near to Emily Dickinson's:

"We outgrow love like other things
  And put it in a drawer:
  Till it an antique fashion shows
  Like costumes grandsires wore."

Even water itself, rain, may by this alchemy be
changed into a substantial image, as it is in this
pretty and feminine "Green Rain."

"I remember long veils of green rain
  Feathered like the shawl of my grandmother—

I remember the rain as the feathery fringe
  of her shawl."

Miss Sitwell would put it:

"Spring comes like a Paisley shawl,"

and her explanation situates "Green Rain" in its
proper *ambiente*. "In after years," Miss Sitwell
says in her *Children's Tales,* "when the bright
visions of childhood have grown dim in the
brains of most of us, the artist still retains the
curious sensitiveness to impressions and mental
atmosphere, the intense yet fantastic seriousness,
which is the main basis of the child's mind . . .
Life still appears to him as a matter of sharp outlines, bright flashing colours, and strange meetings." But, I would add, the outlines, colours

and meetings are intellectualized before they pass
out into adult art to create surprises not experienced in the nursery:

> "Your mouth on mine
> Is fire on stone."

> "It is a night of slaughter:
> But for me
> Meditation."

The thought-image may be extended throughout
a poem, but it is oftener condensed to epigram-
matic terseness:

> "In rainy weather
> Who can tell
> Whether we weep
> Or not?"

> "I shall lie like this when I am dead—
> But with one more secret in my head."

Emily Dickinson wrote:

> "We never know we go—when we are going
>   We jest and shut the door;
> Fate following behind us bolts it,
>   And we accost no more."

Death is a door of departure with Dorothy
Livesay too, who has written her "Testament" in
a manner similar to Emily Dickinson's:

"Should Loveliness come
To show me a flower,
Say I'll be back
In an hour."
(*Dorothy Livesay*)

"If I shouldn't be alive
When the robins come,
Give the one in red cravat
A memorial crumb."
(*Emily Dickinson*)

Metaphysical poets all come by the same route to a solitary place where they muse on this poor mortality; they are not afraid of contemplating the flesh and the bone, of disembodying the spirit. The only one of Dorothy Livesay's poems that causes the reader any difficulty is "Farewell" in which there are three characters: the poet (or her physical body) who says good-bye to the house, her spirit which remains in the house as part of it left behind after the body has gone—her footsteps are echoes only—and, thirdly, the new tenant of the house who thinks that the poet is gone. In "Song of Solomon" she approaches her ideal of dramatic terseness and also "recreates thought into feeling," in the best manner of the metaphysical poets:

"One day's sorrow
Is not much
When there's grief
Still to touch:

> But one day's sorrow
> Drops a stone
> That plunges deep
> Through flesh, through bone."

Flesh and bone—the physical body—are a well. This is not an instance of the romantic and pathetic fallacy as much as an illusion of *optique,* a kinematic interfusion of images.

"Sonnet for Ontario" and "September Morning" will be welcomed by some readers for their human interest and because they are easy to comprehend. "Prince Edward Island" is a little different:

"They do not linger to hear the slow moving of
          hooves,
  The soft breathings of friendly cows among the
          grasses,
  Or the sudden thunder of a young calf, startled
  At wind caressing a groove of birches.

              *   *   *

  They shut out evening from their eyes
  And welcome morning
  With whistling, milking, the drawing of water,
  The sound of voices . . .

  They know not evening,
  These people of the farms."

We feel that the poet is choosing the essentials of a landscape, only the significant essentials that

will convey to us its mood. She abstracts them—
"the drawing of water"—so that they are no longer particularized notations, for time is abolished
as a dimension. The method calls for clear thinking and first-hand observation. The Imagists
accustomed us to it, but the master of it is T. S.
Eliot whose influence, as we shall see presently,
has penetrated Eastern Canada.

It was T. S. Eliot who found the "verbal equivalent" for our spiritual mood immediately after
the war. He saw the human mart and thoroughfare change into a desert; and because his face
shone with that vision he led a numerous band of
pilgrims through a spiritual wilderness which
offered neither bread nor water, nothing but deceptive mirages. That desert experience brought
forth much of the poetry of Smith and Kennedy.
But nearer to our day of writing the depression
has deepened and hardened the notion of bread
and water as the essential realities of life; they
have lost their sacramental value as symbols and
the religious impulse, which manifests itself in a
"tendency to abstraction," fades away as the desert
view changes into a picture of factories and
machines. Although the newer poets were
brought up under Eliot, he can no longer lead
them. The economic and social realities of life
have hounded them, driven them to bay, and they
have had to face them. Now it is from this
courageous facing of our human condition in the

intimate present that Dorothy Livesay's latest poems derive their strength. Here is something not felt before in her work. In the earlier poetry her imagery received its ultimate sanction in her mind; it must now adapt itself to an enthusiastic outlook on life. She has developed beyond her egocentrism to devote herself to a human cause.

The change in the complexion of her poetry is parallel to the change in her outlook on life and literature. It was during a stay in Paris in 1931-2, while she was writing a thesis on "The Influence of French Symbolism on Modern English Poets," that she read Eliot as a present-day representative of the symbolist æsthetic. But her European experiences were to turn her so definitely in the direction of communism that symbolist influence on her own poetry could hardly be anything but negligible. The wind is a symbol in "The Outrider" but her poetry contains no desert imagery or vegetation symbolism. The mood that expresses itself in this language:

"Will this hay last the year—
Where are the taxes coming from—
Must we sell the car?"

whatever relation it may have to Laforgue's *complaintes,* is certainly more real and serious. Looking at the material struggle in Paris, going to working-class meetings in the suburbs, demonstrating with 20,000 in celebration of the Com-

mune, reading *L'Humanité,* she still sensed a
certain isolation and could not yet reconcile that
activity with her other and idealistic existence.
It was only a brief and chance contact with a proletarian poet in London, and the impact of Henri
Barbusse's League of Revolutionary Writers,
that definitely convinced her that she had been
studying with the dead.   But I have an intuition
that her new interpretation of literature owes
something to the writings of John Strachey.
Who, for instance, can read Strachey's strictures
on Proust, D. H. Lawrence and Aldous Huxley
and still retain a tragic view of life or have any
respect for writers who express that view in literature?   All three writers, says Strachey, "confuse
the unavoidable tragedies of human existence in
general, with the entirely evitable, but at present
growing and deepening, tragedies of a specific
system of society in a period of decay." [7]   Strachey's persuasive logic impresses the picture of a
decadent society so forcibly upon our minds that
we cannot resist it.   In the spell of that picture
one sees the art of the symbolist period in relation
to a society in decay and the only way, it seems,
that a living artist might escape death is not to
take refuge in symbolism or mysticism, but to
imitate the dramatist Synge and seek sustenance
from life among the Aran Islanders and the

[7] *The Coming Struggle for Power,* p. 216.

peasants of Wicklow and Kerry. Her reading of Synge and his desire to reproduce the ungarnished folk-speech of the Irish peasant quickened her intuitive impulses, her will to interpret in dramatic form the struggle of the Canadian farmer. "The Outrider" and "Day and Night" are essentially dramatic poems in which the psychological activity results from a particularist view of society and a kind of thinking correlative with that view.

The dramatic interest in "The Outrider" springs from the conflict of two fates and two opposed emotions: the resignation of pioneer farmers and the optimistic struggle of workers in American factories. The local or non-European tone is deepened by the poet's use of the Indian tradition in Canada and the negro tradition in the States. Her debt to the English poets of her own complexion is nevertheless apparent.

In a poem of intriguing elegance from "The Magnetic Mountain,"[8] Cecil Day Lewis uses a no less hypnotizing conceit, the kestrel, a migrant "who yearly changes his tenement of space," to express his yearning for a new territory "somewhere beyond the railheads" in which he will find release for all his human energies.

"Now to be with you, elate, unshared,
My kestrel joy, O hoverer in wind,

[8] *New Signatures*, The Hogarth Press, 1934.

> Swift outrider of lumbering earth
> O hasten hither my kestrel joy!"

That line which Dorothy Livesay has written over her poem, "Swift outrider of lumbering earth," is a marvellous achievement with imagery and wit.

> "Out of the wind and bird flight
> He made himself a song,"

might be said of Lewis as of her own hero. The kestrel or windhover, as it is sometimes called, that denizen of the more outlandish parts of the English countryside is the outrider (scout or forerunner in Dorothy Livesay's language) of the human caravan heavily rolling beyond cities and valleys to conquer new land. In farm environment this "hoverer in wind" is the wind itself which, in the dry season, is significant of life and hope.

> "Wind, lumbering wall, armored tank,
> No slumber for this forerunner
> Who, camouflaged, unmasks the countryside
> Reveals the gash in her deep side. . . ."

"The Outrider," prologue, peripetia and epilogue, tells the story of a farmer's son who went into the city, learned swiftness and returned a

convert to communism to speed up the energies
of his people on the farm.

"He comes with eyes more piercing than before
And scrapes his boots—swinging wide the door."

When the family is united again an old man describes winning the land the year they came out;
the father recounts the hardships of their early
married life and the son remembers being tossed
in his mother's skirts and bouncing high into the
hay but also how he "grew up one evening, much
alone":

> "I would no longer be the beast
> Who ploughed a line straight to the barrier
> And swung back on his steps—my father's son.
> It would take long. But from that summer on
> My heart was set. I raced through swinging air,
> Rumpled my head with laughter in the clouds!"

Then the boy tells how different it was in the
stockyards:

> "It was different, different
> To lift the lever arm
> And see farm beasts revolving by
> The dripping blood still warm.
>
> *   *   *
>
> A thousand men go home
> And I a thousandth part
> Wedged in a work more sinister
> Than hitching horse and cart—

Dark because we're beaten
By a bosses' mind:
A single move uneven turned
Will set you in the wind.

    *   *   *

It was different, different
Because I learned: For this
You plough the fields and scatter
The toil of days and years.

You die in harness and are proud
Of earthen servitude—
While others that live in bond will seek
To shake the rooting wood,

    *   *   *

Others that sell their toil, will put
Possessiveness to shame
And draw you to them in their fight:
The battle is the same.

The blowing silver barley grain
The skyline wide, serene,
These shall be your gift to those
Who wield the world's machine!"

Part III, "Release," is interesting because of the symbolism connected with the outrider and the mingling of factory, agricultural and propagandist terms: union rates, roots, windmills, scouts and enemies. The wind and its purpose are symbols of the boy and his purpose. He has returned to sweep away old prejudices. He can "smell out" the decay. He exhorts the youth among the farmers to work for their release:

> "Not veering with the crow
> But throbbing, conscious, knowing where to go.
> There's time for flying: dig up crumbling roots,
> Eradicate the underbrush and twig
> The snapping thistle and the stubborn sloe—
> Those backward ramblers who insist they know.
>
> Employ your summer-time, at union rate:
> Conveying energy on this green belt
> Of earth assembled, swiftly known and felt.
> Faster! Speed-up is here legitimate."

They agree to push ahead and scout for the enemy capitalists and turn to address reproaches to the old laggards who are afraid of wind:

> "We are ahead of you, with wind persisting.
> Draw us not back—your sleep, your arms,
> Your frigid breathlessness.
>
> Wakeful, we push ahead
> Scouting for enemy lights."

Wind is the energy which alone can move these sleepy, lumbering farmers stalled like

> "so many windmills without hands
> To whirl and drag the water up to air."

The poem ends with a joyful shout at the sight of a new land, not flowing with milk and honey, but a country to be won by hard digging and fertilized with sweat and blood.

> "O new found land! Sudden release of lungs,
>   Our own breath blows the world: our veins,
>   unbound
>   Set free the fighting heart. We speak with
>   tongues—
> This struggle is our miracle new found!"

In that pæan there is no hint of the despair and sense of utter loss tearing an English mother's heart when her son has gone,

> "When an indifferent exile
>   Passes through the metropolis en route
>   For Newfoundland," [9]

but unfeigned joy, joy in lungs and wide open spaces and a struggle for existence which, to a communist, is the miraculous source of vital energy.

A. S. J. Tessimond's brief poem, "La Marche des Machines," [10] which goes:

> "This piston's infinite recurrence is
> night morning night and morning night and

---

[9] Cecil Day Lewis, "Satirical Poems." *New Signatures*, p. 55.
[10] *Ibid.*, p. 97.

death and birth and death and birth and this
crank climbs (blind Sisyphus) and see

steel teeth greet"

will elucidate the title of Dorothy Livesay's poem,
"Day and Night":[11] a tragi-comedy or articulated
pantomime in ten dance diversions representing
the diurnal routine of mechanized human labour
in an American factory. First a solemn parade:

"Men in a stream, a moving human belt
Move into sockets, every one a bolt.
The fun begins, a humming, whirring drum—
Men do a dance in time to the machines."

Then a lively one-step:

"One step forward
Two steps back
Shove the lever,
Push it back."

The foreman too is a machine, merely "arms and
a note-book" in which neither love nor peace are
recorded, so that dreams are cruel jests. One's
companion, "stoking coal in the furnaces," was a
negro—"We were like Buddies, see?"—who
sings this "witty" spiritual:

"Shadrach, Meshach and Abednego
Turn in the furnace, whirling slow.

---

[11] *The Canadian Poetry Magazine*, Toronto, Jan., 1936.

Lord, I'm burnin' in the fire
Lord, I'm steppin' on the coals
Lord, I'm blacker than my brother
Blow your breath down here.

Boss, I'm smothered in the darkness
Boss, I'm shrivellin' in the flames
Boss, I'm blacker than my brother
Blow your breath down here.

Shadrach, Meshach and Abednego
Burn in the furnace, whirling slow."

And the men up in the roller room, swinging steel,
sing:

"We bear the burden home to bed
The furnace glows within our hearts:
Our bodies hammered through the night
Are welded into bitter bread."

Until the hunger, brawn and bones are added up,
put beside the bosses' profit, and hatred bursts
forth like a fiery brand.

"One step forward
Two steps back,
Will soon be over:
Hear it crack!

The wheels may whirr
A roundabout,
And neighbor's shuffle
Drown your shout,

The wheel must limp
Till it hangs still
And crumpled men
Pour down the hill.

Day and night
Night and day—
Till life is turned
The other way!"

Dorothy Livesay's latest work, then, is a "criticism of life"; if we understand life to mean proletarian existence in capitalist society. We may look upon it as an impassioned justification for revolt against tyranny or consider solely the self-value of the work, its intrinsic value as art. As pure literary critics we admire an art which evolves witty adaptations of modern industrial images to dance rhythms and agricultural routine, that excites us to enthusiasm for a cause, moves us with wonder and ecstacy at the sight of a new country and gives to the human tragedy such a poignant and satirical elegance. The work is creative in an artistic sense; it creates new combinations of images:

> "Let the sober
> Days be made
> Ladders through
> A leafy shade."

"Conveying energy on this green belt
Of earth assembled."

"On what agenda
Will you set love down?"

"Where there are silences wind feels them out
Odour of dead fruit he makes known abroad."

"the racing clouds at bay
Rumpled like sheets after a night of joy."

"We were so many windmills without hands."

and, in pantomime, dance and negro spiritual, it
cleverly manipulates the human crisis in action.
Then as communist critics we may find a special
pleasure in conflicts which are Marxist in their
origins. Communist poetry presents social and
economic realities against a background of en-
slavement and war and in this sense a communist
critic would be justified in saying that it was creative. Dorothy Livesay, at the moment of writing
these two long poems, is class-conscious in her
responses to all experience which she apprehends
in terms of exploitation and human or "earthen"
servitude; she sees the urge to win new land battling against a rooted and secure feeling of possession. In this sense too, the communist sense,
her work is creative. It is propaganda and it is
art; although the forms are altogether different
from those complicated geometrical forms spoken
of by Hulme as associated in our minds with
machinery. Hulme was trying to define a geomet-

rical art of the future which would be the result of a "tendency to abstraction" working with machinery as the new material of its environment. In the poetry we have just read we have machinery used, not to create geometrical style or form, but mainly as imagery for propaganda. Instead of a "tendency to abstraction," which is the impulse behind geometrical art, we have a desire for concrete and vital imagery; since the chief aim is to present a fiery, lambent, scorching drama of the mechanization of human labour and the exploitation of men as machines. We cannot study this poetry, as we can study Pratt's, in a detached way, simply as art or as illustrating the invasion of industrial realism into poetry, because it speaks out with such resounding purpose; it sends out a call, it issues a challenge which may well give us pause.

Communist apologetic, as we have already observed, is designed to persuade us that capitalist society is decadent or dead. During her study of "decadent" literature in France the thought that art has its roots in a living society came to Dorothy Livesay as a revelation. Adopting the same connotation of the word *living*, Mr. Michael Roberts can speak of the work of Wystan Auden, Cecil Day Lewis and Stephen Spender as "vigorous living poetry, which shall release our inner energy and turn it to new ends." [12] To an artist who has grown

---

[12] *Critique of Poetry*, Cape, 1934, p. 245.

up in the post-war period, to Dorothy Livesay or
to André Malraux, communism seems to quicken
his creative powers and restore his fertility.   In
bourgeois society he feels estranged, severed from
his ethical roots.   Instead of reaping sterility in
isolation, he wants to live in communion with society and draw out of its struggles, problems and
collective myths power and vision for the creation
of new epics.   And there is a great deal to be
said in favour of this concept of living art; but we
must guard against erecting it into an absolute
criterion of art.   For the purposes of his thesis, an
economist may be justified in speaking of a writer
as singing a "long agonized requiem mass over the
highest expression of human life of which French
bourgeois society under the Third Republic had
been capable," [13] but who shall inform us when art
is dead and who shall sing its obsequies? We have
not done away with Dostoievsky, Pascal, Baudelaire and the rest when we have said that they take
the tragic view of life.   Despite the obloquy of
critics who take an optimistic view the art of those
writers is a living thing, it is there, it remains. The
phœnix raises its head in strange places. Realistic
literature which, in times not long since past, described the condition of the masses as saturated
with sordidness and sadness even now is bright
with heroism and athrob with the vision of a new

---

[13] John Strachey; of Proust.

life. Here, also, is a company of youthful Canadian farmers among whom the lost ecstacy of the Elizabethans, muted and only spasmodically hilarious during the subsequent centuries of territorial occupation, bursts out afresh at the re-discovery of a new found land. How often will it be discovered? Art, in common with every living thing, must breathe the circumambient air, but its roots are among the deep, eternal questionings, joys, conflicts, yearnings in the soul of man. A quixotic spectacle is man, undaunted amid icebergs or tombs, protesting that love never dies! Though all things crumble and decay he shall continue to urge on his lumbering caravan toward the Land of the Magnetic Mountain, that "positively real" El Dorado which, if he finds it, will never again resolve itself into an "earthen servitude."

"O my America, my new found land!"

PILGRIM OF THE ABSOLUTE

A STUDY of the four Montreal poets, F. R. Scott, A. M. Klein, A. J. M. Smith and Leo Kennedy will reveal interesting nuances in their reactions to a new environment. From T. S. Eliot, Edith Sitwell and Elinor Wylie they learned how to express their hamletism, the desert hunger of Petrouchka-like sawdust men. They have a quick eye too on the poets of their own age in England and the States. They have been guided in their reading and in their art. But after that each has tried his own powers and gone his own way. As might be expected of poets reared in the same intellectual and spiritual atmosphere, of poets who are young together, who talk and drink together in the same "Pig and Whistle," get excited together over the new poetry and run off to write their own, they have something in common. Yet, because they are exceptional men, men of vision, each has a distinct and easily recognizable personality. To begin with we must take stock of the disquietude which is common to them all so as to grasp the satire in their art. Although Kennedy was born in England and Scott only came to Montreal when he was twenty-four, yet in a deeper sense they all grew up in the largest city in the Dominion, one of the world's great markets, a stone's throw from

New York, on a magnificent waterway leading out
to England and the Continent. They all have an
experiental contact with the life and thought and
poetry of an age of bourgeois absolutism and spiritual drought. Their souls have shuddered at the
inexpressible vacuity of a pompous industrial day.
Bourgeois industrial society leaves them uncomfortable and nostalgic, it is true, though not, decid-
edly not, because it deprives them of woodland and
agricultural ecstacies but because, in its desire to
reduce everything to the scale of material goods, it
has lost all perception of any higher truth; because
it yawns with the tragic absence of any idea of
spiritual destiny, essential justice, honesty or love.
Their young dreams have broken to splinters in the
vestibules of sky-scrapers. But what matters on
the plane of art is that out of splintered dreams they
can whittle effigies of cold and mystic beauty. From
out the granite earth waters that were slurring underground burst forth and make the hillsides verdant, and voices that might have remained silent,
stilled, when childhood and Eden seemed so remote,
so ghostly, dead, are piercing the desert air with
the stark dissonance of prophetic and haunting
poetry. These poets face their age—we could not
say that of Lampman—and they face it with disciplined passion. They probe among the sand and
bones and ghettos of their disgust with the coolness of scientists eradicating gangrene. Therefore
those acts which the superficial reader might call

sensual and morbid are more correctly ceremonies
of purification. Scott is a professor of law whose
interest has turned in the direction of social re-
form. They all had a hand in bringing Prufrock
to Canada; and Scott brought Sweeney to McGill:
with those Eliot ghosts behind him he satirizes the
social life of the bourgeois from a vantage point
about seven feet above the sidewalk. But he can
write of physical love with the sang-froid of an
anatomist because he is in love with something else
—an absolute. Klein can portray Ghetto life and
character with all its age-long supineness and romance because his lamp is fed by Pinsker's doctrine
of auto-emancipation and Herzl's Zionism; because
he is the parfait troubadour who renders homage
to a Palestinian *Princesse lointaine.* Smith resolutely faces the desert because his progress, when
nothing diverts it, is along the Mystic Way through
purgation to asceticism and religious contemplation. He aspires towards a pure religious poetry
such as Europe lost some centuries ago. And Kennedy, who has had his Catholicism uprooted, can
embalm corpses and ferret among dead bones because he is still gazing with young-eyed wonder
at the Resurrection. His emotionally realistic art,
in the present transitional stage of its development,
has a more intimately social significance because
the vision has been translated into terms of the
human crisis; because at bottom he has known want
and passionately believes in another social order

when this is ended. It is evident, then, that their
satirical mood, to grip the reader, necessitates the
use of contemporary speech, the vehicle which we
have moulded and enriched to express emotions
characteristic of our time. These men are our first
poets to express their thoughts and feelings in
imagery taken from contemporary city life, there-
by introducing a new tone into Canadian verse.
For parallels we must look among the young poets
now coming to maturity in England; to W. H.
Auden, Cecil Day Lewis and Stephen Spender. It
is difficult for a reader still bound by emotional
ties to the English romantics to appreciate this
poetry, partly on account of a new symbolism, and
also because of an unusual energy which results
from a catalytic union of the poet's heart and mind.
Voicing the feeling of his associates regarding the
older Canadian poets, Kennedy writes of Lampman: "For all his careful observation, little in the
form of an emotional climax comes out of it." [1]   It
is precisely because they object, in Eliot's words, to
"the simplification and separation of the mental
faculties" [2] that they differ in technique from their
predecessors in Canadian letters.   There are even
more important distinctions which have their
roots in the souls of men.

F. R. Scott, of McGill University, lived in
Quebec City until he was twenty.   I know nothing

---

[1] *The Canadian Forum*, May, 1933.
[2] *The Nation and the Athenæum*, June 9, 1923.

about the formative influences during those early
years but it will be remembered that his father was
Canon Scott, a familiar name in Canadian antholo-
gies.   It is probable that a decisive force came into
his life when he met A. J. M. Smith in Montreal.
He has something of the keen brilliance and austerity of Smith's mind and temper.   In his lyrics
he is an intellectual man whose emotional nature
is nostalgic for romance which an age of enlight-
enment has despoiled of mystery and wonder.   In
Paradise

> "The clean aimless worlds
> Spun true and blind,
> Unseen and undisturbed
> By Mind,
>
> Till some lively molecule
> Of odd construction
> Learned the original sin
> Of reproduction." [3]

That was "Time's division"; when time was
divided from eternity.   Scott sighs the loss of an
eternal principle; a timeless, pré-intellectual,
integral and absolute Paradise.   Rational philosophy prevents him from ever encountering
l'éternel féminin.   It says you are not that little
man who, at a public dance, was cut "clean away
from his context" and

---

[3] "Paradise Lost."

"swam under water for two days
in green lagoons and red coral caves." [4]

It says you may buy something which parades as
romance on the pavement but you will have no
respect for yourself afterwards; you are trampling
on a dream.

There are two chapters, however, to Scott's
poetry and I purpose keeping them apart. In
the first he is at grips with the peculiar complex
resulting from the loss of Eden; the second is
social satire.

You may know a sunny lake in the Laurentian
Mountains or among the granite rocks of Muskoka.
For a reason, in the depths of winter, you may have
sought that shore again and wondered what had
become of the purple sea, the rusty and yellow-
green rocks and the blue pool the wind had dropped
among the reddish sand, what had become of the
light and the laughter—the rocks now · rounded
with ice, the swishing water congealed into white
superposed planes with wavy edges, the gray sky
hung with sheepskin clouds afloat in a silent magnetic radiance which snapping ice makes ghostlier
still.   The austerity of those winter lakes will lay
hold of you if you stay near them and stab you to
the bone, for it is death; death that stills the dancing heart of Youth.

---

[4] "homunculus on holiday."

FROST IN AUTUMN

"When the first ominous cold
Stills the sweet laughter of the northern lakes,
And the fall of a crisp leaf
Marks the eventual victory of death,
In the presence of granite mountains,
Ice-rounded valleys and rock shores,
I cannot bring myself to your embrace.

For love is an impudent defiance
Flung into the teeth of time,
A brazen denial
Of the omnipotence of death,
And here death whispers in the silences
And a deep reverence is due to time."

That is a typical Scott poem. It is an index of how
he manipulates the complex. Why is love out of
place, you say, in such a romantic valley? Why
does he feel its incongruity with those granite, icy
mountains by the freezing lakes? He repudiates
a "vegetable love" which, at the touch of frost, dies
like a sere and yellow leaf because he is already
in the thrall of an absolute feminine principle
having nothing to do with seasons or the fashions
of an age but eternal, like those granite mountains, defying time and death.

Now with this poem, or as we might say this
compound, on the table in front of us, it occurs to
me that we can best isolate the Scott elements in it

by subjecting it to some literary reagents of fairly recent date.

One of the poems in Verlaine's *Fêtes Galantes* is remarkable because of the vigour of its body, bringing forth new creatures every season. The features of that "Colloque Sentimental" are simply these: two forms have met in an old solitary and icy park, their eyes are dead and their lips are soft.

"—Do you remember our old ecstacy?
—Why would you have me remember?

—Does your heart still beat at my very name?
Do you in dreams still see my soul?—No.

—Ah! The blissful days unspeakable
When our lips clung together!—That may be.

—How blue the sky was and hope how bright!
—But hope has perished and to the black sky fled.

They walked among memories of passionate
    hours,
And night alone heard their words."

Not very precise features, in all conscience! But the emotion bound up with the concept of passion grown cold and dead is fairly prevalent among poets and the poem lives because it enshrines the emotion in perfectly stark, though adequate and apparently immortal tokens: the "Colloque Senti-mental" is the formula for that *particular* emo-

tion. Verlaine squeezed the essence of his sadness into those brief passionless words overheard
by night. It would be difficult to change the
tokens so as to sharpen the impression of strained
melancholy that one has on reading the poem.
They can, however, be modified in three ways: in
the persons, the dialogue, and the background;
other poets have modified and adapted them to
their own ends. For instance, the solitary and
frozen park, in a poet of the Yellow Book generation, becomes "some mysterious dusky grove" or
"darkling glade" in a dream. "The waters of
oblivion" have run over the pallid lips of the two
ghosts who "sought to speak" and "stammered" in
vain.[5] Or again they may manage to articulate
something like a sigh:

" 'How far away the stars seem, and how far
   Is our first kiss, and ah, how old my heart!'

     *   *   *

    'Ah, do not mourn,' he said,
   'That we are tired, for other loves await us.' " [6]

Passion that has romped all day is ready to fall
asleep like a "poor tired child," or limps as the
old lame rabbit limps down the path, or falls
wearily as the yellow leaves fall, "faint meteors in
the gloom." From those decadent depths to which
it had wearily fluttered Miss Sitwell rescued the

---

[5] Ernest Dowson, "Amor Profanus."
[6] W. B. Yeats, "Ephemera."

"Colloque Sentimental" and, with her astonishing
optical genius, not only brought the *décor* back
into focus but also gave it magnificent colour. She
also put a new spirit into the poem; or rather *revived* the spirit of Banville's figurines: Amaryl-
lis, Myrrhine, Titania and Columbine. In her
poem "Rain"[7] two people move aimlessly "beside
the smooth black lacquer sea." The lady is wearing a fluted hat with "ghost-flowers" but her face
seems a "muslined cloud" beneath it; one of the
effects, no doubt, of the "waters of oblivion" that
young man Dowson had made her pass through.
The hour is "silver," "white," "ghostly." "Silence
floats." They are two wandering, lost, disembodied
spirits. The colloquy has changed into a promen-
ade. What was suggestion in Verlaine has become
the form of the ghosts here. What feeling there is
in this poem is evoked by the setting: the unimpor-
tance of the little black dog (for Miss Sitwell can
put in a lame rabbit and bring out a little black
dog) that "tries to catch the white lace butterflies";
the "one curdled sheepskin flower" on the "wide
endless plain" which gives you an irresistible feeling of languor, ennui and resignation, as a plain
always does, for nothing happens there or ever will.
But the figures are fretted and stippled like black
and white Beardsley ladies in a Laforgue drizzle.
Miss Sitwell comes nearer Verlaine in another

---

[7] *Bucolic Comedies*, Duckworth, 1923.

poem, "By the Lake." [8]   But the dialogue is developing rapidly into *style précieux* and, questions of cleverness aside for a moment, the general tone of the poem is that of Pierrot reciting the last rites at Ophelia's grave; the tokens are anxious to dance a minuet, courant, or saraband; Miss Sitwell has stiffened them and shrouded them in her gold brocaded elegance—the emotion is unimportant; Verlaine's whimper has passed out. T. S. Eliot plays a capital rôle at this juncture. In "Conversation Galante," [9] as the title hints, the dialogue attains undisputed predominance; the poet reduces the *décor* to ludicrous insignificance. He salutes the tokens ironically: "our sentimental friend the moon," and

> "That exquisite nocturne, with which we explain
> The night and moonshine; music which we seize
> To body forth our vacuity."

The skeleton is true to type; the ironical spirit, the metaphysical absolute and "l'Éternel Madame" show that it has come through Corbière and Laforgue, but the poem, in its completeness, is rounded out with a serious feeling of the utter inadequacy of the tokens to appease a craving for an absolute which is Eliot's deep need.

> "You, madam, are the eternal humorist,
> The eternal enemy of the absolute."

---

[8] *Ibid.*
[9] *Poems, 1909-1925*, Faber and Gwyer, 1925.

And now we are at the table again with our compound. Scott's poem is a "colloque sentimental"; —or, more correctly perhaps, a "soliloque sentimental." The mood has developed into something deeper than irony but it is evoked by use of a concept which we may term the notion of an absolute. It will be seen now—although it was by no means obvious at first view—that the peculiar and root element of the technique is the notion of an absolute; that is part of Scott's debt to Eliot. I called the poem a compound intentionally: it is a compound of Verlaine and Eliot and Scott. Physical passion, which in Verlaine was dead, is raised to a higher power and transfigured so that it becomes a timeless, integral, absolute and paradisal love. Eliot was able to produce a body of criticism, for example, so remarkable for its cogency and point, so aloof from impressionism, sentiment and all that is particularly characteristic of the feminine soul, because he found, in philosophy and religion, a discipline for his emotions. Woman, the "eternal enemy of the absolute," cannot keep his metaphysics warm, nor can she make him whimper: he is too deeply immersed in his devotional exercises. Woman, the emancipated woman of his own time, is still "l'Éternel Madame" of Corbière and Laforgue and he can only speak of her ironically. At this point, I think, we can lay hold of the significance of Scott's poem. It is this: *l'éternel féminin* is not passion that is subject to death, not a rationalized chameleon to be treated ironically, but something which is eternal and incorruptible in woman, something which the modern age has not stifled but only camouflaged. Scott's is a peculiar case of metaphysical disquietude: he is disillusioned with femininity which is only beauty and prestige and sex-sophistry because his mind is set on something which is not these things but detached from them and which is love. It is interesting to observe, also, that the metaphysical disquietude in such poems as "Frost in Autumn" and "Spring Flame" and others is, in an important sense, transmitted to us through a landscape *décor* and the poem, instead of reproducing the intellectual symbols of poets like Donne, shows, by its discriminating regard for nature, that it has come through a period of vegetation symbolism.

Scott, through these emotional experiences, proceeds in a manner similar to Smith's. While Smith goes into the desert and brings back sand and stone which we have never seen before on our altars, Scott goes into the city and returns with a vanity box. Here are lip-stick and powder, beauty and garish lights; here the prostitution of love. Ointment of spikenard have I none but these I have; I lay them on the altar of our rational god. Then he turns away, still tortured with his nostalgia for a woman's touch, a woman's voice and for the green lagoons of Eden. Many of his poems are concerned with intimate relationships, each of which, by reason of the contrast between his idealism and life's actuality, lead him to pronounce—as I have said of Eliot—the utter inadequacy of them to appease his craving for an absolute.

"He felt the claws of his fears, and rose in a daze
  From the warm wide impenetrable wound of her
      side,
  And looked on the town's bright maze, unsatis-
      fied." [10]

"And on the Monday morning
  By none but poplars seen
  We used our clothes as carpets.
  Less maiden, but more mine

  She lay at rest with shadows
  Beneath a leafy sun." [11]

Miranda, the emancipated girl! A lady's boudoir is but a boudoir of the mind:

"Our conversation has been as personal as lip-
      stick,
  Our intimacies as private as a power-puff." [12]

And since his ideal is inviolate he can say:

"Passionless one, to whom all days are dull,
  Come and intrigue me with your weariness," [13]

---

[10] "Adieux à Deux."
[11] "Miranda."
[12] "Cosmetic."
[13] "Sonnets: i."

or light a cigarette and recline nonchalantly in a
corner:

> "Stand by the window, Tyltyl,
> Stand by the old chintz curtains.
>
> *   *   *
>
> But leave me to blow smoke rings
> In a dusty corner." [14]

Out of the corner of his mind, as it were, he can
watch the drama of love. It is the variable and
ephemeral elements which he is driven to empha-
size. A woman's beauty is a triumphant moment,
loveliness a rose that blooms and is gone;—commonplace ideas, no doubt, but art will never let
them go. Young lovers do silly things, get married,
grow old,

> "And the wife says, as she prepares to go,
> 'Put out the light, John, before you come up to
>   bed.' " [15]

And so the light goes out and night is passionless.

If human passion and physical beauty were all
then the women of these poems, seeing their beauty
gone and passion cold, would cry out and weep like
"la belle heaulmière" and the poet, moved to de-
part this life, would write his "Testament" in the
style of Master François Villon who loved a

---

[14] "Four Moments."
[15] "Young Lovers Old." *The Canadian Forum,* Aug., 1930.

woman's body and knew what sport time made of its members. There is no rage here, but "pity and tears."

> "The body of this woman, flowering once,
>   Made beggars of proud men.
> Now she has paid to tyrant years
> The tribute of her loveliness,
> And she is mistress
> Only to pity and tears.
>
> Dim of eye, with hands
> Unattentive to hair,
> Stooping at shoulder, her step
> Climbing the stair slowly,
> She gropes her way to her room
> For a brief space to dream
> Of towering moments time has overcome." [16]

One of Scott's personal achievements as an artist, it seems to me, is to have manipulated two or three simple tokens in such a way as to move us to pity those lovers in whom passion, though unrequited and hopeless, continues to burn under the dead leaves of accumulated years. In "Evensong" he cleverly infuses Verlaine's melancholy into Prufrock:

> "Shall I then proffer these arms
>   So used to the part of lover?

       *   *   *

---

[16] "Afterthought."

When the sun sets, the stars
Renew the hope and the wonder.
But for two hearts asunder
Through vain repetitive years
The sun sets, and the stars."

And in "Spring Flame" his idea is to dramatize
the ardour of an old passion; the "One of no fear"
of verse two is a man who meets and wins the woman
of verse one:

"Through the glowing dark
    She came
    Like to an arrow-head
    Of flame.

One of no fear
    By a wood
    Spake to the old fire
    In her blood.

And the brimming trees
    Knew the bond
    Between them and those two
    On the ground."

Passion is not dead but reborn and, with the return
of spring, constantly reborn. That is not the only
difference between Scott and Verlaine: Scott has
the advantage of being able to use tokens which
have a distinct power as intellectual symbols. What
are "brimming" trees?

This poet has passed through a period of intel-
lection. You see, by the examples of Dowson and
Yeats, that a man who passes through Verlaine
may come out dripping with ghostly melancholy;
but a mind that passes through Eliot comes out
equipped with intellectual symbols, hungering for
an absolute. The symbols are not yellow but crisp
and hard and do not drip; if at any time they are
weary, it is not with a mauve weariness after passion is spent but weariness of a disillusionment like
Prufrock's or Hamlet's. One of the effects of
Eliot's "The Waste Land" was to convert Sir
James Frazer's *The Golden Bough* into a manual
for young Canadian poets, the interest and strength
of whose poetry is due in a considerable degree to
their possession of a corpus of myth and ritual and
a symbolism of waste land and vegetation gods by
means of which they translate their emotions. All
the vegetation symbolism used by these poets, in
divers manners and to diverse ends, derives from
Frazer. Those lovers who are alone under the
trees symbolize the living principle which is common to man and nature, and this the trees, "brimming" with their spring sap, understand. The
death of vegetation in winter and its rebirth in
spring, which in primitive religions were associated
with the death and resurrection of the god, are in
the present case associated with the death and rebirth of passion. But we are still fairly close to
Verlaine's "frozen park" with our vegetation sym-

bols. Scott's originality consists in treating some as absolutes, some as relatives; his characteristic tricks are to contrast or interfuse them. When he contrasts human love with the inhumanity of granite—in "Frost in Autumn" and "Lone Lover":

> "At my back
> A smooth rock cover—
> This will do
> Till night is over.
>
> Here no touch
> Of limb or lip,
> Woman whisper,
> Dreamy sleep."

—he means that in the presence of mountains, which are tokens of the absolute and eternal, he cannot render homage to an ephemeral gesture of woman, to the flourish which hides *l'éternel féminin*. With lighter heart and Gallic coquetry Paul-Jean Toulet, hanging on his sweetheart's arm in the cemetery, said "Hush! We mustn't speak of love among the tombs." Yet there is an eternal feminine principle; the poet always keeps his vision of it clear.

> "This rock-borne river, ever flowing
> Obedient to the ineluctable laws,
> Brings from the north hills a cold reminder
> Of the eternal lifeless processes." [17]

---

[17] "Surfaces."

The rock-borne river is an absolute; so are rocks themselves, and mountains, the autumn wind, and snow: "eternal lifeless processes." They are contrasted with living things in the vegetable kingdom: trees, leaves, roots and sap which are symbols of the ephemeral:

> "from old hills the wind
> Blows cold, bearing no sound
> Of life striving in leaf,
> Of root probing in ground,
> Water calling, sap lifting." [18]

Whence it follows that "striving," "probing," "calling," and "lifting" are enemies of absolute stillness, utter rest and absolute life;—to abolish the time dimension definite articles are dispensed with before nouns. When he writes:

> "But coned fir trees
> Thrusting high
> To probe the mystery
> Of sky.
>
> Are tall pinnacles
> Erect
> That speak familiar
> Dialect.
>
> Night and thrusting
> Dark tree meeting—
> These be tokens
> Of my mating." [19]

---

[18] "Autumnal."
[19] "Lone Lover."

he is expressing a state of soul by setting relative and vital symbols against an eternal and mysterious life principle.

The Christian Mystics "express states of soul by means of elaborate physical landscape analogies";[20] but Scott's symbols are not mystical symbols. He stands distinct and apart from Smith in this respect. I do not imagine that his notion of love has anything to do with God. His "Calvary" is not a mystical but a metaphysical poem, technically interesting on account of the Scott pattern in which absolute and ephemeral tokens are interfused: Time's sovereignty is broken when Christ's body is pierced:

> "So with the body broken
> blood becomes token;
> Eras are stricken."

The poet's love is a refuge from the scientific view; his complaint is that science has taken away the mystery and enchantment from love. Sex-life is a "cell-colony puffed with vitality," a mode of survival. But that is not love. Therefore he can write of biological love in a passionless, scientific jargon:

> "Let us have carefully to do with touch,
> And measure sensitivity with hairs.

---

[20] T. E. Hulme, *loc. cit.*

*   *   *

You shall lie stiller than a marble nude
And underneath the skin's close coverlet
Compute the quickened beating of a heart." [21]

because he has a vision of a living principle and
dissociates love from the physical body which is
"a burden too heavy to bear."

"The moan of wind over ground,
The low round palpable sound of water
Rolling down upon stone, over and down,
And birches moving in the moving air
Came to me at dawn as I lay woken,
Like the flow and contour of an approaching
          woman,
Like a burden too heavy to bear." [22]

It is this subtle contrast of ephemeral gestures with
absolute principles that makes Scott's poetry so
stark and difficult and gives his satire such swift
and inescapable point.

Since writing the poems we have treated in the
first chapter (1925-9) he has become interested in
socialist movements and his last few poems, together
with various magazine articles[23] and his contribution to *Social Planning for Canada*,[24] are quips or
tirades against bourgeois philanthropy and snob-

----

[21] "Escapade."
[22] "Waking." *The Canadian Forum*, Jan., 1932.
[23] *Communists, Senators, and all that, The Canadian Forum*,
Jan., 1932; *The Trial of the Toronto Communists, Queen's
Quarterly*, Aug., 1932.
[24] Nelson, Toronto, 1935.

bishness, statutory repression of "unlawful" asso-
ciations and government by financial overlords.
The art of his satirical verse, as might be predicted,
is to present the material and corruptible goods to
which the age bows in reverence in a ludicrous
light, in an aura of social contrasts, or juxtaposed
with a notion of an absolute: at their point of maxi-
mum vacuity.   A bourgeois is rushed off to the
cemetery in a motor-hearse which "flaunts a *crucifix* on top." [25]   Do we not quote with pride the
statistics of our tourist trade which is sometimes
our largest annual "export" except wheat?   Do we
not gape at every new machine that is said to be the
last word in comfort and acceleration?   Here, then,
at "tourist time" [26] is a "fat woman in canvas
knickers":

> "Madam,
> The most extraordinary thing in this town
> Is the shape of your legs.
>
> O communication!
> O rapid transit!"

Shall we spend the winter in Florida or California?

SUMMER CAMP

> "Here is a lovely little camp
> Built among Canadian hills

---

[25] "Bourgeois Burial."
[26] *The Canadian Forum*, Oct., 1930.

By a Children's Welfare Society
Which is entirely supported by voluntary con-
    tributions.
All summer long underprivileged children scam-
    per about.
And it is astonishing how quickly they look healthy
    and well.
Two weeks here in the sun and air
Through the kindness of our charity subscribers
Will be a wonderful help to the little tots
When they return for a winter in the slums." [27]

A few shorter selections from this "Anthology of
up-to-date Canadian poetry" will better illustrate
his antithetical method:

NATURAL RESOURCES

"Come and see the vast natural wealth of this mine.
In the short space of ten years
It has produced six American millionaires
And two thousand pauperized Canadian fami-
    lies."

HOSPITAL

"Here the sick and dying are cared for
With the latest scientific skill,
And are visited by those to whom they are dear—
The well-to-do, in their private rooms, every day,
The poor, in the public wards,
From 2 to 5 p.m. on Tuesdays and Thursdays."

---

[27] *The Canadian Forum*, May, 1932.

CHRISTMAS SHOPPING

"It is so nice for people to give things at Christmas
That the stores stay open every evening till ten,
And the shop-girls celebrate the coming of Christ
By standing on their feet fourteen hours a day."

MODERN MEDICINE

"Here is a marvellous new serum:
Six injections and your pneumonia is cured.
But at present a drug firm holds the monopoly
So you must pay $14 a shot—or die."

As a specimen of social capillarity we have this
human embryo which, during the progress of its
auto-affirmation, cultivated the requisite contacts
until it

"Occupies a front pew
In *Who's Who*," [28]

and writes its signature on the frieze of the new
sanatorium or on the "fifty thousand dollar gates"
opening on a college campus.

"The furious games are fought and won,
The Thundering Thousands come and go,
Upon St. James' Street shines the sun
And Ottawa reflects the glow." [29]

---

[28] "Teleological."
[29] "Blumberg comes to McGill." The "Thundering Thousands"
are the college rooters or "rah-rah boys."

In the earlier satires his spleen made him go further than Eliot in the use of scientific terminology
but tricks of language and gesture which are Eliot's
very own—"give promise of more startling sins,"
"to keep their gizzards warm,"—were tantalizing
in a man with such an excellent method. But that
is over and done with. When he relies on his own
dialectic his work is more rapidly corrosive than
purely communist poetry;[30] in a thermo-dynamic
sense, he is like a surgeon removing false impressions with carbon dioxide snow—in a passionless
way. We shall see presently how this caustic com-
pares with the solar wrath of his Hebrew friend,
Klein, facing the ghetto.

It is evident enough that contemporary conditions have induced in us a mood for satire. Forty
years ago Lampman passed through the same mood
and joyfully wended his way up the beautiful Gati-
neau valley. But Scott is a poet of rare courage who
comes into the city—as a pilgrim returning from
the East—and beholds the ignorant devotions of
the multitudes. For are they not Athenians, spending their time hearing or telling or selling some new
thing? Ye men of Athens, I perceive that above
all things ye believe in advertising. As I passed
through your city and came to this mountain I
noticed neon signs in conspicuous corners of markets and intersections rippling as with the magic

---

[30]*Cf.* "Bourgeois Burial" with "The Funeral" by Stephen Spender
(*New Signatures*).

of fabulous profits. And on bill-boards I read em-
bossed posters threatening rebellious heretics with
twenty years in prison. Wherefore I declare unto
you. . . . But it is not necessary to reproduce the sermon *in extenso*; under the arms of that luminous
but despised cross the moral is obvious. When we
are not victims of perverted instincts we yearn for
love, essential justice, freedom to live happily with
our fellows, to enjoy the fruits of earth and our own
minds, to fashion our souls against the evil day.
What is eternal in woman is not class or station,
emancipated rôle or man-like costume or rational
and scientific habits of mind and body—not that,
but more than that, but love in all the wonder and
mystery of a living principle. This poet would
raise us out of the ignoble fictions of our present
economy into the spiritual ether of Eden as it was
before time's division, before the fruit of the tree
opened our eyes and took away all mystery. Once
he could write of a "vagrant" who, after the manner
of Banville's clown, leaped out of a modern city,
out of a "pit of perpendiculars," as Klein describes
it, and fled beyond the stars, beyond the "compass
of his mind," to find a "polar absolute."

> "now you may see him   virginal
>   content to live in montreal."

No, he is neither baffled nor defeated; his pole-
star is still shining, but in the city he has found his

mission: to teach and strive after and transfigure
what is essentially charitable and noble and just in
human relationships. His real significance is that,
in his own way, he describes an episode in the
Odyssey of the modern soul and makes us feel
the distance which separates the relative from the
absolute, the corruptible from the incorruptible
which death, the last enemy, can only glorify.

> "Will it be long, O Death, before
>   I sleep, and sing no more this lay:
> By Manitou's deserted shore
> The homing herons cry no more?" [31]

---

[31] "Villanelle of Manitou."

THE SPIRIT'S PALESTINE

ST. LAWRENCE Main and its tributary streets constitute the Ghetto, one of the three Jewish settlements in Montreal. It is a "warren of small stores and tumbling houses, where large red-faced butchers sire smaller butchers and the occasional poet." Leo Kennedy no doubt had a particular poet in mind when he wrote those lines. Do not infer that Abraham Moses Klein's father was a butcher—he was by profession really a potter—but rather that the poet might have been a butcher or a presser or a cutter or, more probably still, an orthodox rabbi if the soul of this Jewish boy, as all his magnificent poetry and all his multifarious activities attest, had not been illumined, yea fired, with a vision which will never let him rest: a vision of emancipation. The outward and visible environment in which he was reared may well be that described by Kennedy: the Ghetto with its "shabby-derbied and round-shouldered rabbonim twisting syllogistic thumbs at beard level on many a crowded corner . . . with large silk and velvet clad matrons ponderously shoving imported English perambulators, laden till the springs squeak with one chubby Yidel and the week-end's vegetables . . . with over-barbered and under-read 'cavaliers' lurching in and out of pool rooms and

the back parlors of barber shops, where craps and
pinochle are grave pursuits . . . with the bright
white windows of bake shops offering strings of
baigle and loaves of shabbas broit . . . with the pros-
perous and noisy delicatessens wafting out into the
disturbed night their mingled smells of herring,
smoked meat, salami and swiss cheese . . . while
from the kosher restaurants with their insistent
window legends and blue mogen dovids, emerge
high and enervating odours of truly exquisite
borscht, stuffed miltz, and the all-encompassing,
ultimately satisfying incense of pot roast chicken." [1]
But the air the poet breathes is not that. If Klein's
parents had had money they would have pushed
him into the rabbinate; [2] as it is he went through
most of the prescribed readings for love. He knows
his Torah and Talmud and his Graetz. He thoroughly assimilated what the history, literature and
rabbinical erudition of his race could offer his
healthy and inspired appetite. He lives partly on
that and, in part, on the cultural nourishment he
obtained outside the Ghetto. Klein's soul, without
a doubt, is an ardent symbol of the spiritual rebirth
of the Jewish people; the resounding anger and the
prophetic vision, the impassioned lyricism of his
poetry witness to the depth and intensity of Israel's
awakening to a realization of her ancient and splendid destiny, yet one of the rare qualities his poetry

---

[1] *The Jewish Standard*, Toronto, Sept. 30, 1932.
[2] He is now practising law in Montreal.

possesses—although it is not my intention to stress it unduly—is the tone, the mature, the gentle tone due indisputably to a power his soul acquired through intimate association with the literatures of Europe. Klein will not let us forget this. He gives us not only "Designs for Mediæval Tapestry" and the "Ballad of the Dancing Bear" but also the "XXII Sonnets"; not only "Portraits of a Minyan"[3] and "Talisman in Seven Shreds"[4] but also the "Diary of Abraham Segal, Poet"[5]—a long *sirventes* built to Eliot specifications, reinforced at intervals by a line from Moréas or Mallarmé, dramatized, it is true, by "gestures Hebraic" but at the same time spiced with Chaucer and Shakespeare. The various moods of the Jewish mind and its nostalgia are tempered by an æsthetic attachment to Elizabeth and Dante. The poet's pilgrimage to the Holy Land is through a ghetto of bitter herbs for love's sweet sake.

"O love casts roses beneath broken shoes,
And paves this ghetto street with burnished gold." [6]

Chivalry, at any rate the age of chivalry, is a purely Western phenomenon sprung from the soil of European Christian culture.

---

[3] *Menorah Journal,* Oct., 1929.
[4] *Ibid.,* July, 1932.
[5] *The Canadian Forum,* May, 1932.
[6] *Gestures Hebraic.*

"As a nation," says Klein, speaking of his own people, "we were forced to suffer eighteen centuries of stunned amazement before we realized that God helps those who help themselves." [7] After the pogroms of 1880 in Russia Dr. Leo Pinsker published his Zionist classic, *Auto-Emancipation,* which had some effect in recalling the Jews from their "stunned amazement" and inciting them to act. "Among the living nations of the earth," wrote Pinsker,[8] "the Jews occupy the position of a nation long since dead. The whole world saw in this people the uncanny form of one of the dead walking among the living." Klein tilts his lance against all forms of death; he will kill death and all her ministers—in the name of life. Simply to frame some concept by which our minds might grasp the unity in Klein's material we may regard his poetry as the illustration of a knightly outlook on life and all that outlook implies. Zionism is a vision of a return to, and life in, Palestine, the realization of which will lead the poet to war on false prophets, to seek his ship and ultimately—where?

The ghetto is crowded with false prophets who connive with expediency or resign themselves, who keep the letter of the law without raising a finger to remedy their condition, who rant at God, who have lost the spirit of the Jewish epics. There are streets full of them in the "Ballad of the Dancing

[7] *The Judaean,* Montreal, Nov., 1931.
[8] Quoted by Klein.

Bear" and "Ave Atque Vale"; and it is from the
depths of moral turpitude as well as bricks and
mortar and in the present year of grace that Klein
cries "out of a pit of perpendiculars." He faces
them all; the tone with which he treats them makes
clear the essential differences between his nature
and Scott's. Scott's ironical mood expressed itself
in satire which at best was hardly more than a sneer.

There is humour in Klein. He knows his rabbis;
did they not solve for him "each letter's mystic
hook" and " hem his heart with old Jerusalem"?

> "Reb Abraham loved Torah,
> If followed by a feast:
> A Milah-banquet, or a
> Schnapps to drink, at least.
>
> On Sabbath-nights, declaring
> God's praises, who did cram
> The onion and the herring?
> Fat-cheeked Reb Abraham.
>
> *   *   *
>
> And at Messiah's greeting,
> Reb Abraham's set plan
> Is to make goodly eating
> With roast leviathan." [9]

And much wit:

> "two boards are thy horizons; germs
> Thy concubines." [10]

---

[9] "Portraits of a Minyan," *Menorah Journal*, Oct., 1929.
[10] "The Words of Plauni-Ben-Plauni to Job."

"Hope grows great, like three day yeast." [11]

> "lean Reb Zadoc
> Swallowing his fig that tumbled down
> His throat, transparent and ascetic." [12]

His irony is keen; sometimes directly expressed, most often dramatized, as it were, by means of portraits. Reb Simcha, the hair-splitting exegete,

> "Interprets, in some song-spared nook,
> To God the meaning of His book." [13]

Old Mendel, the sweet singer, having neither learning nor riches, hopes to attain Paradise

> "By iterating and re-iterating psalms." [14]

Homunculus, the little Jew,

> "He bore his yoke
> As it were air." [15]

> "Phylactery on brow in lieu of thought,
> rabbi, communing with the hierarch." [16]

One of the best in the category is Reb Levi Yit-schok who, in a different spirit from that of Job or Vigny's "Moses" or "Christ," would reason with the Almighty and cries out:

---

[11] "Ballad of the Dancing Bear."
[12] "Ave Atque Vale."
[13] "Portraits of a Minyan."
[14] *Ibid.*
[15] "And the Man Moses was Meek."
[16] "Talisman in Seven Shreds."

"Where is the trumpeted Messiah? Where
The wine long-soured into vinegar?
Have cobwebs stifled his mighty shofar? Have
Chilblains weakened his ass's one good hoof?"[17]

That is Klein's purpose, not to present a strong
argument against God, but to portray a silly wailer.
Job, indeed, is a neurotic grouser who loves his
pain:

"Bethink thyself again, O Job, again
Consider and give over all these sighs...

*   *   *

That in the tomb there is not even pain."[18]

Gentler pieces of satire are "Preacher" and this
"Etching":

"The sky is dotted like th' unleavened bread,
The moon a golden platter in the sky.
Old midget Jews, with meditated tread,
Hands clasped behind, and body stooped ahead,
Creep from the synagogue and stare on high
Upon a golden platter in a dotted sky."[19]

But in a moment again terror grips the Jewish
heart:

"The leaves rustle. Come, who will now determine
Whether this be the wind, or priestly robes.

[17] "Reb Levi Yitschok talks to God."
[18] "The Words of Plauni-Ben-Plauni to Job."
[19] "Haggadah."

The frogs croak out ecclesiastic German,
Whereby our slavish ears have punctured lobes.
The stars are mass-lamps on a lofty altar;
Even the angels are Judæophobes." [20]

and the oppressor comes down like a wolf:

"The wrath of people is like foam and lather
Risen against us. Wherefore, Lord, and why?
The winds assemble; the cold and hot winds
    gather

To scatter us. They do not heed our cry.
The sun rises and leaps the red horizon,
And like a bloodhound swoops across the sky." [21]

When Klein meets an apostate, his arch-betrayer,
he can flail him with "solar wrath" equal to the
oppressor's. Thaddeus, a very good sample, suc-
cumbs to Christian money and Christian wenches
and, in the capacity of priest and confidant of a
Russian nobleman, Pan Stanislaus, squeezes the
Jews in the villages to provide his master with ale
and amusement. When oppression and extortion
have reduced them to cringing abjection Pan Stanislaus at a banquet one night called for a Hebrew
dancer.

"Jews, cease lamentations; throttle
Sorrow; I will dance, says Mottel.

Lords and barons, dukes and pans,
Seated on their silk divans,

---

[20] "Designs for Mediæval Tapestry."
[21] *Ibid.*

At the banquet-feast prepare
To see Motka dance in air.

Barons slap their Christian thighs
As they see tall Motka rise,

Dancing, waving paws in air,
A pathetic Hebrew bear;

Flaunting his ungrizzly beard,
Ignorant of knaves who jeered.

A huge moujik cracks his whip
Loudly to make Mottel skip.

The bear leaps, he hops, he prances,
Tzithzith flutter as he dances.

Drummers drum, and fiddlers fiddle,
Make a music for the Zhid'l. . .

Happily as a bloated louse
The fat baron Stanislaus

Swills his beer, and munches pork
While he keeps time with his fork.

Motka leaps, he pirouettes,
Gasps and gambols, Motka sweats.

With God's praises on his lips
Motka capersomely skips.

Barons pat their shaking paunches,
Motka rises on his haunches,

Leaps and dances; when behold!
By his rhythms so cajoled,

Even servants drop their plates,
Drop the ducal delicates;

Guardian-varlets leave their stances
And leap into Mottel's dances.

Yea, the butler breaks his bottle
As he strives to out-do Mottel.

Lo! the Pan, sucking a bone,
Suddenly forsakes his throne,

With him in the circle hop
All the lords; they cannot stop. . .

Drummers drum, and fiddlers fiddle!
Make a music for the Zhid'l. . .

For from off her couch she rises,
Paulinka the princess, rises,

No more a bed-ridden cripple,
Tall, her lovely limbs most supple,

Rises, trips toward him, halts,
And takes Motka for a waltz!...

In the hamlet busy Jews
Ply their trades in wonted use.

Thaddeus priest now tells his beads,
While his stone heart bleeds, and bleeds.

Paulinka the princess sings
Of God's unforsaken things.

In Pan Stanislaus's throat
Overbrimming bumpers float.

Motka sells his crystal waters,
Earning dowries for his daughters.

And God in His heaven hums,
Twiddling His contented thumbs. . ."

The sprightly ballad is not only remarkable for
the variety of emotions it arouses and the number
of false prophets it satirizes, but also for the discipline which the figures and emotions suffered as
they passed into art: reading and passion have been
combed and dressed to fit a satiric symbol which is
at once familiar and powerful enough to translate them into art and to stand as a formula for
them. The direct method, which uses the most
obvious vocables:

"Many the provinces I rule but *weariness* rules
over me,

*   *   *

King Solomon on *boredom* sups, and on *satiety*
he dines," [22]

does not provide the formula, does not evoke the
correlative emotions; — certainly not in lyrical

---

[22] "Koheleth."

poetry. The danger is imminent in those pieces which the poet wrote under the influence of an emotion he could not discipline. "The Poet to the Big Business Man":

"Big-bellied dewlapt grand vacuity. . .
You nincompoop, you totally-excess.

*   *   *

You plutocrat of gilded emptiness,
Full guts is your sole teleology . . ."

is gross and ineffectual bombast. But ballads are of their nature heroic, surviving, so to speak, as fragments of older epics, as epitomes of the passion and action of earlier drama. Passages of Klein's writing take us back through Elizabethan drama to the old Hebrew epic.

"Foul deed done! We will avenge! Hence!
Seek the culprit! Wreak the vengeance!
Find him! We will screw his thumbs off!
Pluck his gizzard! Tear his limbs off!
  Be his carcass-remnants fried!" [23]

"Let heathenesse seek refuge in its steel;
Let pagandom invest its coat of mail;
This prayer-shawl is armour to this Jew." [24]

"How, then, and wherefore, despite barbaric wrath
does Jacob swallow sword and fire-brand

[23] "Ballad of Signs and Wonders."
[24] "Scribe."

to outlive every Judeophobic froth?
Is it the finger of the Lord's right hand?
Or is the golem saviour, this rude goth
whose earthy paw is like a magic wand?" [25]

"Rather than have my brethern bend the knee
To images engraved on silver coins,

      *   *   *

I would be glad to see them bow their faces
Into the dust before a solar wrath,
Behold them dance, hurling their wanton phrases,
Unto the hornèd moon of Ashtaroth." [26]

We are in a mood now and hear a language we never
felt or heard in Scott. This dramatic realism and
prophetic wrath, this combination of Shakespeare
and Jeremiah, of blood and brain, is entirely new
to us and entirely Klein's. His brother poets have
no prophets, no persecution of epic proportions,
therefore no anger. Neither have they phylacteries
or many-branched candelabra or unleavened
bread; neither have they spices, figs, dates or
"toothsome" almonds, ointments or choicest orna-
ments, sweet wine or gold from Ophir. But let
us not be dupes of an alluring Orientalism or exotic
religious ritual; let us not gape indecorously at
these quinquiremes from Nineveh. Let us move
warily through the tapestries of Oriental splendour
and accustom our eyes to the hangings on the walls

---

[25] "Talisman in Seven Shreds."
[26] "Rather than have my Brethern Bend the Knee."

and not be afraid of the flutter near the cushioned carved head of a soft couch. We have met her before, this beautiful Shoshannah who is reclining there, even if she have "jet-black hair" and lips "as red as is the core of ripe pomegranates." She is the "fairest daughter of fair Lebanon":

"Thy smile is like the whiteness of the tusk
    Of ivory, my darling one, and thy
Sweet breath is as a waft of powdered musk
    Within a garden when a wind doth sigh. . .
Thy hair is like the coolness of the dusk," [27]

but, rare phenomenon, she is not the Shulamite. Behind the "algum-casemented window" where she dreams of a caravanserai and a Prince who will climb her high lattice wall and carry her away, she is neither the Shulamite nor the Lady of Shalott but related to both; she will not miss the fields of barley and of rye because she will cultivate them where she is in Lebanon. It is a charming art which mingles East and West, Hebrew lyric, Arthurian lay, Provençal *alba,* Gallician *cantigas de amigo,* and weaves a dream of fair women with a polyglot woof of many-coloured silks. "Legend of Lebanon" is the dream of a poet who is at once a Zionist and a Christian knight.

To anathematize the false prophets Klein had to harangue them in the "ghetto-lanes of Prague"

---

[27] "Legend of Lebanon," *The Jewish Standard,* Apr. 14, 1933.

and Montreal; to fight the oppressor he had to encounter baron and burgher in Poland and Russia;
to probe the misery into which Jewry had sunk he
had to grovel in Central European villages after a
pogrom when it was most hideous and revolting.
But what is this?

"Shoshannah, sweet Shoshannah, lovely one,

    *   *   *

Awake, arise."

Not a forgotten spring-song of the great wise
king, not a serenade that Romeo might have
crooned, but the love-song of an exile gazing out
of ghetto-lanes towards orange-groves and distant
Palestinian skies embowering home and love.

From Zionist literature, from the writings of
Martin Buber perhaps more especially, Klein's
mind grasped the concept of a People as a succession of generations growing up and propagat-
ing their kind in harmony, as it were, with the
great cyclic rhythm of nature. The ghetto Jews
have a calendar but they have not life. Nature
is life, the earth is life. As a contrast to the No-
Land of exile, sterile and hopeless, there is a land
where the calendar is blended with the natural
life of the People. That is the vision of a Zionist
in whose heart is rooted the blended notion of land
and home—not a communist complex but an historical belief that God gave the land to His peo-

ple. This Zionist outlook produced such poems as "Cargo"—fruits and prayer-shawls and Torah rolls from Jaffa—and "Sonnet XII."

As the years go by much of Klein's satirical and prophetic verse may lose its savour but the sonnets have an abiding beauty. It is to them that we shall return as to an inner chamber incensed with the tenderness, humility and passion of a poet's soul; passion which still has sovereign power, yet disciplined by study, enriched by learning, gentle and strong.

> "I rise from dreams
> Of you beside me on a garden lawn." [28]

Shelley, yes; but passing on we hear of an *aube* and *envoy* and *serenade* and realize that we are at the day-spring of the sonnet—far away beyond the nature sonnets of Lampman and Wordsworth —at the golden dawn in Italy. We think of Rossetti's love-songs and translations and, through them, of the immortal *Vita Nuova*.

There are evidences of the beginning of that New Life in "Sonnet XX." In a restaurant with his literati friends, "Platos exhaling smoke from cigarettes," "calling one another asses" and "shouting their love for the working-classes," he "toys with a blank menu and a pen" which scribbles:

---

[28] "Sonnet XIX."

"L'amor che move il sole e l'altre stelle."

—the unforgettable line which closes the Divine
Comedy. Is that not the sort of anecdote we
should treasure if it concerned an Elizabethan
coffee-shop or a Florentine street-meeting of
Dante with Guido and Cino or Beatrice? The
poet's pen might have scribbled another line:

"Voi che, intendendo, il terzo ciel movete,"

—you who, by your understanding or love, move
the third heaven, that over which the star of Venus
rules; the star that Dante saw filling the Orient
of his Purgatory with joy and hope. The line
seems to have been Dante's favourite since he re-
peats it several times and notably in the sonnet
which Klein may have had in mind when he wrote:

"Seventy regal moons, with clouds as train,
    Have climbed the marble staircase of the sky,
    Since we in homage first cried 'Suzerain,
    Accept thy lieges.' " [29]

Who is this feudal lady, this "Suzerain" to whom
the lovers render homage? She is the regnant
moon; in the poet's third heaven Queen of Love.

"If there will be a moon to-night, arise,
    Put on your loveliest dress, and take the road

---
[29] "Sonnet IV."

That leads to mountains pivoting the skies.
Regard the moon. Though at the antipode,
And I, upon these lowlands, am as far,
Though I be miles from you, the moon, a mirror,
Silvered and framed in many an angled star,
Will smile your smile, and I will know you nearer.
But if the moon still lingers in Cathay
Or hangs caught in the branches of some tree,
Or has been splintered by a comet-spray,
Or lies drowned at the bottom of the sea,—
Why, I will choose a hill, and sit on grass,
And think of fate, and sigh, Alas! Alas! . . ." [30]

Is there not a remembrance of Beatrice in that
notion of reflected splendour, in that mirror-moon
which smiles her smile? Did ever poet write a
more beautiful "letter" to his beloved? Did Donne
or Dante by whatsoever planetary mechanism
render absence so physically sensible? Or troubadour sigh so hopelessly, deprived of his Lady's
smile? But let her smile, then from her visage
emanates the spirit of love, as when Beatrice moved
her lips and said to the lover's soul: "Sospira."
The smile, the sigh, the humble and charming attitude, the nostalgia, the incantation of the Tuscan
school are all there, and a delicacy of feeling not
anticipated in the satires. The technical significance of the sonnets is that a sweet singer of the
lineage of David has tried to recapture the "dolce
stil nuovo" for Canadian poetry.

---

[30] "Letters to One Absent."

"Amor e cor gentil sono una cosa"

is the definition of Klein's sensibility: love in a
gentle heart.

"Would that three centuries past had seen us born!
 When gallants brought a continent on a chart
 To turreted ladies waiting their return.
 Then had my gifts to you declared my heart!" [31]

His attitude to his Lady is just that, whether as a
Knight in shining armour, "unsullied, clean,"
offering precious gifts to his high-born Lady or as

"a humble thin-voiced Jew
Hawking old clo'es in ghetto lanes, for you."

"Even," he says,

"Even if your heart were stone
 I would be its moss. . ." [32]

A twentieth-century troubadour, whose *terra lonh-
dana*[33] is at the antipode yet close as breathing,
blends with love all the waking and warm emotions
of spring blooms and summer suns. Winter and
death he cannot bear:

"The wind guffawing gusts of vandal song;
 The golden poplars spoiled by noisy thieves;

---

[31] "Sonnet VI."
[32] "Assurance."
[33] Jaufre Rudel: "Quan lo rius de la fontana."

The moon a withered bloom, and all night long
Brown leaves falling, and rain on dark brown
    leaves." [34]

In another tone:

        "what is Spring to marvel at
When Autumn's very leaves are blossoming?" [35]

And in the scholar's tone:

"Lady Autumn in her sleeping walks. . .
Her eyes shine madly with remembered gleams
Of blood upon dead leaves. . ." [36]

Age turns black hair white and chills the blood:

"Let us avow the cup was drained, before
The moon turned blot, the sun a leper's
    sore." [37]

In the springtime of love:

    "Your laugh is joy in blossom." [38]

He calls his love from sorrowing:

"O my beloved, do not sorrow thus.
The moon has lost no lustre, and the sun
No sunlight." [39]

---

[34] "Sonnet V."
[35] "October Heresy."
[36] "Sleep Walking Scene."
[37] "Sonnet IX."
[38] "Sonnet XXII."
[39] "Five Weapons against Death," *Menorah Journal*, Jan., 1929.

Yet, like a parfait knight, he feels another's sorrow:

"Where shall I find choice words to mention
    Sorrow
That Sorrow may not be a pain to you?

    *   *   *

Where shall I find such delicate, such tender
Phrases as will slide off your heart, and not
Open the wound that I had said had vanished?
Where shall I find that soft word, that mild
    thought?" [40]

His vision of a Resurrection is awaking to "hear you weeping overhead." Death to him is the usurpation of powers and thrones by maggots, he wants to be alive: Spring is the season of his "perennial love-madnesses."

If we describe the style of the sonnets as feudal and Elizabethan—and there is no mistaking the ring of these lines:

"His face is as an ancient palimpsest
    Where tears have blurred the versions of a
        sorrow,
    Have blurred the varied versions of a sorrow,
And blurring, made it all more manifest. . . ." [41]

—we have taken no account of the vision, the vision which illumines all the domestic objects in

---

[40] "Where shall I find Choice Words?"
[41] "Portrait."

the Jewish home and makes the poet's heart leap among almond-blossoms and golden oranges crying: "Jerusalem, next year!"

"The candles splutter; and the kettle hums;
  The heirloomed clock enumerates the tribes;
Upon the wine-stained table-cloth lie crumbs
Of matzoh whose wide scattering describes
Jews driven in far lands upon this earth.
The kettle hums; the candles splutter; and
Winds whispering from shutters tell re-birth
Of beauty rising in an eastern land,
Of paschal sheep driven in cloudy droves;
Of almond-blossoms colouring the breeze;
Of vineyards upon verdant terraces;
Of golden globes in orient orange-groves. . .
And those assembled at the table dream
Of small schemes that an April wind doth scheme,
And cry from out the sleep assailing them:
Jerusalem, next year! Next year, Jerusalem!" [42]

Hearing the "still small voice" beckoning intempestively they will start "from out the sleep assailing them" and mumble, perhaps a little crusty: "I will arise and go now." But once aroused to the present reality beyond the window-panes they will exclaim:

"These northern stars are scarabs in my eyes.
  Not any longer can I suffer them.
I will to Palestine. We will arise
  And seek the towers of Jerusalem.

---

[42] "The Still Small Voice."

Make ready to board ship. Say farewells. Con
Your Hebrew primer; supple be your tongue
To speak the crisp words baked beneath the sun,
The sinuous phrases by the sweet-singer sung.
At last, my bride, in our estate you'll wear
Sweet orange-blossoms in an orange-grove.
There will be white doves fluttering in the air,
And in the meadows our contented drove,
Sheep on the hills, and in the trees, my love,
There will be sparrows twittering Mazel
    Tov." [43]

If I were a Zionist I would hang those georgics
in my study and read them every day. As it is I
sit in admiration of that sonnet, its tone, and the
perfect artistry of the first line:

"These northern stars are scarabs in my eyes."

These "northern stars" and *those* "scarabs" have
a magic power of evocation and together make an
optically balanced picture. The very things that
were indigenous in Scott, his very own, and which
he wished to keep fresh and chaste, "unsullied" by
Greek or Roman cult,[44] the "northern stars" of
Canada have become symbols of an alien land in
which a poet suffers and cannot stay. "Make ready
to board ship," he calls to his beloved, "we will
arise and seek the towers of Jerusalem." Let us
watch them go.

---

[43] "Sonnet XII."
[44] "New Names."

On this summer morning the waters of the St.
Lawrence and the hills beyond are bathed in the
glory of a dawn which has put the northern stars
to flight.   An ocean liner is throbbing at the
wharf taking on passengers and baggage for Tel
Aviv.   Groups of Zionists are disappearing over
the hill towards the boat, while Ludwig Lewisohn
and Martin Buber and Edmond Fleg are yet to
come.   Some of the lovers are chatting under the
trees regardless of the dew upon their *escarpins,*
perhaps oblivious of the cardinal's fiery call, while
two, whose going has brought us here, have stopped
upon the brink and turned their heads to say farewell.   They will always stay like that, with their
heads turned, and never go.   They are returning
to Palestine and will never get there; because they
cannot give their whole souls to Israel.   The lure
of Western culture creates a poignant problem in
their consciences and casts a veil of melancholy
over their faces, for it is man's spirit that yearneth.
Dante wished that he could be carried off as if
by enchantment and put upon a boat to sail away
with Beatrice and his friends and spend the days
talking of love.   The Ideal boat, outward bound
on this summer day for Cythera and the spirit's
Palestine, responds to the same emotions through
all the ages of man's history.   Silhouetted against
the Oriental magnificence of Klein's poetry, these
lovers will always linger on the hill, gently leaning
on each other, as in a Watteau picture, their heads

o'ercargoed with alien and knightly romance, their hearts with loon-cries from the northern lakes.

DIFFICULT, LONELY MUSIC

A S I brood over the strained words and subtle
meanings of this young poet, matured by
prolonged study and contemplation, I think of
Milton's Platonist in the tower, and Alastor among
the rocks and cacti of an aëry wilderness, and Axel
d'Auersperg who, refusing to be duped by the
world of appearances, has himself become his soul.
At first I see Smith in the guise of those figures
that cross and recross the mind of W. B. Yeats.
Under the sign of a later poet his effigy changes
again and I see him this time as a spiritual athlete
training his soul as a runner trains his body. After
all this training he has turned his mind outward
upon the present scene.

A. J. M. Smith[1] was born of English parents in
Montreal. During his terms at McGill, from
which he graduated in 1925, he was stirred most
by a course of lectures in seventeenth-century literature given by an Englishman who probably
also put into his hands plaquettes of verse by T. S.
Eliot and Edith Sitwell. The essay on "Hamlet
in Modern Dress"[2] and some of the early poems
prove that he mastered Eliot's mannerisms: his

[1] Assistant Professor of English in the University of South
Dakota.
[2] *The McGill Fortnightly Review*, Nov. 3, 1926.

citation-reminders of other poets, his Hamletesque changes of tone. "Testament," [3] for example, could only have been written by a man who had more than a passing acquaintance with "The Waste Land." "A Hyacinth for Edith" [4] and certain adjectives which occur in other poems betoken his regard for Miss Sitwell's poetry and his mastery of both her earlier and later styles. In the natural course of mental events he studied the work of one writer who is credited by some critics as the beginner of this new poetry: W. B. Yeats. The exercise occupied his mind from 1925 to 1926, in which year he presented a dissertation on Yeats' poetry for the M.A. degree at McGill. Shortly afterwards he went to Edinburgh on a fellowship. When he had to decide on a subject for a doctor's dissertation, he chose to study in more detail the religious poets of the seventeenth century under the direction of Professor Grierson, the well-known authority on John Donne. As a result of his cultivated intimacy with these poets, various images and symbols, epithets and tricks of phrasing passed into his own poetry; they help us appreciably to understand the work, which is stamped, not less patently, with the power and austerity of his own mind.

The earliest poems we have at hand were published in *The McGill Fortnightly Review, The*

---

[3] *Ibid.*, Mar. 10, 1927. *The Canadian Forum,* Aug., 1930.
[4] *The Canadian Forum,* July, 1930.

Canadian Mercury and *The Canadian Forum*.
In 1927 poems begin to appear in American journals and his latest are appearing in England. He
is slowly acquiring prestige among the new generation of poets writing in English. It is only after
what seems a winter's hibernation that he gives
his poems to the world.

Smith's mind, then, was freshly steeped in Yeats,
Eliot, the metaphysical poets and the varied literature which a student is bound to traverse before
he arrives at an accurate knowledge of those poets.
Although an admirer of Yeats' earlier poetry,
where the old legends of Ireland blend with
easily comprehended emotional symbols, it is
Yeats' later poems, webs woven of much more
difficult and intellectual symbols, that Smith has
made his own. And among these the tower is
Yeats' favourite. It is an old symbol but it takes
one's mind back more quickly to Shelley's "Prince
Athanase" and Milton's "Il Penseroso." The
Platonists there represented in their towers Yeats
connected with the signs and shapes spoken of in
another of Shelley's early poems, "The Revolt of
Islam," in the passage where the imprisoned
Cythna tells Laon how she became wise through
subjective contemplation:

"And on the sand would I make signs to range
    These woofs, as they were woven, of my
        thought;

    Clear, elemental shapes, whose smallest change
      A subtler language within language wrought:
      The key of truths which once were dimly
          taught
In old Crotona."

When we see the tower in Yeats' poetry it is, of
course, fashioned after his own myth; otherwise
it would not hold us. The man in the tower on
the Connemara Road in which

    "Benighted travellers
      From markets and from fairs
      Have seen his midnight candle glimmering" [5]

is versed in the strange learning of an obscure race
of Arabs, the Judwalis, and since he was born near
the moon's full, which among the Judwalis symbolizes perfect subjectivity and perfect beauty, he
represents the subjective soul seeking itself. Then,
to progress in harmony with the belief that "all
dreams of the soul End in a beautiful man's or
woman's body," [6] the end of Yeats' dream is a
Bedouin Cythna, perfectly beautiful and versed
in the ancient wisdom of her race, who writes upon
the sand when the moon is full. [7] Another piece
of wisdom (a beautiful soul makes for itself a
beautiful body), borrowed from Spenser's "Hymn

[5] "The Tower."
[6] "The Phases of the Moon."
[7] "The Tower."

to Beauty" or from Castiglione, completes the
cycle of Yeats' thought:

> "The signs and shapes;
> All those abstractions that you fancied were
> From the great treatise of Parmenides;
> All, all those gyres and cubes and midnight
>   things
> Are but a new expression of her body
> Drunk with the bitter sweetness of her youth." [8]

Now we know the meaning of the signs—for Yeats.

In such early poems as "The Moment and the
Lamp" and "For Ever and Ever, Amen," [9] Smith
is working with the symbols of the tower and the
candle and his essay on "Some Relations between
Henry Vaughan and Thomas Vaughan" [10] shows
how Yeats' belief in the *Memoria Mundi* gave
him a clue to the Silurist's hermetical poetry. But
Smith could not follow Yeats over all those strange
frontiers in search of beauty without breaking his
lines of communication with his generation. The
Judwalis are as nothing to him. His problem is
the eternal problem confronting a sensitive mind:
to find significant expression for emotions set up
by contact with the sophistries, the tacit beliefs,
all the impurities that make an age what it is. The
way Smith is trying to resolve that problem, by

[8] "Gift of Harun Al-Rashid."
[9] *The McGill Fortnightly Review*, Dec. 1, 1926.
[10] *Papers of the Michigan Academy of Science, Arts and Letters*,
Vol. XVIII, 1932.

submitting himself to contemporary consciousness, by continued experimentation with technique, separates him from Yeats and brings him into line with poets of his own age in the United States and England.

The end of "For Ever and Ever, Amen,"

> "The Is is the same as the Will Be
> And both the same as before,"

is an early indication of the quality of his mind. He draws back into austere symbols and encloses the poet, creator of immortal shapes, in a concept of Being, after the manner of the great treatise, in a concept of reality, beyond change or dissolution, and turns the key on illusions. The title, which must be included in the poem, brings religion into the meaning of the purely metaphysical terms.

Some philosophical notion may lurk even in the briefest of his poems. In one of eight lines he fares into the country of dreams,

> "Where eternity and time
> Are the two sides of a drum," [11]

that is, where they beat as one, as timeless Being. The thought flashes out from nowhere with the suddenness and novelty of a message received on a

[11] *The Dial*, Dec., 1926.

television instrument, making Emily Dickinson's "finite infinity" more memorable still by illustrating it with a "metaphysical" picture.

Another of them is a miniature in six lines, beautifully composed, beautiful in its simple completeness, which treats a favourite idea among mystical poets, of how the soul, while it is in the body, partakes of a certain privation of life and yearns for union with God. Philosophy again merges into the Christian symbol; the Word made the broken whole. The slow lines of antithetical images so carefully chosen, the naked brevity of them, like symbols in a ritual, saying so much in their solemn silence, yet leaving so much unsaid, so much of ecstatic mystic doctrine, might have been murmured in a dramatic hush during an Easter sermon by a seventeenth-century divine, by Dr. Donne or Bishop Andrewes:

BESIDE ONE DEAD

"This is the sheath, the sword drawn;
   These are the lips, the Word spoken;
This is Calvary toward dawn;
   And this is the third day token—
The opened tomb and the Lord gone:
   Something Whole that was broken."

Donne's gaunt figure may be divined—this time standing in its shroud—behind the veils of another poem, "The Shrouding." [12]

---

[12] *The Dial*, Nov., 1928.

> "Unravel this curdled cloud,
> Wash out the stain of the sun,
> Let the winding of your shroud
> Be delicately begun."

A "curdled" cloud is not a new picture, nor is "wash out the stain," but forced into association with other images called up by "unravel" and "sun" they produce wit, and wit increases a poem's power. To the same end the poet writes, not "dam up the river," that is a commonplace, but

> "Bind up the muddy Thames,"

which condenses into essential brevity two amorphous images: operations in a funeral home and the world's commercial activities. Now it is time to put away worldly affairs and think of death. The last stanza,

> "But stand up in your shroud
> Above the crumbling bone,
> Drawn up like one more cloud
> Into the radiant sun,"

will appear as a "metaphysical" poet's picture of the soul's return to God.

Thomas Vaughan's description of the relationship between Celestial and Terrestrial bodies may help us to understand "Universe into Stone," [13] a poet's picture of stony hearts. "Invert this monstrous world" and stones will become celestial bodies, turn it upside down and stones will be hearts of "peace and lovingkindness" which now have "shrivelled into stone." Christ is the poet who will

> "shape this world of stone
> Into the likeness of a heart
> Of flesh and blood and bone.
>
> I'll take it for my love, and I
> Will joy in it, and sing
> How peace and lovingkindness are
> In many a stony thing,
>
> But not in hearts of flesh and blood,
> And not in living bone,
> That pride and chastity and scorn
> Have shrivelled into stone."

Seventeenth-century readings dart funereal rays through "Prothalamium" [14] during a ceremony which celebrates the body's marriage with the ancient clay. The shades of Webster and Hamlet and John Donne are there, Donne who was "always preaching to himself, like an angel in a cloud, but in none," as Isaac Walton tells. The atmosphere is charged with shadows, cadences and emblems

---

[13] *The Adelphi,* Jan., 1934. Reprinted in Thomas Moult's *Best Poems of 1934,* Cape.
[14] *The Dial,* July, 1928.

of varied provenance; shadows, for instance, from Vaughan's "passive cottage," the emblem of the worm "my sister" from *Job,* a cadence from the Elizabethans,

"Or, reading it, reads nothing to the point,"

a vegetation image of new life in the current style, while "consummation is ushered in" by a night wind from some waste land,

"By wind in sundry corners."

The idea of the poem, as of Kennedy's "Epithalamium," is life in death.

PROTHALAMIUM

"Here in this narrow room there is no light;
The dead tree sings against the window pane;
Sand shifts a little, easily: the wall
Responds a little, inchmeal, slowly, down.
My sister, whom my dust shall marry, sleeps
Alone, yet knows what bitter root it is
That stirs within her: see, it splits the heart—
Warm hands grown cold, grown nerveless, as a fin,
And lips enamelled to a hardness—
Consummation ushered in
By wind in sundry corners.

This holy sacrament was solemnized
In harsh poetics a good while ago—
At Malfi and the Danish battlements,

And by that preacher from a cloud in Paul's.
No matter: each must read the truth himself,
Or, reading it, reads nothing to the point.
Now these are me, whose thought is mine, and hers,
Who are alone here in this narrow room—
Tree fumbling pane, bell tolling,
Ceiling dripping and the plaster falling,
And death, the voluptuous, calling."

Calling to the grand reception, the *Danse Macabre*!
Bleak tokens dressed in the cold participles of the
Eliot period!

The poet is both marshal and celebrant. It is
the latter office for which he is fitted, in preparation for which he sojourned long in the solitude
of his own mind. Under his fingers the words pass
from one to another transformation, out of one aura
of suggestion into another. And this process is
peculiar to Smith, it singles him out from the rest
of his generation, though he has illustrious predecessors; Pythagoras learnt it among the Priests of
the Egyptian desert, Mallarmé was a late adept
and Valéry is still. "This narrow room" is this
life, this body, this grave; "sand," the wall of the
room, the wall of the grave; "sister," is also wife,
sweetheart and again earth, which is pregnant with
new life, with the "bitter root" that "stirs within
her."

Readers not conversant with the new styles in
poetry, and others of a later day, may wonder why
Smith broods so long on death and life in death.

First of all he is a man of the same temper as those seventeenth-century poets who have enjoyed wide popularity in our time chiefly as a result of Eliot's advocacy of wit and erudition and spiritual discipline, men who subjected their bodies to the thought of death, accustomed their minds to the idea of perfect life in a world compared to which this world is but an image in a glass, who spent themselves constantly in the joyful hope of the resurrection. And again because Eliot referred him to *The Golden Bough* and the Grail legend which, at a moment when traditional religions seemed to be crumbling in the general political and social chaos, filled his mind with fitting symbols of decay and spiritual drought, yet fortified him against death by associating the decay and rebirth of Nature with the death and resurrection of gods. Latterly, when nations have been harassed with peculiarly virulent economic disease and poets have had to adopt a social and political attitude, he has assimilated Marx whom he regards as another creator of a myth which furnishes a body of dogma of immense use to the contemporary artist. Those, then, are the literary, religious and social bases of Smith's poetry, and of Kennedy's.

Smith, the most austere and ascetic of the Montreal poets, sternly sets his face towards the desert of contemporary experience. Upon the flowing wells and juicy trees and April emotions, the "girls with pitchers waiting at the well" and the sweet companionship of desert caravans, as so many boyhood mirages, he resolutely turns his back. He defeats the irony of life's illusions by walking straight out into the desert away from human traffic, "unheartened by even the most faint mirage," and relieves his heart by singing difficult and lonely music among the sand and rock which will not "carry it away to blasphemous men." [15]

In some poems he uses emotional symbols to image the sorrow in his heart; it is something apart from all objective phenomena, as the "cat-bird's raucous note" is something apart from Nature's periods.

"He walks between the green leaf and the red
Like one who follows a belovèd dead." [16]

But in the myth which is taking shape he resolves these into intellectual symbols along the same lines as T. S. Eliot whom he resembles as a brother. In desert language this world is a mirage to which he "kisses his hand," for he is "set upon a pilgrimage seeking a more difficult beauty." He bears witness to the disillusionment and despair that have seared the heart of his generation—a lonely and pitiable generation born into a world gone crazy —and driven it into the desert of its own soul, to

<hr />

[15] Yeats, "Ego Dominus Tuus."
[16] "In the Wilderness," *The Canadian Forum*, Apr., 1930; also in *The Hound and Horn*, vol. v, number 2, Jan.-Mar., 1932.

find in desert sand and stone the very real tokens
of its hopeless worship.

"I'm for the desert and the desolation.
  I have kissed my hands to distant trees
  And to the girls with pitchers
  Waiting at the well,
  And I am set upon a pilgrimage
  Seeking a more difficult beauty
  Unheartened by even the most faint mirage.

  I am not I, but a generation
  Communicant with trickling sand
  And grey and yellow desert stone—
  The blood and body of our unknown god." [17]

He teaches a lesson of the renunciation of the
world's pomp in the parable of an old King who
"flung hollow sceptre and gilt crown away" and
wandered off into "a solitude of wind and rain"
to carol like a swan.

LIKE AN OLD PROUD KING IN A PARABLE

"A bitter king in anger to be gone
  From fawning courtier and doting queen
  Flung hollow sceptre and gilt crown away,

---

[17] "Testament." A later version (*The Canadian Forum*, Aug.,
1930) and a final version differ from the early one I have used
here for my own purposes and end as follows:
   "I am not I, but a generation—
     these are the bones of my comrades
     that have found with me, in stony sand,
     the blood and body of our unknown god."

And breaking bound of all his countries green
He made a meadow in the northern stone
And breathed a palace of inviolable air
To cage a heart that carolled like a swan,
And slept alone, immaculate and gay,
With only his Pride for a paramour.

O who is that bitter king? It is not I.

Let me, I beseech thee, Father, die
From this fat royal life, and lie
As naked as a bridegroom by his bride,
And let that girl be the cold goddess Pride:

And I will sing to the barren rock
Your difficult, lonely music, heart,
Like an old proud king in a parable." [18]

The "difficult beauty" which matches the "difficult, lonely music" of the poet's heart is described
in "The Lonely Land" [19] as a "beauty of dissonance": "jagged fir," "bitter spray," "wind-battered
branch," a wild duck's "ragged and passionate
tones."

THE LONELY LAND

"Cedar and jagged fir
   uplift sharp barbs
   against the gray
   and cloud-piled sky;
   and in the bay
   blown spume and windrift

---

[18] *The Hound and Horn.* vol. v, number 2, Jan.-Mar., 1932.
[19] *The Dial,* June, 1929.

and thin, bitter spray
snap
at the whirling sky;
and the pine trees
lean one way.

A wild duck calls
to her mate,
and the ragged
and passionate tones
stagger and fall—
and recover—
and stagger and fall—
on these stones,
are lost
in the lapping of water
on smooth, flat stones.

This is a beauty
of dissonance,
this resonance
of stony strand,
this smoky cry
curled over a black pine
like a broken
and wind-battered branch
when the wind
bends the tips of the pines
and curdles the sky
from the north.

This is the beauty
of strength
broken by strength
and still strong."

In place of fluidity and rhythmical composition, which we have in romantic poetry, there is "a desire for austerity and bareness" and an "attempt to make the organic look rigid and durable";[20] there is a "tendency to abstraction"[21] as in the work of certain contemporary Canadian artists: Tom Thomson, for example. Hulme, who looks at art as the expression of two opposed ideologies, the religious and the humanist, sees in this "tendency to abstraction" a constant characteristic of geometrical art; a tendency which presupposes "the idea of disharmony or separation between man and nature." It is opposed to the tendency, presupposing the idea of harmony between man and nature, that we have elaborated in our study of the naturalistic art of Lampman.[22] Classical Greek art and humanist art after the Renaissance, says Hulme, "having attained a kind of optimistic rationalism, no longer felt any desire for abstraction . . . because they no longer possessed any religious intensity."

The more we ponder on the parable of the old proud King the more its religious intensity grips us. It is the parable of the "Divine Unsatisfied," Christ, the artist, the poet, prophets and desert fathers, saints and seers, lonely and lofty souls who

---

[20] T. E. Hulme, *Speculations*, 1924.
[21] Worringer; quoted by Hulme. The impulse behind geometrical art—a Byzantine mosaic, for instance, as opposed to a Greek vase—Worringer called a "tendency to abstraction."
[22] *Ante*, pp. 34-8.

have forsaken the world to live in the desert with
only their "Pride for a paramour"; intellectual,
holy pride, the *sancta superbia* which is permitted
Catholic monks, a pride "like that of the Magi following their star over many mountains." [28] And
this poet prays for their strength. It is a hard
journey over the desert, a supreme trial of faith
and somewhat disappointing, as the three Kings
realized in Eliot's "Journey of the Magi."

> "We have come a long way riding. Is it this
> Granite overlooking no sweetsmelling vale
> Only to gain?" [24]

And one there is whose every feature signifies lost
joy, his flashing limbs and ruddy cheeks lost in the
sand, "a dark boy at midnight probing a sore" and
crying

> "Jesus, shew me thy grass, thy green,
> Else how shall I keep this thing I have not seen?"

This prayer for wholeness and for faith in Christ's
power prepares the ear for the antiphons and responses of "The Offices of the First and the Second
Hour." [25]

Eliot may have had the strong saints, the "ath-
letes of God," in mind when he wrote of Proust
"as a point of demarcation between a generation

[23] W. B. Yeats, *Ideas of Good and Evil.*
[24] "Prayer at Midnight."
[25] *New Verse,* London, Dec., 1933.

for whom the dissolution of value had in itself a positive value, and the generation which is beginning to turn its attention to an athleticism, a *training,* of the soul as severe and ascetic as the training of the body of a runner." [26] "The Offices of the First and the Second Hour" gives an account of a poet's first exercises in that "athleticism" or "training" of the soul. Apart from the literal significance there is a power in the poem which we could feel if we intoned the lines as though they were part of a religious ritual. That is an added power which the poet knows and wants. To induce the proper mood for these spiritual exercises he has set the poem up to look like a fragment of the Divine Office of the Roman Church which is chanted daily in its seven hour completeness by Catholic monks.

"What is the office of the first hour?

TO ABJURE

To abjure the kindness of darkness, humbly
To concede the irrelevant spite of the spirit,
The nightlike melancholy fleshcase, and the
Romantic unnecessary cape of the naked heart.

Is the rude root and manlike shape
Of articulate mandrake still godlike in this light?

---

[26] *The Criterion,* Oct., 1926.

NAY, WE HAVE GIVEN

Nay, we have given our flesh to the mouth and our
Hearts to the fingers of oblivion. The darkness
Is drained out of us slowly, and these are
No more to us.

What is the office of the second hour?

QUIETLY TO ATTEND

Quietly to attend the unfolding light's stark
Patience, inhuman and faithful like a weed or a
       flower,
Empty of darkness and light."

Darkness is kindly[27] because it permits us to act
without restraint, unseen, and the injunction is to
give up the easy, pleasant, careless ways of those
who walk in darkness, who are immersed in the
here and now, in the flesh which the spirit despises.
"Unnecessary," referring to the "romantic cape of
the naked heart," is perhaps excessive but Smith
is not denying the heart so much as the "unnecessary" display given to it by romantic poets. These
things must be regarded humbly as being irrelevant
to the real spiritual life. If we conform to this
spiritual rule of life is the main tenet of humanism
tenable? Can the fleshly part of man any longer
claim to be godlike or divine? Man can only be

---

[27] The expression is analogous to "the timid sun" in Yeats'
"Lines written in Dejection."

called a "manlike shape," an "articulate mandrake." That humanist vanity is "drained" away
as a result of the spiritual discipline of the first
hour. And now in the second stage, "empty of
darkness" (error, sin), quietly and in patience,
"inhuman and faithful like a weed or a flower," we
wait for the inflowing light (truth, grace), which
is not yet revealed, for the progress ends here.

In these two "hours" Smith has considered two
modes of living or two classes of people: those who
live by the flesh and those who live by the spirit.
It is a way of dividing humanity that a modern
critic might use as an alternative to the Marxian
division which holds so many minds to-day. Saint
Augustine, I believe, was the first to use it in his
City of God. He saw two cities, the city of God
and the city of men and, setting them up in opposition, proceeded to explain the history of the universe in a new way. His work had great success in
his own time and throughout the Middle Ages because it satisfied a spiritual need. "The Offices of
the First and the Second Hour" is preoccupied
with modern heresies, romanticism, humanism, but
the mode of thinking is not new. And there is something in the rambling structure, the intellectual
manipulation of symbols, the utter perishing of
eloquence; there is something in all this and in
word-images assembled frugally with bare Franciscan economy that takes us back to that special
creation of mediæval Christian genius, the Latin

Sequences; those of Adam of Saint-Victor, for example, in which the sacramental symbolism, rich in Biblical reference, is curiously intricate. This expert interplay of symbol is the poet's need. And the pure intellectual bouquet of his poetry—apart from the spirit which is deeper—has a special effect on us. It is like coming upon Góngora after the ballads and *serranillas,* or upon Mallarmé after a rain-pelted lyric by W. H. Davies. After a drenching of pretty nature lyrics in the old style we are revived by the spectacle of a poet playing upon contemporary experience with rare finesse, with ideas brusquely aligned and charged with essential significance.

Villiers de l'Isle-Adam's Axel in his impregnable castle enjoyed perfect economic security and could progress in the life which alone was real to him; but Smith is living under a system that makes it difficult for the inner life of the imagination to flourish. The practical, everyday life he would, like Axel, gladly leave to his servants, but there is no economic security at present and pure poetry as he understands it, poetry which interprets the intensely real life of the spirit, has to give way to propagandist art and satire. The surface life has conquered and now he may "wither into truth." [28] This is the mood in which Smith has written his latest poems. They deal with well-known political and social attitudes and are constructed on

---

[28] Yeats, "The Coming of Wisdom with Time."

original principles. All along he has been striving for precision, hardness, clarity (although the clarity may only be apparent to a reader who has some erudition and poetic experience) and power of evocation. He has learnt his art in whatever school he could. In the latest, the school of Joyce, he learnt to write "This is a theme for muted coronets,"[29] where "coronets" has obviously been attracted by "cornets." He has also gained something by trying out the uses of ambiguity, by squeezing every ounce of meaning out of the various and often conflicting denotations and connotations of words, especially in "Prothalamium" and "The Offices of the First and the Second Hour." This led to his latest experiments with contrapuntal verse[30] in which the emotion is expressed by writing as it were in two keys, by setting two contrasting suggestions, meanings or modes playing against one another. In "News of the Phœnix,"[31] for instance, the disgust results from the incongruous association of the ever-nascent, Phœnix-like flame of the spirit with the commonplace newspaper and bureaucratic mind:

NEWS OF THE PHŒNIX

"They say the Phœnix is dying, some say dead—
Dead without issue is what one message said,
But that was soon suppressed, officially denied.

---

[28] *The Hound and Horn*, vol. v, number 2, Jan.-Mar., 1932.
[30] *Cf.* Julian Bell, Richard Eberhart and John Lehmann.
[31] *New Verse*, Dec., 1933.

I think myself the man who sent it lied,
But the authorities were right to have him shot,
As a precautionary measure, whether he did or
    not."

A member of the older generation to whom the
sufferings of the war are still a vivid memory finds
himself out of touch with the young generations
to whom the war means nothing and who are being
misled into the same patriotic ardour that makes
war possible again.   That is the theme of "A
Soldier's Ghost," which ends with a vision of
these young conformers as so many brother bones
scattered on the battlefield of the next war.   It
was at first entitled "Chorus."

CHORUS

"How shall I speak
  To the regiment of young
  Whose throats break
  Saluting the god

Descending onto the drumhead?
—Each stalled
In his proper stance,
Upholding the service.

We, distilled
Of the polished bone and
The shiftless heart spilled
In the frontier sand,

Pluck at the natty sleeve.
—To what known use?
These young live
Fourth-dimensional to us.

In vain the smoking beeves,
The bloodstained grass!
How, memberless, to touch?
Or, tongueless, tell?"

That is an early draft of the poem. I may be pardoned for giving it here, together with a later version, so that we may observe Smith's austere method of working over a poem, continually straining it in his need of a potent essence. In its published form[32] it reads as follows:

A SOLDIER'S GHOST

"How shall I speak
To the regiment of young
Whose throats break
Saluting the god?

Bones
Distilled in the frontier sand
Fumble
The natty chevron.

Can a memberless ghost
Tell?
These lost
Are so many brother bones.

---

[32] *Poetry*, July, 1934.

> *The hieroglyph*
> *Of ash*
> *Secretes an anagram*
> *Of love.*

And since we are speaking of essence and precision
we might put his "To a Young Poet" [33] against
Verlaine's celebrated "Art poétique" as teaching a
totally different lesson within the same æsthetic
and incidentally calculate our distance from Marjorie Pickthall's imprecision and fluidity.[34]
Now that is the way Smith is trying to express
states of mind familiar to all of us in the present
moment of time. There is a call, undoubtedly, for
poetry which reflects the attitude of masses of
people to-day towards war, armaments factories,
Press Lords, Fascism and the economic order. In
common with proletarians Smith wants a new
ordering of the material bases of life without
which, it is true, the spirit cannot subsist, yet an
insistence on those things will not render the full
meaning of the word life. To be a communist is
still to be immersed in humanism; and Smith
wants to be purged of that error. The English
poets of his own age, coming from the same masters—the later Yeats and T. S. Eliot—but taking
en route a deeper draught of war-mongering and
class hatred, employ a direct style and depend upon

---

[33] *Ibid.*
[34] *Ante*, p. 46.

realistic technique to render their "vigorous living poetry":

> "O there's a mine of metal,
> Enough to make me rich
> And build right over chaos
> A cantilever bridge." [35]

In one sense their poetry is a salute to time. But the only satisfactory way, it seems to me, in which Smith can view contemporary experience is *sub specie aeternitatis*, under the form of his soul's beattude. From his life's star must issue his creative power and under its dominion even myths will suffer change. The extraordinary thing, the miracle, that we expect to witness in Smith's future creations will present itself as a new country in which every breath of doctrine and every beautiful myth is, as it were, "the waving of the robes of those whose faces see God in Heaven." [36] And that, to my mind, is the complexion that really great poetry will have in the future. We have a pre-view of what this may be in "A Soldier's Ghost" where some strange process of abstraction has worked like a spirit's breath upon dry bones and made them live. His later poems all have the essential potency which is the unerring evidence of his touch. His sensibility is inherently mystic, reaching out

---

[35] Cecil Day Lewis.
[36] Cardinal Newman, *Parochial Sermons.*

towards mystic experience, and his mind is balanced on polished agates. His poetry, as a consequence, aspires towards esotericism. That esotericism is the artistic equivalent of his mind's
temper. His verse is not distinguished from that
of Yeats and Villiers de l'Isle-Adam and all those
who intensely cultivate intellect and spirit by anything that has to do with philosophy, but by its
tone, the austerity it has acquired through "an
athleticism, a *training,* of the soul." And it will
be distinguished from the verse of his contemporaries by that same austere discipline. Magnificence
has gone, eloquence has been strained of heavy lux-
uriance; all that remains in the chalice is distilled
essence. The world of contemporary consciousness has shrunk to symbols: to a desert of sand,
cactus, prickly pear, wind, a solitary bird's cry;
to a granite valley with no greenness or fragrant
flowers but strewn with the bones of soldiers who
have died in vain. After a long wandering in that
desert, deceived by the mirages of our own pride,
worn out by the vain expectation of growing into
gods, by the continual drying up of our god-like
powers, empty and weary, shall we still look for
a fugitive caravanserai of Bedouin Arabs and bite
into the cactus and prickly pear until we die; shall
we push ahead and scout for enemy tanks; shall we
pep up our lagging spirits with the prospect of a
new found land over the horizon; or shall we dis-

cipline our souls to reach a timeless Bethlehem?
What shall we do?

"I am not I, but a generation."

As Ernest Psichari, the Centurion, alone in the
immense night of the African desert, so this generation is hungering for "essential knowledge,"
for the "bread of substantial reality." If it cares
to heed, it may learn from Hulme and Eliot and
Smith that its creative powers cannot be regen-
erated and its human grandeur re-established except by the discipline of religious asceticism.
Smith is only beginning his training; yet we are
too far behind in spiritual adventure intimately to
appreciate his art which is a prolongation of his
contemplative life. Many readers, I fear, will
pass it by as unreasonably difficult, over-intellec-
tual, or outrageously unethical, lacking the
warmth of human emotions, and will never know,
perhaps, that they have deprived themselves of
one of this world's chiefest joys: the poetry of a
life consecrated to an austere, lonely and mystic
ideal.

THIS MAN OF APRIL

LEO KENNEDY, poet of the Resurrection, was born of Irish stock in the city of Liverpool some twenty-eight years ago and came to Canada when he was five. His family was not literary and what books were found in the house were brought in by Kennedy who, for seven years, served as a shipping clerk and book-keeper in his father's ship-chandler's business. As a youngster he ran off to sea and spent four months peeling potatoes and washing dishes on a C.P.R. tramp among West Indian ports.

His literary adventures began with his meeting the men who ran *The McGill Fortnightly Review* (1926-28) : Louis Schwartz, F. R. Scott, A. J. M. Smith, Leon Edel and the late Alan Latham. When the *Fortnightly* ceased, *The Canadian Mercury* was launched and continued through six numbers, from December, 1928, to June, 1929; Kennedy was associated with Jean Burton, F. R. Scott and Felix Walter on the editorial board. A little later than the founding of the *Mercury,* he tore himself out of his Catholic environment, went to New York and married. There he experienced many ups and downs. He was by turn book-keeper, book reviewer and newspaper reporter. Then he returned to settle in Montreal.

It is obvious that Kennedy has been more concerned with living than with studying. He is an active and emotional man rather than a scholar; his emotions make his anatomy quiver and jerk. He has written memorable poetry and remarkable short stories where he has been able to translate those emotions into their artistic verbal equivalents. His criticism, on the other hand, is overcast with exuberant emotion. However much he may be preoccupied with the metaphysical poets and their twentieth-century representatives, he is unfitted to write criticism in any way comparable to T. S. Eliot's or poetry like Paul Valéry's, for the simple reason that he is not a metaphysician. Kennedy does not start with philosophical concepts as a basis for his poetry. That has saved him from falling into errors of allusionism and conceptism. His poetry may show an early indulgence in Elinor Wylie ("Reproach to Myself," "Martha and Mary," and the close, smooth grain of his sonnets), and T. S. Eliot ("Rite of Spring" and the sickly "Litany for our Time"), but he feels life intensely enough to be able to nourish his own language without recourse at every turn to the old masters. He can recite pages of Eliot, but if he ever imitates such lost words as

"If the lost word is lost, if the spent word
       is spent,
If the unheard, unspoken
Word is unspoken, unheard." [1]

---

[1] "Ash Wednesday."

he is lost. Take Saint John and Bishop Andrewes
out of those lines and the evening breezes will
blow away the downy seeded milkweed.

There is no immediate cause for fear. Kennedy
has been trying to find life and to find himself;
prospecting for a metal fine enough to surrender
itself wholly to the impress of his emotions; searching for the Word and the Myth which would be
the perfect literary vehicle of his sensibility. He
is very fortunate to have found these things; they
will permit him to unfold his dimensions and reveal his greatness.

Of the contributors to *The Canadian Mercury,*
A. J. M. Smith, especially, was inclined to metaphysical poetry and had something to convey to
Kennedy: a dissatisfaction with the Canadian anthology, an interest in Eliot and seventeenth-
century literature. Eliot naturally led Kennedy
to *The Golden Bough* where he discovered the
Myth. The Myth permeated, became one substance with his Emotion and engendered all his
poems, which are the living figures of his unified
sensibility—a rare possession that present-day
critics have lauded in Donne and the others.

Along a street in Verdun, Montreal, there is a
Funeral Home, easily visible by day and illumin-
ated by night. Donne in his shroud was not nearer
death than Kennedy as he listened to the morti-
cian's details of a modern embalming:

"When washing a body, padding a cheek, or clearing the entrails out of some blue abdomen, Cal-
eb's fingers deftly danced." [2]

"Lid the flat staring eye, as pale as ice;
Bind up the fallen jaw; then fold the palms
Decorously upon the breast."

         "the oaken coffin and the pall. . .
The rented purple hangings in the hall
Over the torn wallpaper . . . and the frail
Blossoms of candles sepulchrally pale." [3]

It may appear on a first reading that Kennedy
moves between the Funeral Home and the Cemetery; that he has built his æsthetic on a passage
from Sir Thomas Browne:

"Now, since these dead bones have already out-
lasted the living ones of Methuselah . . . what
Prince can promise such diuturnity unto his relics, or might not gladly say:

'Sic ego componi versus in ossa velim.'?" [4]

That is no more then a surface impression. He is
faithful to his experience and emotions, but he
has used them as primitive peoples used imitative
magic, to revive life in the ground: as a poet he

---

[2] *Death comes for the Undertaker.*
[3] The quotations are from *The Shrouding*, a volume of poems
published by The Macmillan Company of Canada Limited,
Toronto, 1933.
[4] *Hydriotaphia, or Urn Burial.*

has graced the gruesome paraphernalia of death
and burial in Montreal with the anemones of the
Syrian Adonis.

"Weep not for Adonais."

In that way he has made us look upon present life
as a continuation of the past history of the race;
he has enriched human experience by "widening
the domain of reality," as Eliot has taught us to say.

Living in a country once inhabited by Indians,
Kennedy might reasonably have connected our funeral rites with the ceremonial of death among the
Algonquins and Iroquois.   But the *place* was not
as powerful an influence as the *moment*.   Kennedy
grew up in the relaxing atmosphere which settled
upon our Waste Land after the war and, following
Eliot's lead into Sir James Frazer's immense estate,
he discovered new gods: Attis, Osiris and Adonis.
In *The Golden Bough* he read that the annual
ceremony of the death and resurrection of Adonis
was a dramatic representation of the decay and
revival of plant life, and that the Easter celebration of the dead and risen Christ may have been
"grafted upon a similar celebration of the dead
and risen Adonis . . . celebrated in Syria at the
same season." [5]   That was the link that Kennedy
wanted, for out of the scuttling of his Catholicism,
the thing that he cherished and preserved was the

---

[5] *Adonis, Attis, Osiris*, 1922, vol. i. p. 256.

Easter Cycle (Life—Death—Life), the most amazing thing to him, and in *The Golden Bough* he found its counterpart and origins. So it is that the Myth has fertilized his Canadian sensibility, made it bring forth solemnly beautiful and strangely moving poems which begin and end as resurrection poems. The cycle of life is seen as a bulb bursting, the stem rearing itself up to bud and blossom in spring:

"To rot and burst and climb once more in March."

Kennedy does not dote on flowers in the manner of our older poets. After Flecker he has said in his heart:

> "For one night or the other night
> Will come the Gardener in white, and gathered
> flowers are dead, Yasmin." [6]

From the spring woods he brought back bloodroot, crocus, trillium, and set them before him on the table beside bulbs from a city store. To him the bulbs are symbols of that loveliness, symbols of latent life, "gaunt unresurrected sons of God."

One day during the winter that he wrote advertisements for Simpson's Basement Store he happened to be working with tubers. As he was poking about on the counter, handling and enjoying the bulbs, he was struck by the rather staring

---

[6] *Hassan.*

likeness of the hyacinth root to the papal tiara, gradually conical, with three crowns, and immediately the resurrection idea, always in Kennedy's mind, polarized about the tiara. He had been reading Baron Corvo's astounding story of an eccentric Englishman who became Pope and chose the title of Hadrian VII. In that way the poem acquired its character and appeared, dressed in the wrappings of a poet's fiction, as "Hyacinths for Hadrian."

"He found such pleasure in the roots of things
  That plot a resurrection out of sight."

Klein, I have said, cannot bear death. But Scott, Smith and Kennedy, who were reared in the Christian faith, all see life through the doctrine of the Resurrection and describe succeeding generations of humans by analogy with the cycle of plant life:

"He feels the earthiness of countless peasants
  Stir in loins and sprout like little grain."
                                        (*Smith*)

"Where sapling boys and girls are sweetly aching
  For willow sprouts, and the smell of fresh earth
    breaking."

"And girls now seedlings in their father's reins."
                                      (*Kennedy*)

"But no seed stirs
In this bare prison
Under the hollow sky.
The stone is not yet rolled away
Nor the body risen."
                    (*Scott*)

In all countries, I suppose, from time beyond record, Spring Songs have been sung and Spring Rites celebrated—even in Canada before the Puritan and Victorian occupation. Why was Lampman, who leaned upon the Mighty Mother, so insensible to the flow of sap in his own body? Because he dissociated Man from Nature. Anthropology, the study of man and his beliefs, could not absorb a poet whose sole delight was to get away into the bush. Lampman needed a Myth. We, in our time, are dissatisfied with his Aprils and Octobers after reading Kennedy's "Epithalamium before Frost" and these

WORDS FOR A RESURRECTION

"Each pale Christ stirring underground
Splits the brown casket of its root,
Wherefrom the rousing soil upthrusts
A narrow, pointed shoot,

And bones long quiet under frost
Rejoice as bells precipitate
The loud, ecstatic sundering,
The hour inviolate.

This Man of April walks again—
Such marvel does the time allow—
With laughter in His blessèd bones,
And lilies on His brow."

Marjorie Pickthall, who grieved over love crucified, could move us by the very words of Christ's
passion: *Eloi, Eloi, lama sabachthani?* That, we
might say, was a borrowed power. But Kennedy's
poem is a personal thing, as personal as the beautiful "Burial of the Dead" that Prudentius wrote
fifteen hundred years ago and of which it is the
consummation:

"Nunc suscipe, terra, fovendum." [7]

This Man of April! Open, Earth, and give us
Life. Life out of frozen earth! Life out of
death! One is tempted to soliloquize; in this
"Christian civilization" of Canada we have lost
all grasp of the meaning of the Resurrection.
Henry Vaughan, the Silurist, was conscious of a
"preserving spirit" which caused nature and humanity to renew their being. The hibernation of
bats and dormice was to him a likeness of the
Resurrection. He spoke of "bright shootes of
everlastingnesse" and pictured death as a hidden
but growing flower. But of all the descriptions
of resurrected gods: Adonis, spirit of the corn,

---

[7] Translated by Helen Waddell, *Mediaeval Latin Lyrics*,
Constable, 1929.

Vaughan's "green, immortal Branch," Crashaw's "Rise, mighty Man of wonders"; of all the descriptive phrases that Fray Luis de León meditated upon in *De los Nombres de Cristo* none, I feel, has more power to move our imaginations than that; except Christ's own: "I am the Bread of Life." We may take that little poem apart, unweave the ideas and references, open our hearts to the emotion, and then read it over again to marvel at its subtle perfection. I know of no Canadian poem in which there is such absolute and beautiful blending of thought and feeling, such amazing unity of being.

"April is no month for burials." This young poet, as Adonis, as Christ, dies in order to live. He dramatizes death in order to reveal a sequel: perennial resurrection. He faces corruption and dissolution in order to magnify the immortality of beauty. Job's words are his: "I have said to corruption, Thou art my father: to the worm, Thou art my mother and my sister." But he has espoused Death in order to cry Epithalamium! The paradox is a discovery of startling poetic power.

"Now shall I cry Epithalamium!"

—even while the sap is retreating before the pricking frost.

The title "Epithalamium" in Donne suggested

to Kennedy names for some of his poems. This
one he first called "Sequel":

EPITHALAMIUM

"This body of my mother, pierced by me,
In grim fulfilment of our destiny,
Now dry and quiet as her fallow womb
Is laid beside the shell of that bridegroom
My father, who with eyes towards the wall
Sleeps evenly; his dust stirs not at all,
No syllable of greeting curls his lips,
As to that shrunken side his leman slips.

Lo! these are two of unabated worth
Who in the shallow bridal bed of earth
Find youth's fecundity, and of their swift
Comminglement of bone and sinew, lift
—A lover's seasonable gift to blood
Made bitter by a parchèd widowhood—
This bloom of tansy from the fertile ground:
My sister, heralded by no moan, no sound."

In the old Semitic myths the reproductive energies of nature were personified as male and
female; water was especially identified with the
one power and earth with the other. In Kennedy
the soil is a matrix; "pools of melted snow,"
"water slurring underground" we may consider
the sperm and promise of future life. Spring
shoots will pierce the matrix of the soil,

"Bloodroot and trillium break out of cover,
And crocuses stir blindly in their cells."

Then we may lay them with hyacinths, ragweed
and lilac leaves upon our sorrowing hearts and
bind the April grass about our brows.   One way
of relieving the agony of life's irony, of cheating
death, is to make it give forth life, to fertilize the
desert, make flowers grow out of sand and rock.
Wherever death possesses the land Kennedy grows
tulips and hyacinths, bloodroot and trilliums;
immaculate tokens of new life.   He makes waste
places suddenly burst into flower like the Gardens
of Adonis.

Kennedy moves the idea of resurrection from
place to place with intent to dramatize the revelation.   He finds a Hamlet sinking "beneath the
treason of his esteemèd flesh"; a philosopher moving unwillingly into the "still repository of his
dust"; a widow sitting over her dead husband,
thinking of Christ's "Come forth, Lazarus," and
hearing only "the rattling of a hearse"; a recluse
"wry and arid in her soul" poisoning herself and
quickly realizing that "life was the precious gift."
He finds occasion to write his own epitaph:

SELF EPITAPH TO BE CARVED IN SALT

"His heart was brittle;
His wits were scattered;
He wrote of dying
As though life mattered."

A pleasing subtlety of conception in "Exile

endured," one of his chaste and melodious sonnets, is due to the marriage of his Emotion with the Vegetation Myth:

"I . . .
Who have grown harsh and arid under stone
That shrivels up the heart, and splits the bone!"

"Daughter of Leda" without the Myth would be a Pre-Raphaelite exercise. The Myth has engendered life in the soil of his poetry:

"Afix with gummy maple sap
The tear that widens at each thrust
Of ragweed straining from the dust."

"For all the beauty winter cannot kill."

"gaunt unresurrected sons of God,
Crocus bulbs parched and patient under sod."

"the drip
Of snow water through the dark."

The Myth swells his lines with so much meaning:

"Bind up this heart that splits and bleeds."

"I pass
Among bleached bones of summer."

Kennedy's poetry is not a game played by a

cold brain organized in this or that fashion but a soul's experience, ardent and alive, breathed into harmonious rhythms and rolling chants—the music of a harmonized sensibility. His long lines, which invite comparison with those of the American poet, Archibald MacLeish, have the power and solemnity of great drama:

"Gather the fringes of earth, then draw together
 The parts of this brown wound, and bind them fast
 With measured stitches of your spade, Grave-
   digger."

"Eyes misted with passion, the lids heavily aswoon,
 The nails bruising the palms in ecstasy. . .
 The long shuddering breath, and the ensuing
   quiet."

"And gnash your teeth for rage, and cry relief;
 And weep and curse, and smash your heart to
   bits."

and aspire to the solemn grandeur of Isaiah:

"You shall acquaint the fellowship of grief."

As he found life in death, so he has searched for words which, though old and decaying, have a quick potency in their dry roots, old words that make us mindful of the antiquity of our race, Saxon words (here again we think of MacLeish) taking us back beyond the Elizabethans to the beginnings of our poetry: *leman, charily, cleave, rime*:

"How shall I *cleave* me from my works, indeed?"

He has found the Word, as he found the Myth, and entered into the vital being of it to make it his. The reader is conscious of this reintegration in his best stories (for example, "A Priest in the Family")[8] and in every line of his poetry:

"Now that leaves *shudder* from the hazel limb,
And poppies *pod,* and maples *whirl* their seed."

"And rime surmised at morning *pricks* the rim
Of tawny stubble, husk and perishing weed."

"And the first crocus *hoists* its yellow crest!"

The very rhymes cry out with the vitality of young rams.

Nature's periods thrust themselves into our lives in Canada more violently than in other countries and we scorn them at our peril. Yet what Prince among us has promised diuturnity to his relics by turning his emotions outward among those eternal processes? Worms and moles crawl over the roots of Kennedy's poems, which are flowers of death, April flowers growing out of death, fertilized by fresh water from the deep, hidden wells

---

[8] *The Canadian Forum*, Apr., 1933.

of our language, flowers as precious as orchids, remarkable for the beauty of their funereal colourings.   Dust to dust, says the Priest; vanity of vanities, saith the Preacher:

"All these things endured their time and are
     broken,"

says the Poet—that he might hail the Resurrection.   The Triumph of Life is a trivial word until it illumines the darkness of our flesh.

If we would know the source, the well-spring of his power and of the impression of strength which not alone the subtle artistry conveys to us but which all Kennedy's creative work undeniably possesses, we must enter into the ardent chapel of his soul and gaze in wonder at the Easter miracle. And that was something that remained living and pure, like an altar light, after the edifice of twisted principles and inert dogmas crashed before the surge of a new and life-promising gospel.   When orthodoxy goes out of a man it is to make room for a more urgent and irresistible passion, for he cannot steer himself without a religion.   Wafted by personal circumstance and fresh-arisen winds and the sincere and courageous temper of his mind to new climates of vision he can see human destiny with other eyes and look on it with passion. Human history appeared to him as an ancient succession of fathers who, after bequeathing life

to their children, mingled with chalk and clay
under the sod.   It will always appear to him as a
cycle of life and death but accompanied hence-
forth with a deeper undertone of vital experience.
"To you," he says in his "Testament," [9]

"to you I leave my life which is over and done
          as you are;
to my sons' children your gift to me, the life
          unravelled
and which transmutes as time turns, to your
          portion.

These under my hand in the fall of '34,
these with the breath of life in my body and the
          blood
prompt at the wrist, the eye alert, the wit shar-
          pened by past want."

And that is part of him for ever.   Soon, perhaps,
—for this is a "transitional" poem, which he finds
more and more difficult to write—the complaint
will change into a positive and passionate call to a
new order and a new destiny, the vision of which
he shares with the younger poets on both sides of
the Atlantic.   But the forms will be new; different from any we have yet seen in those poets who
have worked with contemporary conflicts and
realistic technique.   It will be interesting to watch
those conflicts change into living creatures when an

---

[9] *Transitional Poems.*

imaginative current is passed through them in the presence of a religious myth. We know not what the future hath, yet along whatever line his art develops it will always be shaped and toned by Frazer and the great religious writers of the seventeenth century; that heritage of thought and feeling will provide the imperishable symbols and myths. If we reflect on the particular complexion of his poetry, the distinctive feature by which we recognize its creator, we must ascribe it to his assimilation of the myth of Adonis. A new Myth has blown over our white and frost-bound Canadian savannahs that a new Poet might marvel at the miracle of "water slurring underground" and chant the unfailing quickening of New Life and Beauty.

"He shall grow up . . . as a tender plant,
and as a root out of a dry ground."

INDEX

The Ryerson Press are to be complimented on their beautiful presentation of Dr E.K. Brown's book *On Canadian Poetry*. Dr Brown is one of our most promising scholars. He has had the advantage of the best training in this country and in France. He has already given us critical studies of English and American authors. For the time being he is at Cornell living with Americans but he has always been a student of the literature of his native land. As critic in charge of the annual survey of poetry for the *University of Toronto Quarterly* he is fully acquainted with the poetry appearing during recent years in the Dominion.

On Canadian Poetry is the fruit of much study and rigorous intellectual discipline. It is without a doubt the best work that Brown has done. It comprises three chapters: 'The Problem of a Canadian Literature,' 'The Development of Poetry in Canada,' and 'The Masters,' in which he studies the poetry of Archibald Lampman, Duncan Campbell Scott, and Edwin John Pratt. In the first chapter he deals with a subject he has at heart. He expands what he said in *Canadian Literature Today*, 1938, and what he said to the Americans in the Canadian issue of *Poetry*, 1941. It is a brilliant analysis of the economic and social difficulties writers have to contend with in Canada, a complete and exact picture of

Review of *On Canadian Poetry* by E.K. Brown (Toronto: Ryerson 1943) and *At the Long Sault and Other New Poems* by Archibald Lampman, foreword by Duncan Campbell Scott and introduction by E.K. Brown (Toronto: Ryerson 1943). Review published in *University of Toronto Quarterly* XIII 4 (1943-4) 221-9

the colonial spirit, the disguised frontier standards and the puritanism which prevail in our society and which have crushed some of our writers and led others to court an outside public. The second chapter sketches the development of Canadian poetry from Sangster and Heavysege to Anne Marriott and Earle Birney; that is, it covers the whole range of our poetic history. Since it is plainly an historical as well as a critical outline we wonder why author and publisher alike were at pains to inform us that *On Canadian Poetry* 'is not an historical enquiry.' The mind that planned this book, that wrote the opening paragraphs of the study of Pratt, that adopted the social idea which determines some of the judgments brought down in the book is an historical as well as a critical mind. The first chapter might well be a preface to the sound history of Canadian literature which the author knows we have not got. But Mr Brown's real gift is not his historical sense, nor his scholarly curiosity, but rather his ability to scrutinize his material. He collates and examines texts; he searches into a poet's struggles with words and images; he studies influences, traditions, developments, the progress of a poet's art or attitude. The essay on Lampman is a scholar's work. Sometimes we feel that he is a French type of critic working with an idea of the dominant characteristic of a poet's art; the essay on D.C. Scott is such a critic's work. Often we picture him as a disciple already expert in the use of the intellectual instruments of his masters.

During his critical, research, and editorial labours Mr Brown has come under the spell of several master minds, particularly Arnold and Eliot. The shade of his humanism is defined in the terms: 'a literature develops in close association with society' and 'a great literature is the flowering of a great society.' The first chapter of his book is a product of his humanism. The critical instruments he makes most skilful use of in his treatment of 'the masters' are those of the perfect and pure critic as T.S. Eliot understands him. Arnold and Eliot taught us to look 'solely and steadfastly at the object.' Eliot, more austere, reacting solidly against romanticism, against the impressionism which characterized English critical writing a quarter of a century ago, taught us also that a critic 'should have no emotions except those immediately provoked by a work of art,' that 'the end of the enjoyment of poetry is a pure contemplation from which all the accidents of personal emotion are removed.' He taught us that the 'tools of the critic' are two, namely: 'comparison and analysis.' But this austerity was too much even for Eliot. His eye was not so steadfast, his contemplation was not so pure that it kept him from asking himself questions about traditions and reputations and kinds of art. Mr Brown recalls his masters by the nature of the questions he sets himself: 'What are the peculiar difficulties which have weighed upon the Canadian writer?' 'What Canadian poetry remains alive and, in some degree at least, formative?' 'How have the masters of our poetry achieved their success and what are the kinds of success they have achieved?' 'It remains to inquire whether Lampman's reputation at home or abroad is in keeping with his deserts.' Why have the Canadian public and Canadian critics failed 'to do anything like justice to Scott's powers'? He recalls his masters by his use of analysis and comparison; his 'pure contemplation' is the secret of his book's great clarity, its strength and courage. It stands therefore as a new sign marking the end of impressionistic and the advent of scientific criticism. Amateur critics and anthologists will feel uncomfortable in the presence of an eye that looks 'solely and steadfastly,' at our poetry.

293

Mr Brown's comparisons, those drawn from American sources, are new and welcome. But the original kind of comparison he attempts does not consist in placing one author beside another but rather in placing two poems together in one order of value: 'Undoubtedly the poetic beauty of "The Land of Pallas" ... is far inferior to the poetic beauty of, let us say, "Heat" or "The Frogs".' No critic of Lampman could avoid bringing in Wordsworth and Keats whose poetry sang in his head. Such comparisons are not the novel elements in Mr Brown's essay, which wins our admiration by its close study of the development of Lampman's attitude to nature and social pessimism, following upon a scrupulous examination of texts, published and unpublished, and an inter-comparison of the poems under certain orders of value. His analyses are as expert as his comparisons. The best part of his essay on Scott is constructed with the aid of a dominant quality he has isolated and which he calls 'restrained intensity.' He works with it till he finds perfection in Scott, those pieces of his art which express a perfect fusion of intensity and restraint: 'The Forsaken,' 'Powassan's Drum.' But in 'Mission of the Trees'

Scott wished not only to be intense, but also to establish restraint — he was determined not to overdo his effect. The result was too quiet a note. ... Scott was here satisfied with a balance that is mechanical, a balance that was achieved by setting two entities side by side and making sure that they had the same weight. For the greatest effects the balance must be organic: the intensity and the restraint must fuse. This they do not often do in Scott's early or intermediate volumes. When they do his poetry is not to be equalled, I think, by any of the Canadian poets of his generation.